Rosie,
   Best wishes!
      Tonya Royston

D1530901

Dakota had run off, leaving me to my fate…

My eyes adjusting to the darkness, I could see the trees within the shadows, their spider-like branches reaching up to the sky. But my attention was drawn away from them when I heard a faint rustling. Dead leaves scratched against each other from what sounded like something moving through them. "Dakota, please stay. Whatever you do, don't leave me," I begged quietly, but my words dropped away when he charged ahead to the woods.

I sucked in a deep breath as he disappeared. In his hurry to chase off whatever was out there, he'd left me alone, vulnerable and unprotected. I whirled around, prepared to hurry back to the house, but a man stood before me blocking my path to the patio steps.

Fear blasting through me, my heart hammered in my chest. I started to move to one side, but the man stepped with me, remaining directly in front of me. Looking up into his cold, dark eyes, I stopped, feeling like a deer trapped by a mountain lion.

Not sure what to do, I realized I had few options. I could try to run, or I could accept my fate, whatever that might be…

Eighteen-year-old Laken Sumner has just escaped from a stranger and a pack of wolves in the dark rain on a lonely mountain road. Normally, with her ability to communicate with wild animals, who can understand her thoughts, she wouldn't worry about encountering the predators. But these wolves didn't respond to her. She tries to shrug it off, afraid to reveal her fears to Noah, her boyfriend and the deputy sheriff.

But that's not all she's hiding. Drawn to Xander Payne, like a moth to a flame, she warns herself to stay away from him. She's convinced he knows something, and she doesn't trust him. Besides, Noah is the one she really wants. If only she could be sure of that.

When disaster strikes and Laken is forced to confess her secret to Noah, her worst fears are realized as he drifts away from her. Xander is more than willing to step into Noah's shoes with Laken, but she refuses to give in to her feelings for him. Because Noah *will* be back, won't he?

(Twenty-five cents for every print and ebook copy sold will be donated to the Ian Somerhalder Foundation.)

KUDOS for *Silence at Midnight*

In *Silence at Midnight* by Tonya Royston, we get a continuation of the story started in *Shadows at Sunset*. In this book, Laken learns some dark family secrets that make her question who she is. Animals play a big part in this story as they did in the first book, and Laken is put into a situation where she has to confess her "gift" to her boyfriend, the town deputy, Noah. When he starts to back away from her, she is sure it is because of her confession, but he denies it. Meanwhile, Xander is still in the background, vying for Laken's affections. Must be nice to have two hunks after you. (Sigh). Like the first book, this one is well written with a strong, unpredictable plot and charming characters. You just can't help rooting for Laken and wondering how the story will end. ~ *Taylor Jones, Reviewer*

Silence at Midnight is the next book in Tonya Royston's *Sunset Trilogy*. In this second installment, Laken Sumner is still dodging passes from Xander Payne, still talking to animals, and still pursuing her relationship with Noah, the town deputy. But when Laken helps Noah rescue a moose caught in a fence, Noah becomes suspicious and Laken is forced to confess her ability in communicating with animals. Noah seems impressed at first, but then he starts backing away. His rejection leaves Laken questioning herself, especially when she overhears her parents discussing some deep family secrets that she wasn't supposed to know. Royston has crafted a complicated story of a charming and intriguing young woman, whose paranormal gifts are a mixed blessing, if not a curse. *Silence at Midnight* is equally well written and suspenseful as the first one, and you are left chomping at the bit for more. ~ *Regan Murphy, Reviewer*

Silence at Midnight

Book Two of the Sunset Trilogy

Tonya Royston

A Black Opal Books Publication

GENRE: PARANORMAL THRILLER/YA/PARANORMAL ROMANCE

SILENCE AT MIDNIGHT ~ Book Two of the Sunset Trilogy
Copyright © 2016 by Tonya Royston
Cover Design by Jennifer Gibson
All cover art copyright © 2016
All Rights Reserved
Print ISBN: 978-1-626944-17-6

First Publication: FEBRUARY 2016

Published by Black Opal Books **http://www.blackopalbooks.com**

DEDICATION

To my Mom

Thank you for everything!

Chapter 1

It was like something out of a dream. Heavy rain poured down from the black sky, battering the desolate road that twisted through the remote mountains, far from any semblance of civilization. I had just escaped the clutches of a stranger and a pack of wolves—only what they wanted with me remained a mystery.

Rain pelted the pick-up in front of me, slicing through the headlight beams while I stood frozen, unable to move. Beads of water rolled down my slicker, and I shivered. Taking a deep breath, I wiped at the tears in my eyes and shuddered at the memory of the wolves and the man, wondering when—not if—they would find me again. Shaking the images out of my thoughts, I forced myself to smile, realizing I'd have to decide how much to tell Xander about what had just happened, and soon.

The truck opened and he jumped out of the cab into the pouring rain. After slamming the door shut, he rushed over to me, his dark trench coat glistening wet. Water dripped from his hair onto his forehead, but he didn't seem to notice as he stopped in front of me. "Laken! What are you doing out here by the road? Where's your truck?"

My eyes locked with his, and I took shallow breaths, remembering how out of control I felt when the Explorer hydroplaned on the wet pavement and slid into the ditch. "There," I said quietly, pointing to the side without taking my eyes off of him. "I went off the road."

"What? How?"

"I'll explain everything once we get going. I just want to get away from here as fast as we can."

Xander must have recognized the anxiety in my eyes and voice. "Of course. Come on." He wrapped an arm around my shoulders and led me to the passenger side of his truck. Without another word, he opened the door and helped me climb into the warm cab. As I leaned back against the seat, finally feeling safe, my trembling subsided.

"Will you get my book bag out of the Explorer? I didn't think to take it with me." My excuse was lame, but I didn't want to tell him about the wolves and the man or that my book bag had been the furthest thing from my mind as I ran for my life. I pulled my keys out of my pocket. "Here. I can't remember if I locked it."

Xander flashed a reassuring smile as he took them. "No problem. I'll be right back."

"Thanks."

Our eyes met for a quick moment before I looked away, still unnerved by the memory of the wolves and the man. Xander shut the door before disappearing, and I locked the truck. Silence loomed through the dark cab except for the rain pounding on the roof. As I waited, I pushed the hood of my slicker behind my neck and wiped the water off my face, hoping Xander would return soon. I hated to think that the wolves and the man were still out there, and I felt a little guilty for not telling him. But Xander was always so confident and strong. I couldn't imagine even a pack of hungry wolves taking him down.

When the locks clicked open, I gasped, my heart accelerating until Xander opened the door to the driver's seat. "You okay?" he asked as he climbed in, tossing my book bag behind his seat. "You look like you just saw a ghost."

I swallowed nervously, turning my attention to the dark windshield as rain pattered against it. I had hoped he wouldn't notice my anxiety.

"Maybe now is a good time for you to tell me exactly what happened," he said slowly after shutting his door. He started the engine and flipped on the headlights, but instead of pulling out onto the road, he turned the heat to a high setting and then looked at me, his blue eyes waiting.

I glanced at him, hesitant to answer. Taking a deep breath, I summoned my courage. "An animal ran across the road. I didn't see it until it was right in front of me. When I tried to stop, the brakes locked up and I lost control of the truck." I wasn't sure why I cared, but I didn't want him to think I was completely incapable. I had driven these roads ever since I had gotten my license nearly two years ago and never had I come close to being stranded like this.

"An animal? Please tell me you didn't wreck because of a squirrel."

I rolled my eyes, groaning inwardly. "No. Why would you think that?"

"I knew a girl back home who totaled her Hummer, all because she swerved to avoid hitting a squirrel."

I smiled, relieved to know his comment actually had merit. "Well, I assure you it wasn't a squirrel or a rabbit or a mouse." I paused, taking a deep breath. "It was a wolf," I blurted out, my eyes glued to him, studying his reaction.

Mild surprise registered in his eyes, but he seemed to believe me. "A wolf? I didn't know wolves lived around here."

"They don't—or at least they didn't, until now apparently."

"You're sure it wasn't a big dog?"

"Yes, I'm sure. I know the difference. It's not the first wolf I've seen."

Xander watched me intently. "Really?"

I nodded. "Yes. I saw another one twice before tonight. The first time was at the bonfire right before I ran into you."

He drew in a sharp breath, seeming frustrated. "Why didn't you tell me?"

I huffed and turned to stare out the windshield. "I had no reason to tell you. Why would you even ask that?" I shook my head in disbelief, then looked back at him and changed the subject. "Where were you this afternoon, anyway? I waited at that old library for an hour."

"I know and I'm sorry about that. I had to go home. The alarm went off this afternoon."

"Oh," I said with a sigh, trying to be at least a little understanding. "That can't be good."

Xander frowned. "No, it's not."

"Did you find out what set it off?"

"No. We didn't find anything, and we inspected every inch of the house. It may have been a short somewhere. Dad's having a technician come out tomorrow to look at it. Again, I'm sorry. I hope you'll forgive me. I promise it won't happen again."

I smiled reluctantly. "Well, considering you just rescued me from being stranded, I suppose I can. But please don't let it happen again. That library was really creepy. I don't want to go back there alone."

"Creepy?" he asked with a teasing grin.

"Yes. Trust me on this. You'll have to see it to believe it. There were cobwebs in every corner and the books were so dusty, too, like they hadn't been touched in a century. Then a black cat jumped out at me from the shelves and scratched me. So the next time you can't go, I'll skip it and wait until you can."

"Don't worry. I'll be there next time." Turning his attention to the road, he shifted the truck into drive and pulled out, making a sharp U-turn to head back to our town. "Did you talk to your parents? Do they know about your truck?"

"No, I couldn't. I didn't have any cell service up here."

Xander glanced at me curiously. "Then why were you up by the road? I just figured you were waiting for someone to come get you."

"I didn't know what else to do. The only option I had was to flag down the next car. I'm just glad you came along when you did," I explained with a smile, hoping he wouldn't ask any more questions about how I ended up there.

"Yeah. Me, too."

"So I guess we'll have to get a tow truck up here if it ever stops raining," I mused.

"I can take care of that for you. I've got some chains at home. I should be able to pull your Explorer up to the road with this truck as soon as it dries up a bit. If it was a little drier, I bet you could have gotten up the embankment in four-wheel drive. You do have four-wheel drive, don't you?"

"Yes. That was the first thing I tried."

"Well, I think the rain is supposed to move out of here

tonight. If it dries out tomorrow, we should be able to come back to get it on Saturday."

"That would be great. Thanks."

"No problem. I'm glad I can help. I feel partially responsible since I was supposed to drive this afternoon." He tossed another smile my way before returning his attention to the road as he carefully guided the truck around the hairpin turns at a safe speed. "Can I buy you dinner this evening? Make it up to you?"

I sighed, dreading his reaction to what I was about to tell him. "Actually, I'm meeting Noah for pizza. Can you drop me off at Mike's in town?"

Xander's expression darkened, yet he remained calm. "Sure."

He frowned, focusing on the road as silence fell between us, and we rode the rest of the way to town without talking. I leaned my head against the seat, wishing he would say something, anything, to distract my thoughts away from the wolves and the stranger. But he didn't. The only sound was that of rain pounding on the roof of the truck and the windshield wipers moving up and down.

When we pulled into town just before seven o'clock, a misty drizzle was all that remained of the rain. As we passed the shops, bed and breakfast inns, and local bank, I flipped the sun visor down to use the mirror.

"You look beautiful," Xander said quickly while I tucked a few stray strands of hair behind my ear and wiped at the mascara smudged beneath my eyes. My hair had stayed mostly dry, and I didn't look nearly as haggard as I felt.

I snapped the visor back into place as Xander parked the truck in front of Mike's Pizza Shop. "You're too kind," I said, unbuckling my seat belt and tugging on the door handle.

"Hey, not so fast. Do you want me to walk you in just to make sure he's here?"

I had already spotted Noah's sedan among the cars lined up next to the sidewalk under the streetlights. "No. His car is here, so I'll be fine. Thanks again for the ride."

My eyes meeting his icy gaze, I flashed him a grateful smile before hopping out of the truck.

As I pushed the heavy door shut with all my strength, I barely heard Xander's last words. "Don't forget your book bag."

I ran through the mist to the other side of the truck to grab my book bag before heading down the sidewalk to the pizza shop. Xander's truck roared behind me for a moment while he throttled past me. Then the engine noise faded to a soft whisper and the red tail lights disappeared in the distance. My thoughts shifting to Noah, I hurried into the pizza shop, the familiar chime of the bell hanging from the inside door handle announcing my arrival. My eyes adjusted to the bright lights in the dining area as I scanned the randomly seated guests. Roughly half the tables were vacant, and yet the buzz of chatter rang out through the restaurant.

Within a few seconds, I saw Noah wearing blue jeans and an untucked beige shirt rise to his feet at a table in the back corner. Our eyes met, and I recognized the concern in his expression at once. He rushed toward me as I crossed the dining area to meet him halfway. Without a word, he raised his hand to my chin and gently kissed me. When he lifted his lips from mine, a warm glow rushed through me, and I momentarily forgot about being chased by the wolves.

"I'm sorry I'm late," I murmured.

"What happened? I was starting to get really worried. Come on, let's sit down." He took my hand in his, leading me to the corner table he had claimed while waiting for me. Two sodas, one half empty, sat upon the red and white checked tablecloth. "I ordered you a Diet Coke, but the ice may have melted a little."

"Thanks." I peeled off my stiff raincoat and hung it on the back of a chair. It had dried on the ride back to town but now glistened with a film of moisture from the mist. After dropping my book bag on the floor by my feet, I sat down across from Noah and sipped my drink. "I had an accident," I explained, toying with the straw in my soda.

"What kind of accident?" Noah asked. "Laken, I don't like the sound of this."

My gaze shifted to the tablecloth. "I slid off the road somewhere between here and Littleton," I said with a deep sigh. "The Explorer's stuck in the mud. Xander came along right after it happened and gave me a ride."

"What? How did that happen?"

"An animal ran out in front of me. Another wolf," I admitted, glancing up at him.

"Another one?" Noah asked, his jaw gaping open.

"Yeah. This one was white, so it isn't the same one I saw at the bonfire."

Noah frowned. "This is becoming a big problem. I'm starting to wonder if we should tell your father."

"No!" I gasped, surprised he would even suggest it. "Right now, I seem to be the only one who has seen them. He'll either think I'm crazy or he'll put me on lockdown and I won't be allowed out of his sight unless someone is with me." I paused, looking at Noah as an unsettled thought crossed my mind. "You don't think I'm crazy, do you? You believe me, right?"

"Of course I believe you," Noah replied. "I heard at least one of them last weekend. There's no doubt in my mind something's going on out there. But like you said, as far as we know, you're the only one who has seen them."

Fear crept up my spine as his words sank in. It would be one thing if other people had reported sightings of wolves roaming the woods, but the wolves had seemed to have singled me out. I was sure it had something to do with the stranger, but I didn't want to worry Noah by telling him about the man I had seen up by the road tonight. He would certainly tell my father, and I wasn't sure I was ready for that. Besides, then I'd have to I explain how I'd gotten away, and I couldn't tell him a moose charged out of the woods to protect me. "So what do we do?"

Noah leaned back in his chair and folded his arms across his chest. "I don't know, but I sure wish I did. Until tonight, you've been safe. It's a good thing Xander came along when he did, but next time you might not be so lucky."

I nodded. "I don't think I'm going to drive outside town again, at least not until things settle down. And I'm definitely not going back to that library alone."

"That's a start, but it's not a long-term solution." Noah sighed, lifting his eyes away from me as Mike's full-time waitress, Katy, approached. In her forties, she kept her long reddish-brown hair secured in a ponytail, her brown eyes warm and welcoming. Smiling, she pulled a notepad and pen out of her apron.

My stomach growled at the thought of food and I realized I was pretty hungry after using so much energy to escape from the wolves. We ordered a medium pizza, only resuming our conversation after Katy left. "I feel like a sitting duck," I admitted. "And there's nothing I can do about it. This all started when Ryder was taken. Do you think there's a connection?"

Noah shook his head. "There's no way to know. But speaking of Ryder, I have some news about the guy who took him. That's why I wanted to meet you tonight." He smiled sheepishly. "Well, it's one of the many reasons I wanted to see you tonight."

My heart swelled from his comment. It was nice to know he had been looking for an excuse to see me again. "What did you find out?"

"The FBI has been working this case and they found out that our guy received a pretty big bank deposit the week before Ryder was taken. Ten thousand dollars."

"What? I thought people stole kids to hold them for ransom. How could the money have something to do with Ryder?"

"They don't know. They're trying to find out if he had any other deals going at the time. The money could be completely unrelated to Ryder unless—" His voice trailed off.

"Unless what?" I asked, curious to know where he was going with this.

"Unless someone paid him to take Ryder."

"Why would anyone do that? That's crazy." I paused thoughtfully. "Of course, so are a bunch of wolves roaming New Hampshire that seem to only appear when I'm alone. What else is the FBI doing? Are they following up on the money to see if they can find out where it came from?"

"Yes, but they're notoriously slow. Since Ryder was found safe and the guy died, it's not high up on their list of priorities. It may be a while before we learn anything else."

I shuddered at the memory of Ryder's abduction. It wasn't that long ago that I felt completely safe in these mountains. Now I couldn't go anywhere alone. Not for a hike in the woods or to the library in a neighboring town. We even locked our doors now, a first for me. My world was crumbling at my feet, and I didn't know how to stop it.

Noah reached across the table to grasp my hand. "It's going to be okay, I promise."

I met his gaze and smiled weakly. "I hope so."

The pizza arrived a few minutes later, and we dug into it while Noah changed the subject, asking about my classes and the plans for homecoming weekend. I couldn't have been more grateful to have something other than my accident to talk about.

After dinner, he drove me home through the misty rain. When we pulled into my driveway, the lights in the windows shone like bright beacons in the dark, but that didn't stop a feeling of dread from washing over me. My parents would be waiting inside, and I would have to tell them the Explorer was stuck in a muddy ditch halfway between here and Littleton. The only problem was that I couldn't tell them about the wolves. I'd have to blame my accident on something else like a moose, and I hated lying to them.

Shifting into park, Noah turned to me with the motor running. "Would you like me to walk you to the door?"

"Yes, always. But I'm going to take a rain check for tonight. My parents are probably waiting for me and I just want to get this over with."

"Okay. But the next time I bring you home, I'm walking you to the door like a proper gentleman. And I'm not taking no for an answer."

Smiling, I unbuckled my seat belt and released the strap over my stiff raincoat. As soon as I was free to move, I leaned toward him. "Good. When will that be?"

"Saturday night? If you're free, that is."

"I am. Maybe we can pick up where we left off last Saturday night before we were so rudely interrupted."

"Be careful what you wish for," was all he said before kissing me. When Noah pulled away, he grinned. "For the record, I'm just glad you're okay tonight. I don't like hiding all of this from your dad."

"I know. Neither do I. But I know he'll overreact." I gazed at him, meeting the concern lurking deep within his eyes. Without looking away, I placed my hand on the door, poised to open it. "Call me?"

He nodded. "I will. Good luck with your parents tonight."

"Thanks." I shot him a faint smile before reaching for my book bag on the floor by my feet. Then I pushed the door open and slid out of the car. Waving, I crossed through the headlight beams on my way to the sidewalk. When I reached the front door, I paused, darting a quick look across the lawn into the darkness and wondering if the man who had been with the wolves a few hours ago was nearby. A chill racing down my spine, I realized I would never know.

Trying to push the memory of him out of my thoughts, I reached into my pocket for my keys. I unlocked the door, hoping my parents were home because the last thing I wanted was to be alone. Even though I dreaded telling them about the accident, dealing with that would be a walk in the park after what I'd been through tonight.

Chapter 2

The next morning, bright sunshine amidst a deep blue sky greeted me when I opened the curtains after climbing out of bed. Sometime during the night, the rain had cleared out just as the forecast had predicted. The trees, now entrenched in their transformation to yellow, orange, and red, glistened with leftover beads of rain.

The clear sky helped me put the memory of the dark rainy road from last night behind me. At least my parents had remained calm when I had told them about my accident. As planned, I blamed it on a moose in the road. I hated that I couldn't tell them the truth, but the fewer people who knew about the wolves, the better. My father had frowned at the thought of the Explorer left up in the mountains and assured me he'd check on it today. He knew a local tow truck driver who might be able to pull it up to the road if the ground was dry enough. If not, then it would have to wait another day.

Still wearing my pajamas, I turned away from the

window. Dakota barely moved from his bed, his black fur looking like a dark shadow on the fleece cover. He sighed as I straightened the comforter, extending his legs and gently scraping his nails on the wooden floor. Once I finished stacking my pillows against the headboard, I walked across the room to my closet. I studied my jeans folded over the hangers, suddenly bored with them. Then I scanned my meager selection of rarely worn skirts and settled on a purple one. As I pulled it out of the closet and laid it on my bed, I paused, scolding myself. *A skirt for school? You almost never wear skirts to school. You're just dressing like this today because Xander's giving you a ride this morning.* He had texted me after I arrived home last night and offered to pick me up this morning. In spite of how we had left things when he dropped me off at the pizza shop, I accepted without hesitation.

I studied the skirt which happened to be the shortest one I owned and made my legs seem even longer than they really were. Before I could make a final decision, I sensed a pair of judgmental eyes watching me. I glanced at Dakota who now sat up, his gaze locked on me. "Don't look at me like that. I can dress up a little if I want to. Besides, Noah might stop by after school and I want to look my best." I knew it was a weak excuse, but I wasn't trying to convince Dakota, I was trying to convince myself.

"Screw it," I said quietly. "I'm going to wear what I want to wear, and I don't care what you—" meaning me, "—and you—" I shot a glare at Dakota. "—think about it."

Twenty minutes later, dressed in my purple skirt, a black sweater, and black boots, I clamored down the wooden stairs, my keys in one hand and my book bag in the other. My hair hung loose, wispy strands hiding the silver earrings I had chosen to wear with the diamond necklace my father had recently given me for my birthday.

The kitchen was still and quiet since my mother had already left for school. As I poured coffee into a silver thermos, I heard the unmistakable rumble of Xander's truck in the driveway. I rushed to the refrigerator to grab some creamer, not surprised when Dakota stormed down the stairs and charged into the kitchen. The hair on his back was ruffled upward, a deep growl rolling out of his chest. He scrambled to keep his balance, the tile floor slippery like ice against his nails as he turned the corner and made a mad dash into the entry hall.

Ignoring him, I plucked a granola bar from the pantry and my black leather jacket from the coat closet. Then I hurried back into the kitchen to gather my book bag, coffee, and keys before running to the front door.

I was about to rush outside when I noticed Dakota in the family room, standing at the edge of the window where he poked his nose around the sheer curtain. He quietly stared outside, the hair on his back now lying flat and his head tilted to the side.

"Make up your mind, Dakota," I said with a chuckle before slipping out the front door.

Sometimes, I truly wished I could read that wolf's mind like he could read mine. Smiling to myself over Dakota's change of heart, I pulled the door shut behind me and locked it.

I turned and started down the sidewalk, pulling my jacket tight against me in the cool morning air. Before I reached the driveway, I stopped when I saw Ethan jogging across the front lawn. As usual, he wore jeans and a denim jacket over a T-shirt. His book bag was slung over his shoulder and his thick dark hair swept across his forehead. He glanced at me, a curious look in his eyes as he approached with a spring in his step.

"What's going on here?" he asked, halting beside the sidewalk as the truck engine shut off.

"Hi. I didn't have a chance to call you last night. I kind of got the Explorer stuck in a ditch on my way home from the library. It's about halfway between here and Littleton right now."

Ethan smiled faintly. "Way to go," he teased. Then his grin faded. "Seriously, though, are you okay? What happened?"

"It's a long story, but yes, I'm fine. Xander was on his way to the library when he found me and gave me a ride back to town. He offered to drive us to school today since I obviously don't have any wheels." I squinted up at Ethan, nearly blinded by the bright sun peeking over the distant treetops behind him. Out of the corner of my eye, I noticed the truck door open before Xander climbed down from the driver's seat wearing black jeans, a tight gray shirt, and dark sunglasses. I felt his stare on me, causing butterflies to dance in my stomach when his sexy blue eyes flashed through my mind.

"Good morning," he said.

"Hey, Xander," Ethan called. "Thanks for giving us a ride. It sucks about her truck, but I guess those things happen."

"No problem. Go ahead and hop in. The door's open."

Ethan nodded at him. After shooting me a knowing look, his eyebrows raised, he approached the truck and jumped into the back seat. Ignoring him, I nervously fumbled with my coffee thermos as I walked toward the truck. Stopping short when I nearly ran into Xander who stood in my way, I slowly looked up at him, surprised to see he had removed his sunglasses. Our eyes met, and I noticed an all too familiar intensity in his expression. "Good morning," I said shyly, feeling awkward.

"You look really nice today," he complimented. "You

should wear skirts more often." A wide grin broke out across his face. "On the other hand, it's awfully distracting. I may not be able to concentrate today, so maybe you should go back to jeans next week. You just look— very—tempting."

I felt my face heat up and took a deep breath. "I'll take that as a compliment. Thank you." I started to walk around him, but stopped when we were shoulder to shoulder and tilted my head up to flash him a teasing smile. "You look nice today, too. I'm sure Marlena will be pleased." I raised my eyebrows at him before walking away.

After a few seconds of silence in which I knew I'd caught him off guard, I heard his quick footsteps as he jogged around the truck to catch up to me. He passed me before opening the heavy door to the front passenger seat. Turning around, he blocked me again. "Hey, listen, about that—"

"You don't have to explain. It's none of my business."

"Then why'd you bring it up? Are you jealous?"

"Don't flatter yourself," I scoffed indifferently. The fact was, I *was* jealous, and the only time I seemed to forget about him lately was when I was with Noah.

His arrogant grin fading, his eyes softened. "I'm just trying to figure you out, that's all."

"Then I'll make it very easy. All I want right now is to get to school on time," I stated quietly. "So it would make me very happy if you would move out of my way so I can get in the truck."

He nodded and stepped aside without a single word, his eyes meeting mine for a moment. When I tore my gaze away from him to look at the truck, my confidence faltered. Getting in and out of his monstrous pick-up was quite easy in work-out pants and jeans. But I hadn't considered how I would get into it when I had decided to wear a skirt this morning.

As I hesitated, Xander laughed softly. "Would you like some help?"

I shot him a glance, expecting to see arrogance written across his face. To my surprise, he smiled warmly.

"Yes, that would be great," I replied.

I slid my keys into my pocket and tossed my book bag onto the floor. With the coffee thermos in my left hand, I reached for his palm with my right one. His touch was strong and warm, sending a tingle up my arm. Focusing on keeping my balance rather than my fluttering heart, I gripped him firmly. With his support, I managed to climb into the truck, painfully aware that a single misstep would send me falling backward into him. I couldn't afford another close call with him. His every touch, every look, hypnotized me, making me forget Noah and everything else around me.

When I plunked down on the seat, Xander shut the door as soon as he released my hand. I closed my eyes, fighting to find my composure and my sanity. When I opened my eyes with a deep sigh, I remembered Ethan in the back seat. Sipping my coffee, I glanced into the rearview mirror to see him practically drooling over the truck.

As Xander climbed into the driver's seat, Ethan poked his head between the two front seats. "Wow, man. This is a really cool truck. How long have you had it?" he asked.

Xander slid the key into the ignition and fired up the engine. He smiled across the cab at me, catching my eye for a moment, before buckling his seat belt and shifting into reverse. "A couple weeks," he replied, backing the truck out of the driveway. "We bought it after we moved up here to get around in the snow and ice. We didn't need anything like this back in California."

"How do you like it so far?" Ethan asked.

"It's awesome. I can't wait to see how it handles in a snowstorm." As Xander rambled on about the truck, I tuned him out and buckled my seat belt. Then I spent the entire ride to school fidgeting in my seat, wishing I could pull my skirt down to my knees when it rose several inches up my thighs. Every so often I caught Xander looking at me from behind his sunglasses. Each time, I turned my attention back to the window, pretending the trees we passed were much more interesting than his stolen glances.

We pulled into the school parking lot with fifteen minutes to spare before the homeroom bell would ring. Eager to find Brooke, Ethan said a quick thank you to Xander for the ride and hopped out of the truck. He hurried around to my side as I unbuckled my seat belt and opened the door. "I'm going to catch up with Brooke. Does she know about your accident?"

"No," I confessed. The truth was I'd been too shaken up last night to call either one of them. Going over the events of the night with my parents had been enough. "I didn't have a chance to tell her."

"Great. Then I'll have to. You know she's going to lecture you, right?"

I rolled my eyes. "Yes. Will you please tell her everything is fine and make sure she doesn't worry about me? I just don't want to talk about it anymore today."

Ethan smiled. "I'll try, but you know Brooke. She's very protective."

"I know," I said, a pang of guilt for not telling her whipping through me.

"Well, I'll do my best." Ethan inched his book bag strap toward his neck. "See you in homeroom."

"Okay."

I flashed him a grateful smile and watched him disappear between the cars and trucks on his way to the school. Then, hoping no one was watching, I grasped the door handle and contemplated the running board. I hesitated for a moment, my coffee thermos still in my other hand. Just as I realized getting out of the truck in this skirt was no easier than getting in, Xander appeared. He took one look at me and silently extended his hand. Letting go of the door to take it, I lost my balance. The thermos fell out of my grasp, hitting the pavement with a loud clanking noise while I reached both hands out to him. He grabbed my waist, steadying me as soon as my feet touched the pavement. Instinctively, I reached up to grab his arms, not letting go right away.

My heart nearly skipped a beat from the feel of his strong hands circling my waist. He anchored me against his chest for a moment even though I stood firmly in place. Embarrassed, I looked up at him, wishing he hadn't removed his sunglasses because his eyes mesmerized me, sending my senses into a whirlwind.

"Thank you," I muttered. "I don't know what I was thinking when I decided to wear this skirt today."

He gazed down at me, his eyes smoldering. "Me, neither. But for the record, I'm glad you did."

Confusion muddling my thoughts, I wondered if he was about to kiss me and I tore my gaze away from his. Shaking my head, I pulled away from him and looked down at the asphalt, searching for my thermos until I saw it tucked against the rear tire. Without hesitating, I rushed toward the back of the truck, grateful to get away from Xander.

A cool breeze swept across the parking lot, taming the heat Xander sparked inside me. It felt refreshing as I bent down to pick up my coffee, or at least what was left of it. After standing up, I started to head toward the front of the truck to retrieve my book bag, but I didn't get very far. I stopped dead in my tracks when I saw Marlena approaching Xander while he reached into the truck for my book bag. As always, she looked stunning in tight jeans, tall boots, and a black leather jacket over a matching sweater. Her long blonde hair swayed as she walked, her cold blue eyes glaring at me. I frowned, hoping she hadn't seen me fall against Xander in my botched attempt to get out of the truck.

Her narrowed eyes remained on me as she sauntered up behind Xander, throwing her arms around him. She leaned in toward him, resting her chest against his back. Finally taking her gaze off me, she gently nibbled his earlobe. "Guess who?" she whispered in a seductive voice.

Jealousy ripped through me when Xander smiled. He dropped the strap of my book bag without lifting it and spun around. Then he kissed her passionately, possessively, as if I wasn't standing less than ten feet away. When he lifted his mouth from hers, he grinned at her. "Good morning, gorgeous."

A wave of nausea shot through me and I silently chided myself for caring. There was nothing real about the way he looked at me if he could turn around and flash Marlena the same sexy smile seconds later.

I desperately wanted to disappear, but I still needed to get my book bag. I cleared my throat loud enough to get their attention, causing Xander to pry his eyes away from her. Mustering my courage, I put one foot in front of the other until I closed the gap between the three of us.

"If I can just get my bag, I'll leave you two alone," I said, stopping in front of them.

"Sure. Of course," Xander replied.

Draping an arm over Marlena's shoulders, he grabbed my book bag with the other one and handed it to me.

I snatched it from him, meeting his gaze for a moment. I thought I recognized an apologetic glimmer in the blue depths of his eyes, but my alter ego ruined that fantasy at once. *Stop imagining things!* I scolded myself. *He's not sorry for kissing Marlena in front of you and he shouldn't be. He only went out with her after you turned him down for the dance. So don't act like he should still be chasing after you.*

In spite of my rational thoughts, I shot him a quick look of disappointment before turning away. Then I rushed across the parking lot to the school, fighting back the tears that welled up in my eyes.

දංද

I kept my distance from Xander that day, dreading the afternoon ride home with him. During lunch, I received a text from Noah, reminding me about our date Saturday night, and the confusion Xander caused all but disappeared. My earlier jealously of Marlena gone, anticipation of seeing Noah again filled my thoughts for the rest of the day.

The ride home that afternoon was far less eventful than the morning disaster even though Ethan took off with another friend, leaving me on my own with Xander. I managed to get in and out of the truck with a quick hand from him, keeping my balance this time before rushing away after a brief thank you in the driveway.

As soon as I got up the next morning, I dressed in faded blue jeans and a gray sweatshirt. I secured my hair up in a ponytail and slipped it through the back hole of a navy baseball hat. After tying the laces of my hiking boots, I grabbed my keys, sunglasses, and phone, then hurried downstairs to the kitchen to wait for Xander who had promised to pull my truck out of the ditch. My father had driven up to it yesterday, but the ground had been too soggy from the rain to pull it up to the road.

I was about to make a beeline for the coffee on the counter when Dakota trotted through the kitchen, passing my parents who lounged at the table with their newspapers and coffee. Without a single glance their way, he disappeared through the doorway leading to the entry hall. Curious, the coffee forgotten, I left the kitchen and found him parked in the family room at the corner of the window, his nose poking around the edge of the curtain as he stared outside. I shrugged, feeling as though I'd stepped back in time since Dakota had assumed the same position just yesterday morning when Xander had shown up. As odd as it seemed, I dismissed his interest in Xander and returned to the kitchen to grab some breakfast while I still had time.

Looking up from his newspaper, my father shifted sideways in his chair while I poured myself a cup of coffee. "Is Xander on his way?" he asked.

After adding a dash of creamer, I leaned against the counter, my hands circling the warm mug. "Yes. He should be here any minute."

He pursed his lips together for a moment. "Do you think he knows what he's doing?"

"You mean pulling the truck out of the mud?"

My father nodded.

"I suppose so. His truck is huge, so it must be strong enough to get the Explorer back up to the road." Somehow, I couldn't imagine Xander offering to do something he wasn't completely sure he could handle.

"Okay," my father said, sounding unconvinced. "But if it doesn't work, call me and I'll have Sam go get it with his tow truck."

"Thanks, Dad." Leaving my coffee on the counter, I walked across the kitchen to the pantry and grabbed a breakfast bar. Before I could rip it open, Dakota whined from the other room. Seconds later, the familiar rumble of Xander's truck echoed through the house. He was early, just like the morning he'd picked me up to go hiking. "I hear him, Dakota. Bye, Mom. Bye, Dad," I said, grabbing my things before rushing to the front door. When I reached for the handle, Dakota circled me, his tail wagging and an eager look on his face.

"What's gotten into you?" I asked, shoving my loose items into my pockets so I could stroke the fur between his ears. He glanced up at me, then stared at the door knob. "Oh, no," I said with a chuckle. "You're not going anywhere. I'm not about to let Xander know about you. The less people who know, the better."

He shifted his gaze to me, his amber eyes solemn, before charging back into the family room, supposedly to watch out the window. I shook my head, surprised at his reaction to Xander. Dakota generally didn't like or trust people he didn't know. His initial reaction to strangers was usually a warning growl with the hair along his spine standing straight up. He had always stayed up in my room or disappeared into the woods behind our house when company arrived. But I got the distinct feeling it was different with Xander. Dakota seemed to like something about him. Of all people, Xander was the last one I expected Dakota to like and trust right from the start.

Shrugging off Dakota's odd behavior, I slipped out the front door into the morning sunshine. I slid my sunglasses on, noticing that the maple tree in our front yard had completed its transformation to red. The mountains in the distance rippled with color, mostly shades of orange and yellow. A crisp chill lingered in the air, and I wondered if I should run back into the house to grab a jacket. But as I followed the sidewalk out of the shadows and into the light, I realized that wouldn't be necessary. The morning sun promised warmer temperatures were on the way.

I hurried over to the truck waiting in the driveway, the

engine rumbling. Xander remained in the cab, tapping the steering wheel to the beat of music that echoed from within.

I was both relieved and disappointed when he didn't get out to help me. Fortunately, I really didn't need help as long as I was wearing jeans and hiking boots. After pulling the door open, I climbed up into the passenger seat beside him while he shut off the music.

After closing the door, I buckled my seat belt before turning to him. "Hi. Thanks again for helping out with this."

He looked at me, his eyes hidden behind his sunglasses. He wore an open black shirt over a matching tank top, the shark tooth pendant hanging above the neckline. "No problem. It's the least I can do since I never made it up to the library," he replied, his voice low and raspy. Then he reached for the coffee thermos in the cup holder and took a swallow.

"Tired? Late night with Marlena?" I asked before I could stop myself.

He flashed a subtle smile. "I thought you didn't care about that."

"I—I don't," I shot back. "I'm just making conversation."

He shook his head with a grin and put the thermos down, about to shift into reverse when a knock tapped on the window. He rested his right hand on the gear shift, and we both turned our attention to the side to see my father's bearded face. Xander immediately rolled down his window. "Good morning, sir," he said in a voice that lacked the fatigue from seconds ago.

"Good morning, son. I thought I'd introduce myself before you headed out. You're Xander Payne?"

"Yes, sir."

"I hear your father bought the big place up on Glacier Drive."

"That's right."

"Tell him to stop by sometime and introduce himself. This is a small town and I like knowing the residents. It helps in my line of work."

Xander nodded. "I'll pass along the message, but I can't make any promises. My father likes to keep to himself."

"That's no big deal. We have plenty of folks around here who like their privacy." My father scanned the truck with approval. "This is quite a rig you've got. You sure you're going to be able to get the Explorer out?"

"I think so," Xander answered with confidence. "I've got some heavy duty chains and the transmission in this truck is about as strong as they come."

My father nodded in agreement. "Yeah. You can't go wrong with a Dodge Ram. It's a beauty. I see you've already got your snow tires." He paused thoughtfully before continuing. "You should be fine today, but, if you can't get the Explorer out, I've already told Laken I can arrange for a tow truck to head up there."

"Thank you, sir."

"No problem. It was nice meeting you, Xander. Next time, don't be a stranger. You're welcome to come in for a few minutes."

"I'll remember that. It was nice meeting you, too, sir."

Without another word, my father turned away from the truck and headed for the house. Xander rolled up his window before shifting into reverse.

"Your father seems nice," he commented as he backed the truck toward the road. "I wasn't sure what to expect from the town sheriff. He seems reasonable."

"Of course he is," I scoffed. "What did you expect?"

After looking both directions, Xander swung the truck

into the road and then guided it forward along the curves cutting through the woods. "Let's just say I'm not used to police officers who are nice. The ones I knew in California were mostly guys who just wanted to carry guns and push people around."

"It sounds like you're speaking from experience." I raised my eyebrows, wondering how I could get him to tell me more about his past.

He kept his eyes glued to the road. Gripping the steering wheel with one hand, he reached for his coffee with the other. "A little."

I opened my cereal bar, searching for the right way to ask more about him. Before I could come up with a question that didn't sound nosy, he returned his coffee to the cup holder between our seats and promptly changed the subject. "What do you say we try to hit that library again this week?"

A chill raced down my spine as the creepy library, suspicious librarian, and graveyard across the street flashed through my thoughts. In spite of it all, I had to admit I was eager to explore the books I had found from the Underground Railroad era, as long as I wasn't alone. "Sure. But I am not driving up there alone again, so you can't bail this time."

He flashed a quick grin my way. "I won't, I promise."

From that point, we wound our way through the mountains, talking mostly about the History assignment and other classwork. I was grateful the conversation didn't stray to more unpleasant topics, such as what had happened to cause me to lose control of the Explorer—or, even worse, Marlena.

We arrived at the site of my accident in about thirty minutes. The road and woods looked far less threatening in the daylight than they had in the dark rain. The Explorer remained exactly where I had left it, facing into the

woods down the short, steep embankment. Bright sunshine greeted us when we hopped out of the truck onto
the shoulder of the road.

Several cars whizzed by, the license plates from Mas-
sachusetts, Connecticut, and New Jersey, to name a few
states, indicating that the autumn leaf-peeping season had
begun.

As a shiny black SUV breezed past me, I shimmied
along the side of the truck to meet Xander at the back. He
now wore only the tank top, his tanned muscles gleaming
in the sunlight while he dropped the tailgate. He reached
into the bed and pulled two heavy chains to the edge before turning to me, his blue eyes no longer hidden behind
his sunglasses. "I'm going to need you to get into the Explorer and put it in reverse when I tell you to. Just let me
get set up first."

I nodded. "Okay. Can I help with anything?"

"Nope. I've got it." He studied the distance from the
Explorer to the back of the truck which was parked as
close as it could get without rolling down the embankment. After pulling one of the chains out of the truck,
Xander let it fall to the ground. Bending down, he attached it underneath the tailgate. I found it impossible to
pay any attention to how he was setting things up since I
was too busy admiring his arms and shoulders. Somehow,
everything about him, from his piercing eyes to the dag-
ger tattoo branded on his arm, still mesmerized me.

Xander dragged both chains to the back of the Explorer and connected them, the center section falling to the
ground. Then he strolled back up the hill and approached
me, a sheen of sweat glistening on his skin. "Ready?" he
asked.

"I guess. How hard do you think this will be?"

He shrugged. "Not sure. I think I can get you up the
hill. The ground has dried out a lot, but it's still a little

soft. First, let me pull out to tighten the slack in the chains. I need you to watch and let me know when to stop."

I carefully stepped over each chain as he led me a few feet down the embankment. "Just raise your hand when I need to stop. I'll never hear you if you yell. Okay?"

I met his questioning gaze and nodded. "I think I can handle that."

"Good." He whipped around and walked back up the hill to his truck. After he climbed into the driver's seat, the truck roared to life. The chains rose slowly in the middle as he eased the truck forward. When they were almost straight, I raised my hand and he stopped. He left the engine running, jumped out of the truck, and hurried down the hill to inspect them. "Perfect." He looked at me. "Now it's time for the fun part. I need you to get in the Explorer, turn on the engine, and put it in reverse."

"That doesn't sound too hard."

"Well, it's probably going to feel a little weird when it starts to move. But it should only take a minute or so to get you back up to the shoulder."

"Okay. Do I need to give it any gas?"

"Maybe a little. Just make sure your foot is off the brake."

"Got it." Jingling my keys, I hopped over the chains and headed for the Explorer, eager to get it out of the ditch. Then I could head back to town and away from Xander. All I wanted was to focus on my date with Noah tonight, and every second I spent with Xander this morning would make it that much more difficult to forget him.

As soon as I hopped in the Explorer, I turned on the engine and rolled down my window. Then I shifted into reverse and eased my foot off the brake just as he had instructed before motioning a thumb's up signal out the window.

The pick-up roared as Xander started to pull the Explorer up the hill. The chains caught almost immediately, and the Explorer lurched backward. Xander was right. It felt very strange to be moving, but not controlling it. Within seconds, the Explorer bumped onto the shoulder of the road and leveled out.

Xander returned to my door as I put the truck in park.

"Wow. That was fast," I said.

A satisfied grin slithered over his lips. "Piece of cake. How did it feel?"

"Weird, just like you said. But it's a huge relief to get it out of there."

"I'm sure it is. Well, wait here for a minute. I just need to unhook the chains."

After he disappeared from my window, I stepped out of the Explorer onto the dirt shoulder. Looking down the embankment, I saw deep tire ruts carved into the hill where I had tried to back up that night. I shivered at the memory of being stuck down there in the cold, dark rain and wondered how I would have gotten home if Xander hadn't come along when he did. Not to mention what would have happened if the man and the wolves had returned.

Pushing the horror of that night out of my mind, I walked to the back of the Explorer as Xander stood up from unhooking the chains. "You're all set. You can take off now. I'll finish up here."

I looked at him, noticing that his eyes were almost transparent in the blinding sunlight. "Thanks. I really appreciate this."

He shrugged. "It's nothing."

"No, it's not. I owe you one."

In a flash, he leaned toward me, trapping me between his arms as he pressed his hands against the Explorer. "Then have dinner with me."

"What, like a date?" I asked in surprise.

He smiled eagerly, the look in his eyes daring me to accept his invitation. "Yes."

"What would Marlena think if she knew you were asking me out right now?"

"I don't care."

"Well, I do. She and her friends almost clobbered me once because of Noah, and now, thanks to you, she's completely forgotten about him. I'm not about to rock that boat."

"And if she wasn't in the picture?"

I nervously glanced down at the dirt. "If you must know, I have a date with Noah tonight. So my answer hasn't changed. Why do you keep pushing this?"

Xander dropped his arms to his sides, stepped back, and took a deep breath. "I like you, that's why. And I don't like it when I can't have what I want. I'm not going to give up. I can be very persistent."

"You think?" I asked sarcastically.

He chuckled. "You haven't seen anything yet."

Shaking his head, he turned and headed back to his truck while a car buzzed by on the other side of the Explorer. After its hum faded in the distance, I heard the clanking of chains being dragged along the ground. Resisting the urge to tell Xander one more time that I wouldn't change my mind, I returned to the driver's seat of the Explorer, eager to return home and spend the rest of the day dreaming about my date with Noah.

Chapter 3

Noah picked me up at seven o'clock that evening. When I heard the doorbell ring from upstairs in my bedroom, I grabbed my purse packed with my keys, phone, and lip gloss, then raced down the stairs before passing my parents in the kitchen.

"I've got to go. I'll be home by midnight," I muttered, hoping they wouldn't drill me with questions.

Fortunately, they didn't call me back into the kitchen or follow me to the door to ask about my evening plans. They knew I would be with Noah, and that seemed good enough for them.

I hurried to the front door and slipped outside, grateful to escape without another embarrassing farewell from them like the night Noah and I had gone on our first date. As soon as I shut the door behind me, I relaxed and smiled at Noah.

He looked particularly handsome in blue jeans and a white button-down shirt. Behind him, the falling sun cast purple streaks across the sky. The temperature had dropped considerably, the warmth from earlier in the day now gone.

Noah hadn't told me where we were going, but at my insistence, he had at least explained it would be casual and suggested I wear jeans. I followed his lead, choosing a burgundy sweater with a folding neckline to go with them. A short double-stranded silver necklace and teardrop earrings partially hidden by my loose blonde curls completed my look tonight.

"Hi," I said, a little out of breath after racing through the house. "Just one minute. Let me lock up."

I turned, twisting the key in the door before dropping it into my purse. Locking our doors had become second nature lately, but at this moment, I did it more to keep my parents inside than to keep anyone out. The last thing I wanted was for them to step outside as Noah and I were leaving.

I turned back to him, took a deep breath, and looked into his soft brown eyes. "Okay. I'm ready."

"Good. You look beautiful," he said, reaching an arm out around my waist and pulling me toward him in a swift movement.

I reached my arms up around his shoulders as he leaned in to kiss me. His lips grazed mine, and I closed my eyes, my senses lost between the taste of him and the spicy scent of his aftershave. He pulled me closer, one hand moving up my back and the other one sliding lower until his palm rested on the back pocket of my jeans. A few moments later, he lifted his head with a guilty smile and released his hold on me.

"Sorry," he said. "I think that's what I'm supposed to do when I drop you off after our date, not when I pick you up. What can I say?" He paused, leaning toward me. "You're irresistible," he whispered in my ear.

His breath blew softly when he spoke, making my

heart flutter, a warm glow spreading over me before reality set in. At this rate, we'd never leave my doorstep. As much as I would have loved to stay in his arms for hours, my stomach grumbled and I reminded myself that my parents were just inside the front door. "So are you," I replied with a smile as he lifted his head. "But my parents are home right now, so maybe we should get going."

A serious expression crossed over his face as he seemed to realize his boss could walk outside at any moment. "Say no more. I'm going to have to be a little more careful. You're dangerous, did you know that?"

I laughed softly. "I've never been called that before."

Smiling, Noah took my hand and led me down the sidewalk to his car. After walking me around to the passenger side, he opened the door like a true gentleman. I settled into the seat, buckling my seat belt as I waited for him. He hopped in on the other side, secured his seat belt, and started the car.

"Where are we going?" I asked.

"Laconia," he said, backing out of the driveway before pulling onto the road, the headlights shining in the twilight shadows.

"Laconia? That's forty-five minutes away. What's in Laconia?"

"First of all, it's well out of my jurisdiction which means there's nothing I can do if a couple drunk kids come in, stirring up trouble. And secondly, I found a pretty cool place down there when I first moved here. A band plays every Saturday night. They're really good. I think you'll like them."

"Hmm, dinner and music with no interruptions. That's definitely worth the drive." I grinned, pleasantly surprised at his plans for the evening. If I had any luck at all, there would be a dance floor and I wouldn't have to wait until homecoming next weekend to dance with him.

"Have you been to Laconia?" he asked.

I nodded. "A few times when I was younger. It's a lake town and insanely crowded with tourists all summer. Us locals try to stay away."

"Yeah. It was pretty crazy when I was down there last month. I hope it's a little less crowded now that summer is over."

"Oh, I don't know. The fall tourists seem to be around this weekend. I went to get the Explorer today and there was a lot of out of town traffic."

"That's right. I forgot you were going back there today. Everything go okay?"

I hesitated, remembering Xander's attempt to get me to go out with him again. But I knew Noah really only meant getting the Explorer. He had no idea how my feelings for Xander tortured me, and I had no intention of ever letting him find out. "Yes. Xander pulled it up to the road with his truck. I think he felt guilty for bailing on our first trip to the library."

Noah raised his eyebrows, briefly glancing at me before focusing his eyes back on the road. "He should feel guilty. If he'd been with you, you never would have ended up stranded all alone. I still don't like to think about what could have happened. Did he tell you why he didn't show up?"

"Yes. He said the alarm at his house went off. He went home to help his dad look for what triggered it, but they didn't find anything."

"Hmm. It seems kind of odd that they have an alarm system to begin with. There doesn't seem to be a lot of crime up here, at least not usually. And so far, I haven't been called out to any break-ins."

"That's what I thought. It does seem weird, doesn't it? I didn't think to ask my dad if you guys got called up to their house when it went off. Did you?"

"No," Noah replied, shaking his head, his lips pursed together as he focused on the road. "Unless your dad took the call and didn't tell me."

"That's odd. Aren't most alarms set up to contact the police when they go off?" It was more of a rhetorical question than one I expected him to answer. "But it's really none of my business." I shrugged, not wanting to talk about Xander, his father, and their unexplained paranoia. "So what's good to eat at this place you're taking me to?" I asked, deliberately changing the subject.

Noah took the hint. "Just about everything. Burgers, sandwiches, appetizers, and even pizza."

"Sounds great. I'm starving."

Noah turned onto the highway and we cruised south for about a half hour. I pointed out various towns and landmarks we passed on our way, practically feeling like a tour guide by the time he pulled into a gravel parking lot in front of a log building. A bright neon sign at the top center read *Blue Moon Restaurant and Bar*.

Noah found a parking space under a street lamp next to a few motorcycles, and I released my seat belt as he shut off the engine. "Those are some pretty tough looking motorcycles. Is this a biker bar?"

It wouldn't have surprised me if it was. Laconia held Harley Davidson rallies from time to time and was a popular biker town.

"Not that I've been to many biker bars, but no, it's not. You're going to like it here, trust me."

Noah stepped out of the car, immediately coming around to my side. After he opened the door, he extended his hand down to me. Taking it, I stood up and scanned the parking lot as a leather-clad stocky man with a scruffy gray beard rode past us on his rumbling Harley.

Noah shut the door while I watched the man park his bike, swing his leg over the seat, and saunter toward the double-door entrance. I hesitated beside Noah's car, wondering if everyone inside the restaurant looked as rough as this guy.

Noah turned to face me while I leaned against the car. "Are you okay?"

"Yes," I said a little too quickly. "Are you sure this place won't be full of a bunch of tattooed bikers?"

Noah smiled and stepped toward me, resting his hands against the top of the car on each side of me. "After what you've been through with those wolves roaming the woods, I'd think a few bikers would be the last thing to scare you. There's nothing to worry about. No one's going to bother you."

"Yeah. I guess you're right. It's silly to worry about this." Even as I relaxed, a vision of the man in the woods and the wolves chasing me flashed through my mind. *No. No, no, no,* I thought. *You're not going to let them ruin tonight. So stop thinking about that and focus on Noah and having a good time.* I looked up at Noah, trying to smile. "Shall we go in?"

"Um, now I'm not sure," he murmured, moving closer to me and twirling a finger in my hair. "I kind of like being with you out here."

I swallowed nervously, noticing the heat simmering in his eyes. "Well, I'm hungry, so maybe we can go get a table."

"Not so fast. I just want to enjoy the moment."

I choked out a smile, trying to lighten the mood. "What? Outside in the parking lot?" Gazing at him, I was surprised that his expression displayed a mixture of guilt and disappointment. Reaching up, I gently touched his neck. He flinched, his gaze shifting away from me, and I dropped my hand back to my side. "What is it?" I asked.

Noah looked at me, an unmistakable longing in his eyes. "When I moved here, I never thought I'd meet someone like you. You have no idea what you're doing to me."

"No, I don't. Maybe you should tell me," I whispered as another loud motorcycle rumbled by, breaking the tension between us.

Noah's head shot up and he backed away from me. "Sorry about that," he said when the motorcycle engine's noise faded across the parking lot. It cut off, sending the dimly lit parking lot into silence. He held his hand out to me. "You're right. Let's get some food."

I took a deep breath and reached for him. Hand in hand, we walked across the parking lot to the front door.

Noah broke away from me to hold it open before I walked into the restaurant. Inside, a bar lined one of the cedar log walls. Stained glass decorations and beer plaques hung on the walls. Dining tables were scattered around an open floor space facing a small stage. A group of guys in T-shirts and jeans, several with tattoos, were setting up instruments and microphones on the stage. A few men at the bar wore leather jackets with bright silver zippers, and one in a leather vest had tattoos inked up and down his arms.

The other guests seated at the tables were mostly couples, young and old, waiting for the band to start as they ate dinner and sipped their drinks.

An older man with a gray beard wearing jeans and a blue plaid shirt greeted us from behind a podium. "Two for dinner?"

"Yes," Noah answered.

"Okay." He grabbed a few menus. "Right this way."

We followed him through the restaurant to a table for two in the corner near the edge of the stage. As we sat down, he handed the menus to us.

"Enjoy your dinner," he said before heading back to the entrance.

I smiled at Noah, the flickering flame of the single candle in the center of the table reflecting in his brown eyes. "This looks pretty nice. I'm glad you brought me here," I assured him.

We studied the menus for a few minutes, only raising our eyes when a brunette in jeans, a tight white shirt, and dangling gold earrings appeared beside our table. She pulled a pencil and notepad out of her back pocket, sighing tiredly while she studied us. "Either of you two have IDs?"

I glanced at Noah before looking up at her. "I'm just having a Diet Coke."

"And iced tea for me," Noah told her.

She smiled at him, interest shining in her brown eyes. "You sure you don't want a beer or somethin' a little stronger?"

He paused, considering her suggestion. Temptation flashed through his eyes before he answered, "No, thank you. Just iced tea. We've got a long drive home."

Sighing with relief, I watched her walk across the restaurant to the bar. "That was interesting. She must be wondering what you're doing here with me."

Noah shrugged, then grinned. "Don't be silly. Besides, you could easily pass for twenty-one."

"Really? Only twenty-one?" I asked with mock disappointment.

"Okay, maybe twenty-two. But don't tell your dad I said that. He'd probably kill me."

My smile fading, I looked across the table at him. "You don't have to worry about that. I don't tell my dad anything you say—or do, for that matter. In fact, I really don't see him much now that school started."

Before he could comment, the waitress returned with our drinks. Then we placed our orders and handed the menus to her.

After she left our table, I sipped my soda while the musicians started testing the sound system with an occasional guitar chord and drum beat.

"Are you looking forward to homecoming next weekend?" Noah asked, setting his iced tea down.

"Yes, but only because I'm going with you."

"That can't be completely true. Don't girls like to get dressed up no matter who they're with?"

I raised my eyebrows. "Maybe some girls, but not me. Dances aren't really my thing."

"Yeah? What is your thing? Raising wild animals?"

"What?" I gasped, nearly choking on my soda. "Why do you say that?" I suddenly wondered how much he knew about me. He couldn't know, could he?

"Dakota?" Noah said. "Remember him?"

Relief washed over me. Of course, he was only thinking about Dakota. "Yes. I guess I don't really think of him as wild." The other wolves from the rainy night, on the other hand, were definitely wild.

"So back to the dance. Do you have a dress?"

"No, not yet. I'm going shopping with my mom and Brooke tomorrow. Why?"

"I just wanted to know what color it is so I can get you a corsage to match."

"Then I'll have to let you know what I find."

Noah laughed softly. "I can't believe I'm going to a high school dance."

"Why? Is it uncool?" I teased with a grin.

"No, not at all. I'm really excited to take you. In fact, I'm sure it will be a lot better than my last high school dance."

"Really? You mean you weren't a popular jock who dated the prettiest girl at school?"

"Hardly," he scoffed. "I had some issues at home with my mom, so I kept to myself most of the time. I think I went to two, maybe three dances while I was in high school. I missed out on a lot of things most kids take for granted."

A wistful look swept across his face, and I realized how much I still didn't know about him. "Well, now you get to be the coolest guy at the dance," I told him.

"Yeah, right. Oldest maybe, but I'm not so sure about cool. Those kids I hauled down to the station a few weeks ago probably won't be too excited to see me."

"They're a bunch of jerks, anyway," I said, remembering how they harassed me in the hall just days after Noah busted them at the bar. As tempted as I was to tell him all about that, I chose not to. No good would come from dredging up their threats, especially since that's all they were. "I don't care about them. But I'll be the envy of every girl there because I'll be with you."

Noah leaned across the table toward me. "Now you're just trying to make me feel better about my sorry high school days."

I smiled at him, meeting his warm eyes. "Nope. I'm just being honest."

Our food arrived just then, a cheeseburger for him and a veggie burger for me, both plates piled high with French fries on the side. We ate in silence as the band began to play a country song with a catchy tune.

By the time we finished our burgers, a crowd had gathered on the floor. The only open seats were those left by guests who had gotten up to dance. Half-empty glasses cluttered the tables and jackets hung on the backs of chairs. The band was led by a dark-haired guy with a thick beard, an earring, and a cross tattoo on his upper arm. Listening to the music, I realized this was the closest Noah and I had come to having a normal date that wasn't interrupted by two drunk boys or a wolf and a stalker in the woods.

Don't get your hopes up. The night isn't over yet, a sarcastic voice rolled out in my head before I shoved it away, refusing to let my fears ruin the night.

When the music slowed to a ballad, the lights dimmed. The crowd coupled up, and those left alone wandered back to their seats. Noah stood up and stepped to the side of the table, holding his hand out to me. "May I have this dance?"

I nearly knocked my chair over behind me as I rose to my feet and took his hand. "Of course." As soon as his fingers wrapped around mine, he swept me onto the dance floor and into his arms. I leaned against him, savoring this moment with his chest pressed against mine and his arms wrapped around me. One of his hands rested on the small of my back while the other slid up higher until his fingers grazed my neck, pushing a stray lock of hair behind me. Resting my cheek against his shoulder, my face inches from the collar of his shirt, I closed my eyes, wishing the song would never end. I felt safe in his arms. Safe from the wolves and the stranger...

I whipped my eyes open, silently scolding myself for letting my thoughts ruin this perfect moment, and took a deep breath to settle my nerves.

Noah stiffened, looking down at me. "Are you okay?"

"I've never been better," I whispered with a smile. "So far, this is our best date yet. You're still here, and I doubt any strange wolves will come after me in here."

"I guess the third time's a charm."

Sensing him relax a little, I sighed and leaned my cheek back against his soft shirt.

We stayed at the restaurant and bar for a few more hours, dancing to all the slow songs and even a few of the faster ones, despite my inept attempts to keep up with the rhythm. When it came to dancing, I had two left feet. But I managed to get through the night with only stepping on his feet twice. Around eleven o'clock, I started to feel drained. When I let a yawn slip out, Noah paid the check and ushered me out to the car, insisting we leave in time to get back to my house by midnight.

On the way home, the full moon darted in and out of view from behind the mountains and trees. I leaned back against the seat, the music echoing in my mind. Smiling, I remembered being in Noah's arms for each song and how his warm embrace made me feel as though I had escaped into my dreams.

As the car sped along the highway, I felt myself being lulled into a light sleep. Growing stiff in the seat, I shifted to my side, facing Noah's direction and resting my cheek on the headrest. I sighed when I felt him reach over to touch my hand where it rested on my thigh. Briefly opening my eyes, I saw shadows dance across his face before drifting back to sleep.

After what seemed like only a few minutes, the car jerked to a stop. Still groggy, I waited for it to move again. Instead, I heard Noah's soft voice when he touched my shoulder. "Laken, wake up. We're home."

I opened my eyes to see the familiar shadows of my house in front of me. A single light shone from behind the sheer white curtain in the family room window, and shadows stretched across the front yard, making the sidewalk barely visible. "Hmm," I said. "What time is it?"

"Five minutes to midnight."

"Good. Then I'll get up in five minutes." I let out a contented sigh, hoping he knew I was only teasing.

"No way. I'm bound to get extra points with your parents if I get you home early. Come on, I'll walk you to the door." Without giving me a chance to object, he hopped out of the car.

"Brown-noser," I joked.

Reluctantly raising my head, I unbuckled my seat belt and started to get out just as Noah approached, offering his hand to me. My purse in one hand, I reached for him with the other and stood up. After shutting the door behind me, he walked me to the house. The chilly night air nipped at me through my clothes, a bitter wake-up call compared to the warm car.

"Do you think your parents are still up?"

"I doubt it. It's pretty late, and I don't think they're particularly worried about me because I'm with you."

A devilish grin lit up Noah's handsome face. "They should be," was all he said before cupping my chin in his free hand and pressing his lips against mine. His fingers traced a line along my jawbone until they wandered behind my neck and played with my hair. I melted against him, responding to his kiss with slightly parted lips. After a fleeting moment, Noah pulled away. "I'd better let you get inside."

I nodded as he dropped my hand. "Okay. I am pretty tired."

"At least one of us is. I think I'll take a cold shower when I get home."

I suddenly imagined him in the shower, beads of water rolling down the curves of his muscles.

Damn, girl! Looks like he's not the only one who needs a cold shower tonight, I thought, hoping he couldn't see the blush setting fire to my cheeks. "Good night, then," I said with a deep sigh. "Thank you for a wonderful evening."

"You're welcome. Why don't you get inside? I want to make sure you're behind locked doors before I leave."

I nodded, fumbling around in my purse until I found my keys. Then I unlocked the door, opening it with a single click. Stepping inside, I turned, hoping for one last kiss, but Noah had backed several feet away, seeming eager to be on his way. I caught his eye and waved.

"Good night, Laken. Call me tomorrow after you get a dress for the dance. I want to hear about it."

"I will," I promised.

After one last glance his way, I gently shut the door behind me and locked it. A smile permanently etched on my face, I crept through the quiet house. Aside from the family room, the rest of the house was swallowed up by darkness.

I tiptoed up the stairs and down the hallway to my room where Dakota greeted me with a gentle nudge and a wagging tail. I gave him a quick scratch between the ears before heading straight for my bedside table to turn on the lamp. As Dakota sank onto his bed, I wandered back to my dresser on the other side of the room. I took off my necklace and earrings, gently placing them on the wood surface. Then I backed up to the edge of the bed and sat down, lifting my feet to yank my boots off.

As I pulled the second one off, Dakota jumped to his feet and charged out of my room with an eager whine. *What in the world?* I wondered, rushing after him, my socks slippery on the hard wood floor. I flew down the stairs, my right hand clinging to the railing for support while I thought I heard Dakota whimpering at the front door. Before I reached the bottom, a pounding sound drowned out his whining. It wasn't until I crossed through the kitchen to the entry hall that I realized someone was banging on the front door. My eyes narrowed suspiciously, I ran to it and flipped on the outdoor light. My pulse raced with fear as I peeked out the peephole, not sure I even wanted to know who was on our doorstep at midnight.

My heart nearly fell into my stomach when I saw Xander waiting anxiously on the doorstep.

Shaking my head in disbelief, I flung the door open.

"What are you doing here? Do you have any idea what time it is?" I whispered angrily.

Xander stared at me, his eyes dark in the dim light and his black jacket blending into the midnight shadows behind him. "I could ask you the same question."

I huffed, about to scold him for his blatant lack of common decency when Dakota wormed his way past me and lunged at Xander. Standing up on his hind legs, he threw his paws up against Xander's shoulders.

"Dakota! Down," I ordered as quietly as I could.

He pushed off of Xander, dropping his front end to the ground.

Shocked, I snapped my gaze back to Xander. "I'm so sorry about that. He usually doesn't react to strangers like this. I don't know what's gotten into him."

The surprise in Xander's eyes faded to a look of awe. "It's okay." He knelt to the ground and rubbed Dakota's chin. Dakota nuzzled him, planting a sloppy wet kiss on his ear. Xander wiped at his ear, a huge grin forming on his face. "At least one of you likes me. Who is this? Is he a—"

"Wolf? Yes. And his name is Dakota."

Xander rose to his feet and studied me, a curious expression in his eyes. "Wow. He's really cool. How come you never told me about him?"

"Why would I tell you about him? Hardly anyone knows about him, so I'd really appreciate it if you kept this quiet."

"Of course. I won't tell a soul."

"Thanks. Because if this gets out, he could be taken from me," I said gravely.

"I wouldn't want that to happen."

"Good. Neither do I." I paused, my irritation at his unannounced midnight visit returning. "Why are you here? I didn't even hear your truck."

"I parked down the street so I wouldn't wake up your parents."

I laughed sarcastically. "You didn't think banging on the door would wake them up?"

He ignored my question. "I just wanted to make sure you got home safely."

Frustrated, I let out a loud huff. "I told you I was going out with Noah. He's a cop for Christ's sake. How much safer could I be?" I asked between clenched teeth.

"Being a cop doesn't mean a damn to me."

"Well, it does to me," I said. "At least it's a hell of a lot better than you sneaking around here in the middle of the night."

He drew in a sharp breath. "I suppose that's how you would see things."

"How long were you waiting out there?" I asked, cringing when I imagined him watching me with Noah. Maybe he really had been in the woods behind my house the night Noah brought the pizza over. And maybe he had also been with the wolves in the pouring rain.

"As long as I needed to."

I huffed again. "Are you keeping tabs on me?"

"Can you blame me after Thursday night? I'm worried about you. You should be thanking me."

"It's not your job to look out for me. I can take care of myself." I looked him square in the eyes. "If you follow me one more time, I'll have my father put a restraining order on you faster than you can blink. So stop with this insane nonsense and leave me alone."

Without waiting for him to respond, I spun on my heels and rushed back inside the house. I desperately wanted to slam the door in his face, but instead I shut it quietly. After clicking the lock into place, I turned, leaning my back against the door. Then I dropped to my knees and studied Dakota's amber eyes, my nerves still on edge. I hated to admit it, but as each day passed, I grew increasingly suspicious that Xander had something to do with the wolves and the man in the woods. I had no idea how he was connected to them, but I hoped the truth would be revealed before it was too late.

Chapter 4

I rolled out of bed the next morning around ten
o'clock at Dakota's insistence. He had started nudging my arm with his nose ever since the sun had
edged up over the horizon, but it wasn't until he licked
my ear that I slid out from under the comforter. Without
changing out of my red flannel pajamas, I pushed my
bare feet into a pair of slippers and wandered down the
stairs. Dakota trotted behind me, seeming eager to escape
the confining bedroom. Still sleepy, I padded across the
empty kitchen and opened the back door.

I followed Dakota outside, pulling the door shut behind me. Cold air nipped at my ankles as I folded my
arms across my chest and walked across the patio, watching Dakota stroll through the wet grass before stopping to
relieve himself. Reaching the edge, I stood, not wanting
to sit on the steps or one of the chairs that dripped with
the same morning dew covering the yard.

I stifled a yawn and admired the blue sky and trees
shimmering with yellow, orange, and red hues. Another

picture perfect New England fall day was upon us, one where everything seemed right at the moment. It was hard to believe that anything sinister had passed through the woods behind our house. The figure from the night Noah had brought the pizza over flashed through my mind for a moment. As I frowned at the memory, Dakota lifted his dew-covered nose from the grass. He paused halfway between the patio and the edge of the forest, scowling at me as if scolding me for my dark thoughts.

I sighed, knowing he was right. I should be thinking about what was good in my life, like last night with Noah and the homecoming dance, instead of worrying about a stranger who hopefully wouldn't dare show up in broad daylight.

Just as I started to relax, the leaves on the forest floor rustled in the distance and my heart jumped while I looked at the woods in the direction of the noise. Dakota focused his attention in the same direction, his low growl barely audible over the breeze whipping through the trees. *Oh no,* I thought with dread. *Not again, and not on such a beautiful morning. What is it now? The wolves or the stalker?* I gulped in fear, unsettled once again as the rustling sound grew louder.

I stared beyond the trees, searching for any movement. My pulse quickening, I contemplated running back to the house, but before I turned around, a deer weaving through the woods caught my eye. Sunlight filtered down through the thick canopy overhead, casting a dust-filled ray diagonally between the trees. The deer leaped through it, charging ahead like a frightened gazelle running for its life from a predator. Dakota's keen eyes honed in on it, and he watched it for a moment, his body as still as a statue.

As I expected, Dakota couldn't resist the chase. He shot across the yard, his powerful legs propelling him forward in long strides. Within seconds, he disappeared.

I wanted to call after him, but I didn't. I knew better than to think he'd give up the thrill of chasing a deer to return. *Just stay safe, Dakota,* I thought. *I don't need to lose you now after everything that's happened.* I only hoped he would return safely before the sun set tonight. With a deep sigh, I walked across the patio and returned to the house.

After working on a little homework that morning, my mother took me and Brooke shopping for our homecoming dresses. We browsed in store after store for hours, finally finding dresses that matched our styles and price ranges. Brooke chose a short black dress while I bought a floor-length burgundy gown with a slit that reached just above my knee on one side.

When I returned home that evening, I hung the plastic-covered dress in my closet. After tucking the box containing new sparkling shoes on my cluttered closet shelf, I slipped out of my sneakers, my feet aching from the afternoon of nonstop walking.

As I pulled my socks off, I spied the stack of textbooks on my desk. Frowning at the long night of homework ahead of me starting with an English essay due in the morning, I sighed. I was too wound up from shopping and the anticipation of the dance to start my homework just yet.

Then I spotted Dakota's empty bed while the gray sky darkened outside the window over my desk. I longed to have him home, but I also knew how much he craved the freedom of the mountains. It didn't surprise me that he was still out, and I reminded myself that he might not return before I went to bed. In fact, it could be several days before he returned, and there was nothing I could do to change that.

Pushing Dakota out of my thoughts, I reminded myself that I had homework to do. But before committing to any of my assignments for the rest of the night, I grabbed my phone and marched over to the bed. Propping myself up against the pillows, I switched on the bedside lamp. I had promised to call Noah once I had a dress for the dance, and calling Noah ranked much higher than my homework.

I found his number in my call log and tapped on it. The other end rang five times before dumping into his voice mail. Sighing with disappointment, I left him a message. "Hi, Noah, it's Laken. I was just calling you like I promised. We had a great time shopping today and I got a dress for the dance. But I really wanted to let you know that I had fun last night." I paused, hoping I sounded light and carefree. "Anyway, call me back if you can. I'll be up pretty late doing homework. Talk to you soon." After hanging up, I stared at the dark screen for a few minutes, hoping he would call back right away.

When I realized that wasn't going to happen, I glanced at my textbooks. Reluctantly, I slid off the bed and walked the few steps to my desk. Then I sank into the wooden chair and opened my English notebook. Determined to keep Noah and Dakota far from my thoughts, I picked up a pencil, prepared to finish the homework I had put off all weekend.

ᘔᘓᘔ

Noah never returned my call that night, but Dakota came home safely. Although Dakota's presence comforted me, I wondered all night why Noah hadn't called me back. I barely managed to finish my homework including the assignments due the next day as insecurities rolled around in my head. *Maybe he's having second thoughts. Maybe he's decided I'm too young for him and now he's changed his mind. Maybe he's going to break our date for the homecoming dance.* My eyes clouded over with tears several times, and I vigorously wiped them away so I could continue working. If only clearing the doubts from my mind was as easy.

The next day, my classes came as a welcome distraction. Between second and third period, I returned to my locker, the chattering students swarming in the hallway drowning out my thoughts of Noah. I shoved my Calculus book on the shelf, grabbed my Physics book, and shoved it into my bag.

Out of the corner of my eye, I saw Brooke emerge from the crowded hall, her red hair bristling against her black turtleneck sweater and her long skirt swaying around her boots. She grinned, her blue eyes full of suspicion as she stopped beside my locker. "Laken, honey, did you forget to tell me something yesterday?"

I turned my attention to her as I slid my book bag strap over my shoulder. "Maybe," I said with a lingering smile. "Why?"

"Ethan told me you had a late night visitor on Saturday."

"Oh yeah, that," I mused. On the way to school this morning, I had confided in Ethan about Xander's surprise visit Saturday night, curious to know what Ethan thought. He'd agreed that it was odd but, at the same time, he brushed it off like it wasn't a big deal.

Brooke drummed her fingers on the book bag at her hip. "Why didn't you tell me about this yesterday?"

"What? With my mom around? She doesn't know. Neither of my parents do, and I'd like to keep it that way. Not to mention that I was really just trying to forget about it. I don't know what to think about him." I shook my head, my smile fading.

"You don't? I think it's pretty obvious. He's totally

hot and, clearly, he has a thing for you. He can show up on my doorstep anytime." Brooke paused, scanning up and down the crowded hallway. "I probably shouldn't say that too loudly. We don't want Marlena to hear any of this."

I rolled my eyes at that thought. "That's all I need right now. This is just creeping me out. He's so weird. One day, he's a perfect gentleman, and the next, he's acting like some stalker."

She wrinkled her eyebrows. "Yeah, I guess that is kind of creepy. But maybe he's just worried about you." Even as she defended him, she didn't seem convinced that his intentions were innocent.

"He shouldn't be. My father is the sheriff and Noah is his deputy. Could I be any safer? I'm telling you, I don't buy it. And now I have to do this History project with him, so I can't avoid him."

"Well, maybe it was a one-time thing. Or maybe, he's so obsessed with you that he can't stop thinking about you, and the very thought of you out with Noah was driving him crazy," Brooke teased, lightening the mood.

She grinned, and I couldn't help smiling. "I wish he would just forget about me," I said, knowing I didn't really want that. "I would have thought Marlena would have him kissing the ground she walks on by now."

"I don't know about that," Brooke said skeptically. "He doesn't strike me as the type who lets a girl, even a girl as beautiful as Marlena, turn him into a lovesick puppy."

"Yeah, maybe you're right. Because if he was, he probably would have been with her Saturday instead of watching my house all night. Oh, and guess what? There's more."

"More? Okay, spit it out. You're killing me with all these secrets."

"Xander met Dakota Saturday night."

"Oh, no. What happened? Did Xander live to tell about it?"

"Actually, yes. Dakota loves him. He was jumping all over him and giving him kisses. Even Friday and Saturday morning, he whined at the window when Xander picked me up. It's really weird. I don't get it. He usually hates strangers. He's still a little leery of Noah."

"Hmm." Brooke pursed her lips before breaking out into another smile. "Well, I guess you have your answer. Xander can't be all bad if Dakota likes him."

"Who does Dakota like?" Ethan asked as he appeared behind Brooke, gently resting his hand on her shoulder while he caught her last few words.

Brooke turned to him, a bright glow in her eyes. "Xander."

Ethan huffed in wonder. "Really? You're kidding. It took like a month for that wolf to trust me, and he likes Xander?" He paused thoughtfully. "Wait a minute, how did that happen? I thought you kept Dakota away from everyone except us," he said, leaning toward me, his worried brown eyes darting around us as though making sure no one was within earshot.

"Saturday night. Dakota pushed his way out the door before I could stop him when Xander showed up. And you're right, I don't want anyone knowing about him. I don't like this at all. What if someone turns us in for having a wolf? My dad would kill me," I said, frowning.

"I hardly think Xander's going to turn you in. Something tells me he's not the type to worry about bending the law. Didn't you tell us he stole a car?" Ethan asked.

I nodded, but Ethan's reminder didn't reassure me. "He might not turn me in, but he could use it against me," I mused.

"I doubt he'll do that," Brooke said. "Maybe you need

to give him a chance. I bet he's not that bad. You said yourself he has a nice side."

I shook my head. "I still don't trust him."

Ethan watched the students milling about the hallway before turning back to us. "He's headed this way. Do you want us to stay?"

I sighed, knowing I'd have to deal with him sooner or later. "No," I muttered reluctantly. "You guys go on. I'll see you in class in a few minutes."

"You sure?" Ethan asked skeptically. "'Cause you don't sound sure."

"Yes, I'm sure," I answered with a reassuring smile. I had handled Xander on my own several times when we were alone. Surely I could deal with him in a crowded hallway. "I'll be fine."

Brooke smiled. "You're telling us everything he says at lunch."

With that, she and Ethan turned and headed down the hall. As they disappeared into the crowd, Xander emerged, his eyes studying me. His gray shirt hugged his shoulders, the sleeves rolled up to his elbows and the bottom hanging untucked over his blue jeans. The lighter colors somehow made him seem less threatening and creepy, but certainly no less handsome.

He greeted me with a hesitant smile as he stopped inches away. "Good morning, Laken."

I backed up slowly until my shoulder blades touched the cold metal locker. "It was," I replied sarcastically, my eyes meeting his.

I glared at him, wishing he would take the hint and leave me alone. My heart pounding, I hoped I could resist any attempt he might make to apologize for scaring me Saturday night.

"So you're still mad at me," he mused.

"No," I said. "I'm not mad. Creeped out, confused,

and maybe even a little scared would be more like it."

He shook his head. "You've got it all wrong."

"Really?" I challenged him. "Because I seem to recall you watching my house until I came home Saturday night. Seems pretty creepy to me."

"I was making sure you got home safely. I saw a car pull into your driveway, but I couldn't be sure you made it into the house."

Heat raced across my cheeks as I remembered Noah's goodnight kiss outside my front door Saturday night. Just the idea of Xander watching us the whole time rattled my nerves, and I tried to push that thought out of my mind. So what if he saw Noah kissing me? Maybe he should get a good look at me when I was with Noah to see how happy I was. "Let me get something straight. Noah's a police officer. It doesn't get any safer than that."

"Like the time he left you at the restaurant in town?"

"There were extenuating circumstances beyond his control that night."

Xander shook his head. "I don't care if he's a police officer. That doesn't mean I trust him."

"I do. And frankly, I trust him more than I trust you."

A sly smile tugged at his mouth. "What about Dakota? Does he trust Noah? Because your wolf sure seemed to like me, even in the middle of the night when you'd think he'd attack anyone at your door."

I scanned the hallway to make sure no one was listening. Fortunately, students were filtering into the classrooms and the hall was starting to clear out. "What's that supposed to mean?"

"Wolves are smart and intuitive. Maybe you should pay closer attention to his signals. I mean, if *he* likes me, how bad can I be?" he smirked.

As much as I couldn't argue with Xander's rationale, I wasn't about to admit I agreed with him. "All I can say is that it's a good thing Dakota likes you. Without that, you'd have nothing, and I'd be asking Mr. Jacobs for a new History partner."

"About the project," Xander said, changing the subject. "Are you up for another trip to that library this week? I was thinking we could check it out Wednesday or Thursday after school."

I tried to think of an excuse to get out of it, but I came up empty. The last thing I wanted was to be alone with Xander in that dusty old library, but I didn't see that I had a choice. "Fine. Either day works for me. But you're driving, and if you can't go again, I am not going by myself."

"What happened last week shouldn't happen again. But if anything else comes up, we'll just go another time." He paused and slowly smiled. "So are we good now?"

My eyes meeting his, I deliberated my answer. I was willing to put his midnight visit to my house aside for now, but I wasn't ready to let it go altogether. "Only if you stay out of my relationship with Noah and, even then, it's going to take some time."

Xander leaned toward me, placing his hand against the locker beside my shoulder. "No problem. As I've said before, I have plenty of time. You'll realize the mistake you're making sooner or later."

His breath blew gently against my neck, and I trembled. I frowned, frustrated by both his persistence and the butterflies I felt every time he was near. I narrowed my eyes. "You're talking in code again. I don't know what that means. But mark my words, regardless of what happens with Noah, the one mistake I won't make is going out with you."

"Someday, you'll see how wrong you are." He pulled back, dropping his arm to his side. "See you in History."

Then he turned and walked down the half-empty hallway, leaving me flustered and frustrated. I shook my head as I watched his retreating figure, wondering how I would ever survive this History project.

Drawing in a deep breath, I shoved all thoughts of Xander to the back of my mind and focused on my next class. I was about to step away from my locker when Carrie approached, a warning look buried deep in her brown eyes. "Laken, you're looking a little cozy with Xander today," she said, her voice dripping with sarcasm.

I glared back at her. The last thing I wanted was to have to defend a conversation I'd been forced to have with someone I didn't even like. "If you must know, I'm stuck with him as my partner for the History project. I'm not exactly happy about it," I told her truthfully.

Her eyes narrowed in disbelief, Carrie stood blocking my way, her arms folded across her purple sweater. "Sure, you aren't."

"Whether you believe it or not, it's true. Why do you care, anyway?"

"I don't, really. But Marlena does. She told me to give you a message. Play with fire and you're bound to get burned."

"Why don't you tell Marlena to deliver her own messages?"

"Whatever." Carrie shrugged and unfolded her arms. Then she turned on her heels and strutted away, her mission complete.

With a frown, I shook my head. *Unbelievable! I don't want Xander's attention any more than I want Marlena's threats. Doesn't he realize the trouble he's causing? Why won't he just leave me alone?*

The bell rang out through the almost empty hallway, cutting through my thoughts. The few lingering students rushed into classrooms, leaving me alone. Huffing, I realized I was now late to my next class. Without another thought wasted on Xander or Marlena, I pressed my book bag against my hip and took off down the hall in a mad dash to class.

❧❧❧

The week dragged by slowly. As Monday became Tuesday, and Tuesday passed to Wednesday, Noah still hadn't called. Not a single message was left by him. Not one voice mail or even a quick text. I resisted the urge to call him again, assuring myself that he knew how to find me and he would do so when he was good and ready. But as the week wore on, my mood darkened with the suspicion that his feelings for me had changed since he'd brought me home Saturday night.

By Wednesday night, I finally gave up on my futile attempts to finish my Calculus homework. I dropped my pencil on the desk and pulled my jean-clad knees up against my chest. Resting my heels on the edge of the seat, I stared blankly at my open closet. The white plastic cover hung over my homecoming dress, but I could see the burgundy satin underneath. The thought that Noah would break our date for the dance caused a stray tear to roll down my cheek.

Dakota got up from his bed, his nails clicking on the wood floor as he approached me. He nudged my legs with his nose, his soft eyes appearing worried.

"Thanks, big boy," I whispered, wiping at the tear on my face.

I dropped my feet to the floor, letting Dakota rest his chin on my lap while I stroked the fur between his ears, wishing he could tell me Noah would call soon. But all I could do was enjoy his silent company and hope I would hear from Noah soon.

I tossed and turned that night. The midnight hours crept by, feeling like an eternity. By early morning, I felt tired and rundown, and I dreaded the day ahead. I was completely unprepared for my classes or another trip to the old library, this time with Xander. No good could possibly come out of today.

I managed to get through my classes with little consequences from skipping my homework the night before. When I finally exited the massive double doors of the school after the last class, I yawned. All I wanted after my sleepless night was a nap, and yet I had promised Xander that I would go to the library. Even the bright afternoon sunlight glinting off the side mirrors of the cars and trucks in the parking lot couldn't perk me up. I stopped at the edge of the sidewalk, oblivious to the other students who passed me on the way to their cars. As I waited for Xander, I aimlessly kicked at a pebble on the cement, my heavy book bag feeling like a ton of bricks because I'd had to pack a few extra books to catch up on the assignments I had skipped last night.

The sun was warm, but fall afternoon temperatures were tricky. Stand in the sunlight and I found myself peeling off my jacket, but the chilly shadows made that same jacket necessary. The denim jacket I wore over my black shirt was versatile enough for the fall weather and matched my blue jeans. My diamond necklace rested against my chest, the pendant cold to the touch. My hair fell over my shoulders, the golden ends shining in the sun.

When Xander finally walked out of the school, he wasn't alone. Marlena clung to his arm, her face glowing with a brilliant smile from something he said. Her dark skirt and sweater matched Xander's black shirt and pants, her light blonde hair seeming almost white against all that black.

My mood darkened as they approached. Marlena's smile faded, her icy blue eyes glowering at me. I ignored her, gazing with disappointment at Xander as I wondered why he had to drag her along to meet me. But I wasn't about to ask him what his purpose was. "I'm going to put some books in my truck before we leave. I'll meet you in the parking lot," I said.

Without waiting for an answer, I hurried away from them. Shaking my head and looking down at the pavement, I rushed between the cars and trucks. *He better not bring her with us to the library. That's all I need, to be with the happy couple when I don't even know if I still have a date for the dance.* A lump formed in my throat at that thought. Tears threatened to spill from my eyes, but I held them back.

I emerged from between two cars and stopped as a white SUV rolled past me. After it disappeared, I looked both ways before continuing across the lot. When the Explorer came into view, my jaw dropped at the sight of Noah standing beside it, watching me with a soft smile.

My heart swelled with relief and I couldn't stop a tear of happiness from escaping the corner of my eye. I wiped at it before he could notice as I walked toward him slowly, hesitantly. He smiled, his eyes appearing apologetic when I met his gaze. Even in his light blue deputy shirt, he looked gorgeous.

Swallowing nervously, I stopped in front of him. "Hi," I said quietly.

"Hi."

An awkward silence loomed between us, the voices and cars around us fading out as if the world stood still. Finally, I asked, "Where've you been? I was starting to wonder a bit."

"I'm sorry about that. Some things came up this week that I had to deal with. But everything's good now and I wanted to see you rather than call."

I desperately wanted to ask him what could have prevented him from making a quick phone call or sending an even quicker text, but I held back. "Are we still on for the dance this weekend?" I asked.

A reassuring smile softened his solemn expression. "Of course. I wouldn't miss it for the world. I hope you know I'd never let you down like that. You didn't think I was going to break our date, did you?" he asked incredulously.

I shrugged with uncertainty. "I didn't want to think so, but I wasn't sure. The thought crossed my mind."

"Well, you have nothing to worry about." He reached up to touch my neck under my hair before kissing me.

He gently brushed his lips against mine as he wrapped his other arm around my waist. My heart skipped a beat and all my nerve endings tingled. Longing to reach up around his shoulders and pull him to me, I hesitated, still a little unsure about him. He ran his hand down my arm until his fingers found mine, and I melted against him, savoring his touch and responding to his kiss.

A few moments later, he pulled away. I looked up at him, expecting to meet his gaze, but he wasn't looking at me. Instead, he stared beyond me, clearly focused on something else. "Looks like I have some competition," he whispered.

Curious, I whirled around to see Xander approaching. Sparks shot out from his eyes, and a scowl lingered on his face. This wouldn't be pleasant. "I don't think you two have met. Noah, this is Xander, my History partner. Xander, Noah, the town deputy."

They nodded at each other as Xander stopped a few feet away. "Laken, we should get going. So maybe you can wrap things up here."

"Okay. I'll be right there."

He glanced at his watch. "You said they close at six, right? We need to hurry."

"And I said I'll be right there," I repeated, my tone warning him to back off.

"I'll be waiting in the truck." Xander's icy blue eyes met mine before he whipped around and walked away.

"Hmm," Noah mused. "He seems nice."

I groaned. "He's extremely moody. It's exhausting."

I kept my explanation short. I could spend hours dwelling on Xander's unpredictable mood swings and endless attempts to get me to go out with him even while he was dating Marlena. But Xander was the last person I wanted to think about when I was with Noah.

"If I didn't know any better, I'd think he has a thing for you," Noah said. "I guess I'd better call or stop by more often. I don't want him stealing you away from me."

A smile tugged at my mouth. Maybe a little competition wasn't such a bad thing after all. "Good. So don't leave me waiting next time, okay?"

"I won't. Well, I'd better get back to the station." Noah lifted my hand to his lips and kissed it. "Where are you going with him?"

"Back up to the library in Littleton to work on our History project."

"Oh, that's right. The infamous project. Well, have fun and call me when you get home. I still want to hear about your dress."

I made a face at him when he told me to have fun. "First of all, fun is not exactly how I'd describe this project. And secondly, you call me. I should be home by seven."

Noah released my hand. "Seven o'clock, then. Make sure you have your phone with you." He flashed one last smile before heading back to his police car.

As I unzipped my book bag to get my keys, a smile lingered on my face. The dark cloud hovering over me for the last four days had finally vanished. A warm glow took its place as I realized my date with Noah for the dance was still on. My mood brightening, I opened the back door of the Explorer to dump my books on the seat before leaving for the library. After locking up, I headed across the parking lot, my sights set on Xander who waited beside his truck. Suddenly, an afternoon with him at the creepy library didn't seem so awful.

Chapter 5

I don't trust him." We hadn't even rolled out of the school parking lot before Xander started in on his anti-Noah speech.

"You pretty much said so Monday morning. Well, I didn't care then, and guess what? I still don't. *I* trust him, and my parents trust him. And that's all that matters." I leaned against the headrest of the roomy leather seat, admiring the red maple trees that lined the sidewalk while Xander pulled out onto the street. I avoided his glances darting my way as he appeared to steal every chance he had to gauge my expression. Instead, I studied the blue sky peeking out beyond the branches overhead.

"I wouldn't expect you to say anything different, at least at this point in time. But mark my words, I don't like him."

I huffed. "You don't even know him. He's a nice guy. I think he's a little lonely since he doesn't have any family around here."

Xander emphatically shook his head. "No, that's not it. There's something else wrong with this picture. I mean, how old is he? And he's dating a high school student? That's just weird."

I turned in my seat to face Xander, rolling my eyes at him. "Ouch," I said, insulted. "Now that was just mean."

"I didn't mean anything against you," he explained. "Of course not. Any guy would be a fool not to go out with you if given the chance," he said, staring straight ahead.

I looked away, feeling a blush fire across my cheeks while he continued. "I just meant it's a little odd that he's not going out with girls his own age."

"Okay, now I see exactly what you mean. Dating someone a few years younger, yes, that's a reason not to trust someone," I said, mocking him. I shook my head, frustrated. "Your argument is really weak. And I don't think we should keep talking about this. You're beginning to make me wonder if I'm going to have to keep you two separated at the dance on Saturday."

"Don't worry. I'll be civil to your date if you can be civil to mine."

I raised my eyebrows. "I think you have it backward. You should be asking Marlena if she can be civil to me," I muttered, remembering the warning Carrie had delivered to me on Monday.

He glanced at me, a frown consuming his smile while concern registered in his blue eyes. "Why? Is she bothering you again?"

"No," I lied. "I think she's forgotten that I exist since you swept her off her feet. It's actually been a big relief, so if I haven't thanked you for that lately, thank you."

Xander's smile returned. "You're welcome, then. At least I've done something right."

"I don't know if I'd call dating Marlena right, but it has served its purpose." I studied his profile as he focused on the road cutting through town. "So tell me, what's it like to date the most popular sought-after girl in school?"

Xander shrugged indifferently. "If you must know, it's kind of a drag. She may be easy on the eyes, but there's no depth. Skin-deep beauty doesn't do it for me. She has no heart, unlike you." He glanced at me, appearing interested in my reaction.

But I didn't give him one. Instead, I watched him with a blank stare, waiting for him to continue.

"You have a good heart. Your way with animals is very unique. It says a lot about you."

I looked away, staring back out the window at the reflection of red and orange leaves in the glass. "I don't know what you're talking about."

"Sure, you do. You have a wolf, Laken. Not just anyone can tame a wolf."

"He was born in captivity. He didn't know any different when I got him."

"Doesn't matter. He still has wild instincts. And you're a high school student, not some wolf expert who knows how to work with one. But you did it anyway, successfully I might add." He paused thoughtfully for a moment. "He's the stray dog that found the missing little boy, isn't he?"

I huffed, wondering if he really needed me to answer that. "What do you think? Of course he is. I'm surprised you had to ask."

Memories of that fateful night when Dakota and I had set out into the mountains to find Ryder came flooding back to me. It seemed like a lifetime ago, even though it had only been about six weeks.

"See. I knew it wasn't some random stray dog."

He flashed a smug grin, triggering my memory of the night at the bonfire when he'd challenged my story about finding Ryder.

I glanced at him, meeting his gaze for a moment before he returned his attention to the road ahead. "Does it really matter?" I asked.

He slowed the truck and turned onto the road that would take us to Littleton. "Yes, it does. I don't want any secrets between us."

"Well, now that you know mine, maybe you should tell me yours." I knew he was hiding something, but I held little hope that he would indulge me just yet.

"Okay, I'll tell you a secret if you promise not to tell a soul."

Rolling my eyes, I had a sneaking suspicion I was about to get a snide, sarcastic confession out of him about something I probably didn't even want to know. "Okay, I promise," I groaned.

"I'm only using Marlena for sex."

Damn! Sometimes I hated being right. I scowled, letting out a deep sigh. "Good for you," I said flatly. "But quite frankly, you're going to have to come up with something better than that if your secret's going to be even with my secret."

I hoped he bought my act as I pretended to be bored. Meanwhile, jealousy stirred deep within me as a vision of Xander and Marlena kissing earlier that afternoon flashed through my thoughts and I fought hard to push it away. *You have no right to be jealous!* I scolded myself. *Noah is taking you to the dance just like you wanted. It'll be perfect, as long as you stop caring about who Xander's with.* As I tried to convince myself, I looked back at Xander, wondering what his kisses and his touch felt like. A part of me admired Marlena's confidence. I could barely get past kissing Noah, and she had already taken it all the way with Xander.

Forcing myself to think about something else, I suddenly realized how tired I was from my sleepless night of tossing and turning.

"Am I boring you?" Xander asked.

"A little," I answered, watching the trees as he skillfully guided the truck up the mountain road. "I'm going to rest a little until we get there. Can we listen to some music?"

"Sure. But I'll need you to tell me where to go once we get to Littleton."

I nodded. "Just wake me up when we get there." I leaned back, closing my eyes while he turned on the radio and music filled the truck.

I must have dozed off because the next thing I heard was Xander's voice waking me up. "Laken," he said as I felt something tap my thigh.

When my eyes peeked open, I noticed his hand resting on my leg. I bolted upright, jerking away from him as if burned by his touch. "I'm awake."

Xander lifted his hand, holding it up in the air for a moment. "All right, chill. I didn't mean to scare you."

I flashed my eyes at him, meeting his calm, relaxed gaze. *Except that's all you ever do,* I thought, wanting so badly to say it out loud.

But I held my tongue and sighed, scanning the town we were passing through on our way to the library. Unlike last week when I had driven through the deserted rainy streets of Littleton, the town bustled with activity. Cars drove by, and pedestrians, including hordes of school children, made their way along the sidewalks.

"You didn't scare me," I finally replied, relieved to see him return his hand to the steering wheel. "I was just startled, that's all."

"Bad dream?"

"No. But once we get to the library, it's going to be like reliving a nightmare," I muttered.

"Why's that?"

"You'll see," I promised, my eyebrows raised. The

street we needed to turn onto came into view. "Slow down. You'll need to make the next right."

He slowed just in time to cut the corner, passing between two brick storefronts. Within a few blocks, the rows of businesses ended. Victorian homes sat back from the road behind perfectly manicured lawns surrounded by white picket fences. After passing them, we entered the woods and headed farther away from town. As soon as we reached the bend in the road where the trees disappeared on both sides, I recognized the library's gravel driveway across from the cemetery, but neither one seemed quite so haunting on a sunny day.

"There it is," I said, pointing to the opening between the picket fences with peeling white paint.

Xander eased the truck into the driveway and stopped beside the sign. "Littleton Library, Established 1825," he read. He swept his gaze out across the distance until it landed on the tiny library of white paint-chipped planks. "This is it?" His jaw dropping, it was the first time I'd seen him rendered speechless. After a long pause, he said, "You weren't kidding. It doesn't look like much."

I laughed softly. "You think it looks bad now? You should have seen it last week in the rain and fog."

He tore his eyes away from the dilapidated building and looked at me. "I can't imagine what you must have thought when you got here." Returning his attention to the driveway, he drove the short distance to the parking lot where he eased the truck to a stop under a tall yellow maple tree. A single car sat out front, the same one I had seen last week.

"I almost didn't even go in," I told him.

Xander shut off the engine. "Can't say I blame you."

We remained in our seats as a breeze blew through the tree above us, rippling a shadowy reflection of leaves across the windshield.

After a minute, I unlatched the seat belt and reached for my book bag at my feet. "Come on. I can't wait to introduce you to the world's friendliest librarian," I teased.

"Lovely," he muttered, unhooking his seat belt with his keys in hand.

I opened the door and climbed down from the truck, my boots grinding the gravel stones together beneath them. After shutting the door, I circled around the front of the truck to find Xander at the back door reaching for his bag. I stopped, waiting patiently for him to gather his things as I shifted my book bag strap higher up my shoulder.

A few seconds later, Xander pulled away from the back seat and shut the door, a black book bag in his hand. "I'm ready if you are."

I nodded. "Maybe we should come up with a plan before we go in. That librarian is really mean. She'll probably kick us out if we make a sound."

Xander smiled mischievously. "Then we'll just text each other."

I rolled my eyes. "That seems a little inconvenient."

"Don't worry. This will be fun. I love ruffling feathers." Trouble brewed in his clear blue eyes.

"I'm so glad you find this amusing. I knew I never should have brought you here. Please behave."

"Why? Sometimes it's a lot more fun not to behave. Oh, I know what we should do. Let's get caught making out between the bookshelves. Now that'll really drive her nuts."

I sighed, shaking my head at him. "In your dreams. Well, come on, let's get this over with. And no messing around!" As I turned on my heels and headed toward the library, Xander's footsteps echoed on the stones behind me.

When he reached my side, he casually draped his arm around my shoulders. "Figures you'd take all the fun out of this."

I wiggled out from under him, silently cursing the unwelcome tingle rushing through me. "Are you going to be serious at all? Do I have to remind you we're here to get some work done?"

"I know that. I'm just trying to get you to lighten up, that's all."

"Well, save it for Marlena."

As I reached the front steps to the library, a feeling of dread overwhelmed me. Remembering the librarian's stern stare, I wondered what she'd think of Xander.

Fortunately, Xander ceased his constant teasing while we made our way up the wooden steps. I tossed him a knowing look, my eyebrows raised, before pulling the front door open. The musty smell of old, leather-bound books greeted us inside the library's entrance. The front desk was empty, as were the rows of cluttered bookshelves extending behind it. My relief lasted only a moment before I heard the teetering footsteps of the librarian's rubber-soled black shoes. She ambled into sight from one of the aisles and stopped at her perch behind the front desk.

Leaning her elbows on the counter, she looked over the top of her glasses at us. I stood still, almost afraid to breathe until her black cat leaped up onto the counter, startling me.

"You," she spat out, suspiciously eyeing Xander at my side. "You're back and I see you're not alone. Well, you know the rules. No talking. This is a library, and keeping quiet is of the utmost importance."

"I remember," I whispered.

Xander leaned against me, wrapping his arm around my shoulders. My pulse quickened, but I couldn't tell if it was from the librarian's harsh stare or Xander's touch. "Who exactly are we keeping this place quiet for?" he challenged as I elbowed him under his ribcage.

The librarian narrowed her eyes at him. "You're going to be trouble, aren't you?"

I stiffened my back and stepped forward, putting some distance between us. "He didn't mean that. He's always kidding around. We'll be quiet, I promise."

The librarian's stern expression softened, barely. She drew in a deep breath. "Very well, then. But I close up at six o'clock sharp. I expect you to be done and out of here by then."

"Yes, ma'am," I replied.

With my hand on my book bag, I headed around the desk toward the bookshelves, leaving Xander to follow.

But when the librarian spoke again, I stopped dead in my tracks. "One more thing," she said. "No hanky panky back there, you two. This is a library, not a motel."

I groaned inwardly, shaking my head. I should have known she wasn't going to let us in that easily. "Yes, ma'am," I repeated obediently.

Xander slipped by me as I stood reeling from the librarian's presumptions. He shot me a teasing smile, his eyebrows arched and a devious twinkle in his blue eyes.

After a few moments, I glanced back at the librarian to see she had buried her nose in a book. Relieved she had something else to do other than throw more unnecessary warnings at us, I hurried off between the bookshelves to find Xander who had disappeared down an aisle. By the time I found him at the table in the back corner, he had placed his book bag on the scratched surface and stripped off his jacket. His black shirt strained across his broad shoulders, outlining the contours of his shoulder blades and thick upper arms. Cursing silently, I pried my eyes away from his masculine backside. This was going to be a very long project. I only hoped I'd be able to focus on our research and not let my thoughts wander to his perfect shoulders, strong arms, and sexy eyes. Avoiding his gaze, I approached the table and dropped my book bag next to his. Then I peeled off my jacket, hanging it on the back of a wobbly chair.

Without a word, I turned toward the bookshelves, but I only managed to take a single step before Xander grabbed my wrist. Drawing in a sharp breath, I stopped and spun around to face him. "What?" I whispered, my eyebrows raised as I met his stare.

He slowly uncurled his fingers from around my wrist. "Shouldn't we discuss where to begin?"

I whipped my hand back to my side. "Shh," I whispered, putting a finger up to my lips. Reluctantly, I moved closer to him so he could hear me. "The books are organized by date. The Underground Railroad occurred primarily in the first half of the eighteen hundreds, so we have about fifty years to comb through. I'll show you where to start."

I tried to turn away from him, but he caught my wrist again, his intense blue eyes studying me as I tried unsuccessfully look away from him. "I love it when you wear your necklace," he said, releasing my wrist and lifting his hand to trace the diamond-studded pendant resting above the neckline of my black sweater.

"Then perhaps I need to leave it at home every so often," I replied, realizing I would do anything to get rid of his unwanted attention.

His fingers grazed my skin before he slowly pulled his hand away. "No, please don't do that. It looks like it belongs on you."

My gaze met his, his eyes holding mine locked in place, causing my breath to catch in my throat. Refusing to let him unsettle me, I took a deep breath. "We should get started," I whispered, breaking away from his stare and turning to explore the closest aisle.

Xander followed, and I sensed his presence behind me as I fought to forget his touch. Focusing on the task at hand, I quickly found books dating from the early eighteen hundreds. Xander began pulling them out at random while I tried to find the memoir I had been forced to leave behind last week. The vaguely familiar books with their plain, nondescript blue, brown, and green covers all looked the same, so I had to guess where to start.

I stopped about halfway down the aisle, sinking to my knees to scour the bottom two shelves where I remembered finding the memoir. I pulled books out just far enough to read the titles and then slid them back into place. As I rummaged through them, the black cat that had jumped out at me last week flashed through my thoughts. At least today, it was up front and wouldn't scare me again.

Within fifteen minutes, I found two books that looked promising. One was about a slave family who had escaped through the area with the help of local residents who opened their homes up to them. The other one had been written by a southern bounty hunter who had spent years tracking escaped slaves throughout New England. I was about to carry the books back to the table in the cobweb-filled corner when I located the memoir I had found last week.

Holding the three books, I stood and crept down the aisle, hoping to slip around Xander without touching him—or worse, making eye contact. Of course, I couldn't get so lucky.

Xander noticed me approaching and turned from where he'd been studying the shelves. He held a large book in his hand as he stepped into the center of the narrow aisle, blocking my way.

"Find anything good?" he asked quietly.

I nodded without a word and lifted the books to show him. He tucked his book under his arm and took the top one off my pile.

As he reached for it, his hand barely touched mine, but it was enough to send shock waves through me. Trembling, I nearly dropped the other two books, but I caught them, awkwardly slamming them against my thigh before they could fall to the floor.

"You okay?" Xander asked, reaching his hand out to help steady the books in my arms.

"Yes, I'm fine," I whispered curtly, lifting the books against my chest.

Xander nodded before redirecting his attention to the book he'd taken from me, his eyebrows raised as he read the title. "Cool. A bounty hunter's stories. This should be interesting."

"What did you find?"

He reached for the large book tucked between his arm and rib cage and flashed the black cover in front of me. "The coroner's log from eighteen thirty-seven."

"Really? How does that relate to the Underground Railroad?"

Xander shrugged with an amused smile. "I don't know. I just thought it looked like a good read."

I huffed. Boys! They were so easily distracted. "Sounds morbid. Well, these three that I found should keep us busy until six. Remember, she won't allow books to be checked out, so we have to take a lot of notes before we leave."

"Man! I feel like I stepped into a time warp here. So much for downloading our research off the internet and copying it into a paper."

"This is authentic research. I think Mr. Jacobs will be impressed. Do you want an A or a C?"

With a knowing look in his eyes, Xander leaned toward me. "What difference does it make?" he asked, his voice a whisper. "My future has already been planned, and nothing's going to change that. It's not like my grades matter." Then he pulled back, his eyes catching mine once again, locking my gaze to him like a magnet.

The moment ended when we heard the librarian's footsteps approaching the aisle entrance behind me. As much as I wanted to avoid her, I was grateful her presence saved me from Xander's mesmerizing stare. Without another word, we hurried to the back table where we'd left our book bags and jackets before she could say anything.

I sat down at the table and pulled a notebook out of my bag, trying not to care that Xander had chosen the seat next to me rather than the one across from me. *Great,* I thought. *Now we'll be bumping elbows. That's all I need.* With a frustrated sigh, I forced myself to focus on the books. I started with the memoir that described in detail how the woman had opened up her home, providing food and shelter for escaped slaves. She and her husband had built hiding places within the walls and basement of their home, often answering the door to bounty hunters while the slaves hunkered down in the cellar. I read quickly, scribbling notes by hand. The woman, Josephine Kramer, had risked her family's safety to help people she didn't even know escaping a life of captivity and torture. Her story fascinated me, keeping me occupied until six o'clock, the other books I had pulled from the shelves forgotten.

"We should get packed up here," Xander said quietly, sliding his notebook into his bag.

I nodded without lifting my eyes from the book. "Okay. Give me one minute."

As Xander rose to his feet and slipped his jacket on, I skimmed the rest of the page before flipping through to the end. I was about to snap the book shut when I noticed a picture of a woman from the waist up on the inside back cover. I held it open, studying the faded black and white photograph. She appeared young—I guessed in her twenties—and she wore formal clothing, a dress I assumed, with long sleeves and a collar that reached up to her chin. Her light brown hair had been swept up into a bun, a few spiraled locks framing her pretty face. My eyes traveled down, locking on something familiar, and I drew in a sharp breath at the sight of my necklace.

Frozen, I stared at the pendant of intertwined circles, questions racing through my mind. Was the necklace in the picture the exact same one hanging around my neck right now? If so, did that mean I was related to her?

"Come on, Laken. We need to get going."

Xander's voice broke me out of my thoughts. I nodded slowly, unable to tear my eyes away from the faded black and white photograph. As I sat mesmerized by the picture, Xander hoisted his book bag up over his shoulder. Then he stepped behind my chair, looking over my shoulder. "Fascinating," he commented sarcastically. "It's a woman. Can we please go before the librarian chases us out of here?"

"Look closely. What do you see?"

"It's a—" His voice dropped away and, immediately, I knew he saw it. "It's your necklace."

"Yes. Do you think it's the same one?"

"I don't know." Xander leaned down behind me, studying it closely while I turned to watch his expression. He stared at the picture, his eyes locked on the necklace. "Probably. Wow, that's unbelievable. I'm sure you weren't expecting that."

"No way. Her name was Josephine Kramer. My father

told me this necklace is a family heirloom. I wonder if it means we're related to her."

Xander straightened up, resting his gaze on me. Before he could say anything, I said, "You never told me if your dad found anything out about it."

An uneasy look crossed over Xander's face before his usual confidence returned. "I don't know. I haven't asked him."

"Would you? Ask him for me, that is?"

Xander shot his gaze to mine and smiled. "Only if you hurry up and get ready to go. Because if you don't and that librarian decides to hunt us down back here—" He leaned down toward me, resting his hand on the table. "I'm going to have to kiss you just to see her reaction."

I huffed at him, shaking my head. Then I took one last look at Josephine Kramer before snapping the book shut and rising to my feet. "You just don't give up, do you?" I muttered as I tucked my notebook and pen into my bag, zipped it up, and scrambled into my denim jacket. "Ready."

"Damn. You're no fun," he said with a smirk, gesturing for me to lead the way.

I held my tongue, not wanting him to see how much his teasing unnerved me. I also didn't want to talk as we passed the librarian on our way out. With my bag hanging from my shoulder and the library books in my hand, I led him down one of the narrow aisles to the front.

The librarian perched behind her desk, the black cat sprawled out in front of her. "I was just about to go looking for you two," she said.

I smiled faintly, but stopped at once when she glared back at me. "Here are the books we pulled."

I set them on the counter, and Xander placed his on top of mine. Then I turned toward the front door, feeling her stare on my back as I walked away. Xander followed me out the front door into the cool evening air.

The colorful leaves now looked like black shadows against the purple sky above the parking lot. Our footsteps on the stones were the only sounds in the silence as we walked toward his truck. I hurried around to the passenger side and climbed up into the seat as soon as Xander unlocked the doors. Briefly remembering my drive home last week, I was relieved that I had Xander to drive me home this time. No wolves or stranger would chase me tonight. No matter how uneasy Xander made me feel, I trusted he would at least get me home safely.

I buckled the seat belt and leaned back, my book bag tucked next to my feet on the floor. As Xander started the truck and drove out of the gravel lot, he rambled on about the stories he had read in the bounty hunter's book. He didn't seem to notice that I tuned him out as I watched the trees pass by. My thoughts were focused on one woman, Josephine Kramer. I didn't know who she was other than a real-life hero, and I didn't know if she was related to me, but I was determined to find out.

Chapter 6

When I arrived home, I couldn't stop thinking about Josephine Kramer. I quickly fixed a salad topped with hard boiled eggs and cottage cheese, grabbed a can of ginger ale out of the refrigerator, and carried my dinner up to my bedroom desk. Placing the dishes next to my computer, I hoped I would soon learn the answers to my questions.

I sat at my desk, glued to the internet for hours. At first, I looked up my parents' ancestry, but I didn't find anyone named Josephine Kramer. As I clicked on website after website promising centuries of family trees, I squeezed in a few bites of my salad. Occasionally, Dakota rose from his fluffy bed and walked over to me, his nails tapping on the hardwood floor. Each time he nudged my lap, I reached down to scratch between his ears, my eyes never leaving the monitor. As time ticked by, I picked at my salad and sipped my soda, barely finishing half of my dinner.

When I finally gave up looking for Josephine Kramer

in my parents' families, I started over with a search on her name. She came up right away and I spent nearly an hour tracing her descendants. Interestingly, none of them were related to my parents that I could tell. The trail dead-ended with a girl named Ivy Jensen who grew up in Lincoln around the same time as my parents. I stared at her name on my computer screen, drumming my fingers against the desk and wondering where this left me. Disappointed, I frowned as I traced my necklace pendant, my mind churning with questions. Could there be two identical necklaces and I just stumbled upon the wrong one in the picture from the library book? Of course, anything was possible, but was it likely? I shook my head, feeling as though the deeper I dug, the more questions I had. The only way I might get answers would be to ask my parents if they knew anything about Ivy Jensen and why an ancestor of hers named Josephine Kramer had worn my necklace.

I wasn't sure how much time had passed when my phone buzzed from where I'd left it next to the keyboard. Breaking my attention away from the computer, I reached for it, reading the caller ID at once. Noah. My heart fluttering, the ancestry website instantly forgotten, my thoughts shifted to him and I closed the internet. "Hi, Noah," I said, lifting my gaze up from the wolf image on the screen to stare at the black sky outside the window.

"Hi, Laken. Everything okay?"

"Yes, of course. Why wouldn't it be?"

"I thought you were going to call me when you got home and it's almost ten," Noah explained.

"Oh wow!" I gasped, glancing at the time in the corner of my computer screen. Nine fifty-five. I had completely lost track of time. Although, as I remembered it, he had promised to call me at seven. But that didn't matter now. All I cared about was that he was on the line, so I played along. "Sorry. I got home a few hours ago, but I've been working on something."

"The research project?"

"Sort of," I admitted. "It's actually something I found while we were at the library today." From that point, I launched into an explanation starting with the book I had found written about Josephine Kramer and ending with my ancestry research that had come to a screeching halt with one name, Ivy Jensen.

"I guess you've been pretty busy," Noah said after a long pause when I stopped talking.

"Yeah. I didn't realize it was so late. And I still have about an hour of Calculus homework to get through. It's just so fascinating. I mean, to think that I might have an ancestor who was a real life hero all those years ago. That's really cool, but now I can't prove it."

"Well, like you said, maybe your parents will know how you ended up with her necklace."

I reached up to touch the pendant one more time, as if feeling the cool metal and diamond-studded surface reassured me it was real. "Yeah, that's probably my only shot to figure this out now."

"Not to change the subject here, but do you remember why you were supposed to call me tonight?"

I forced my thoughts back to reality and smiled dreamily. "My dress."

"Yes. So are you going to tell me about it or not?"

"That's very sweet of you to be interested, but all I'm going to tell you is that it's burgundy. Other than that, you'll have to be surprised."

"I can live with that. I like surprises, at least good ones. Will a white or almost white corsage work?"

"Anything you pick will be perfect." My heart glowed at the thought of the dance. He didn't even need to give me a corsage. All that mattered was that he was taking me. I had never looked forward to a school dance as much as I was looking forward to this one, and it was only because of him.

"It's more important to me that you like it. I want Saturday night to be special."

"It already is," I murmured as a yawn slipped out and I realized how tired I was.

Noah must have picked up on my fatigue. "I'd better let you go before you fall asleep on me," he said.

"I would never fall asleep with you on the phone. But I really should go because I haven't even started my Calculus problems yet."

"Good night, then. I'll pick you up at seven Saturday night."

"I can't wait. Good night, Noah."

I hung up and placed the phone on my desk. Sighing, I leaned down to pull my Calculus textbook out of my bag. I flipped the book open to the seventh chapter and grabbed my notebook and a pencil. Pushing away all thoughts of Josephine Kramer, Ivy Jensen, Noah and the dance, I began the homework I should have started hours ago.

ᴄ⁄ᴈᴄ⁄ᴈ

Xander approached me at my locker the next morning while I was organizing my books.

"You look tired," he commented without bothering to say "hi" or "hello." He casually leaned against the neighboring locker, his dark green shirttails hanging over the waist of his jeans.

"I was up late," I replied, focusing on my books and avoiding his stare.

I knew the dark circles under my eyes that no amount of make-up would hide gave me away. I'd woken up late this morning after turning off the alarm in my sleep. In my mad rush to get ready, I had grabbed a red sweater and jeans, barely finding enough time to pull my hair up into a ponytail before rushing out the door.

"Doing what?"

I shook my head. "God, you're nosy," I said sarcastically. "Why do you care, anyway?"

"If I tell you why I care, will you go out with me?"

"Ugh!" I groaned, whipping my eyes toward him.

Suddenly aware of the buzzing voices around us, I wondered if Marlena or any of her friends lurked close enough to hear our conversation. I hadn't forgotten Carrie's warning from earlier in the week. Even though I had no choice but to work with Xander on the History project, I suspected we would be watched any time we were together at school. "No, nothing will make me go out with you, and I would really appreciate it if you would quit asking, especially here," I whispered angrily.

He laughed softly, infuriating me even more. "I'm only going to stop when you say yes."

"Look, if you must know, Marlena has made it quite clear you belong to her and her alone. She's already threatened me once this week."

Xander's teasing smile immediately disappeared as anger flashed across his face. "What? She threatened you? You told me yesterday she wasn't bothering you."

"I lied."

"What did she say to you?"

"She didn't say anything. Carrie gave me a message from her the other day warning me I'll get burned if I play with fire. The point is, she's watching us. She obviously doesn't like…whatever you might call our relationship."

"Friends?"

"I'd say more like study partners. My friends don't show up on my doorstep at midnight without at least calling first."

"You're never going to forget that, are you?"

I shrugged, not bothering to answer him.

Xander sucked in a deep breath. "Okay, look, I'm glad you told me about Marlena's threat. I'll take care of her. She shouldn't threaten you again. But if she does, I want you to tell me right away."

"Fine," I agreed reluctantly.

"Because I'm not going to let her dictate who I can talk to or be friends with."

"Maybe you should just tell her she has nothing to be jealous about."

Xander stared at me, his sober eyes meeting mine. "I'm not so sure about that."

I tore my gaze away from him and slammed my locker door shut. Picking my book bag up off the floor, I slid the strap onto my shoulder.

Then I turned back to him, ready to end this conversation. "I need to get to homeroom." I started to walk away but stopped when he grabbed my upper arm. "What now?"

"You have a few minutes before the bell rings and, in case you've forgotten, we're in the same homeroom." He smiled softly, releasing his hold on me. "I just wanted to ask if you found anything out about the woman in the picture who was wearing your necklace."

"I tried, but I really didn't find anything," I replied, wondering why he even cared. "There's no Josephine Kramer in my parents' ancestry, and when I researched her descendants, I got as far as someone named Ivy Jensen."

"Ivy Jensen? Who's that?"

"I have no idea. All I know is that she grew up here in

Lincoln. I bet she knew my parents. They're all about the same age."

"Really? Where is she now?"

"I don't know. But it doesn't matter. Clearly, she's not related to us. I stopped once I realized she was the last descendant of Josephine Kramer. It was kind of disappointing. It would have been really neat to be related to a woman like Josephine Kramer. I can't even begin to imagine the risks she took to help people she barely knew."

"But that doesn't explain the necklace. Your father said it was an old family heirloom, right?"

I nodded. "Yes, he did." I remembered him telling me it had been in our family for centuries. "So there must be two or even more just like it. That's the only possible explanation."

"Or maybe you have to dig a little deeper. Find out who Ivy Jensen is."

"Yeah. I thought I'd ask my parents if they knew her. If she grew up around here, I'm sure they would know who she was. But there's still the chance that the necklace in the picture isn't the same one. Maybe I'm just on a wild goose chase that will get me nowhere."

"I'll ask my dad if he thinks there could be two identical pieces, but from what I've learned, the older a piece is, the less likely it is to have identical copies. Years ago, jewelry was made by hand, not mass produced in factories. It was more like artwork back then. Once a jeweler finished something, they moved on to new creations. So I doubt there are duplicates. Which means you need to find out who Ivy Jensen is. Maybe you have a long lost aunt out there. Or maybe, she's a crazy relative who's psychotic, and your parents have hidden her from you to protect you."

I huffed at his wild imagination. "I'm sure if I had an aunt or a cousin around here, I'd know about it. First of all, my parents don't keep secrets from me. And secondly, it's a small town. They couldn't hide a relative from me if they tried."

"I'll buy your second point, but how do you know your parents have never kept a secret from you?"

"I just know. Now can we please go to homeroom? Or, if you're not ready, can you at least let me go?"

Xander took a deep breath, appearing to read the frustration in my voice. "Sure. But I'll meet you there. I have to take care of something first." His gaze shifted to focus on something behind me. I suspected it was Marlena, but I didn't dare turn around.

Without another word, I rushed away from him and hurried down the hall, dodging the other students. My thoughts centered around one name. I hated to admit it, but Xander was right. I would only find out how Josephine Kramer's necklace ended up in my family if I asked my parents about Ivy Jensen.

ᏣᏒᏣ

The next morning, I woke up late. Not bothering to change out of my red plaid pajamas, I wandered down to the kitchen where my father sat alone at the table with a magazine and a mug of coffee.

Still sleepy, I padded across the kitchen, Dakota at my heels. "Good morning, Dad," I said while I unlocked the back door and opened it.

A cold draft blasted into the house when Dakota charged outside. Instead of following him as I often did, I shut the door behind him, opting to stay in and take advantage of the morning to ask my father if he knew Ivy Jensen. Searching for the right way to broach the subject, I turned and headed for the gurgling coffee pot on the counter.

"Good morning, Laken," my father replied, lifting his attention from his magazine. "You're up late today."

"I know." I nodded, searching the cabinets until I found a white mug with the Lincoln Police Department shield on it. After filling it with coffee, I turned. "Brooke and I stayed up late talking about the dance. She's really excited about tonight." I was also catching up on my sleep from my late night of research and homework the night before, but I conveniently kept that to myself.

The mug still in my hand, I gathered a cereal bowl from the overhead cupboard and a spoon from the silverware drawer, then carried them to the empty seat beside my father. As I reached for the box of Cheerios on the table, my father closed the magazine, pushing it aside. "Where's Mom?" I asked.

"She ran out to the store." He paused for a moment. "Are you looking forward to the dance tonight?"

I looked up from pouring the cereal to meet his steady gaze. My father didn't ask me about boys often, and I sensed he felt awkward talking about tonight. I shrugged, smiling faintly as though the dance wasn't a big deal. "I am, but I've had something else on my mind for the last few days." I reached for the milk and splashed some into my bowl. "Dad, did you know a girl named Ivy Jensen when you were growing up?"

My father nearly choked on his coffee, spitting what was in his mouth back into his mug. "Where did you hear that name?" he gasped.

I twisted the cap back on the milk container, watching my father's wide-eyed reaction. His face turned a ghastly white as he stared at me. "I didn't," I answered slowly, my cereal forgotten when I noticed the alarm in his eyes. "I kind of stumbled upon her. I think she may have something to do with the necklace you gave me."

He took a deep breath, meeting my gaze. "What makes you think that?"

"She came up in the research I was doing on my History project," I explained before scooping a spoonful of cereal and taking a bite.

"Really? I thought your project was on the Underground Railroad."

"It is." Between bites, I told him about the picture of Josephine Kramer wearing my necklace and my online research that traced her to Ivy Jensen. "I'm just curious to know how the necklace ended up in our family," I explained as I finished.

My father leaned back in his chair. "Fair enough. I can understand your curiosity."

"So you know her?"

"Yes, I *knew* her," he admitted slowly, emphasizing the past tense. "A long time ago." A wistful look swept across his face, but he didn't offer any more information.

"Is she a relative? And if she is, how come you never told me about her? I'd certainly like to meet her. Where is she now?"

"Whoa, Laken. Slow down. That's a lot of questions. Yes, she has something to do with your necklace." He dodged all of my questions except the one that had haunted me since Thursday night.

I dropped my spoon, my cereal forgotten, and stared at my father, feeling as though I hadn't really known him for the last eighteen years.

"Am I related to her?"

He looked away from me, nodding as he confirmed my suspicions. "Yes, you are."

"How? Is she an aunt or a cousin? And can I meet her?"

He sighed, meeting my imploring stare. His lips quivered, his eyes glistening with tears. "I'm sorry, but that's not possible. She passed away many years ago."

"Oh," I said with a sigh, my hopes suddenly deflated like a balloon being popped. "I'd still like to know about her. How was she related to us?"

Once again, my father nervously scanned the room. For several seconds, he avoided my gaze. Before he could answer, the garage door rumbled, signaling my mother's return. My father abruptly stood, pushing his chair out behind him. "That's your mother and I don't want to talk about this in front of her." He grabbed the milk and carried it across the kitchen to the refrigerator.

"Why would she care?" I asked, my eyebrows raised as I shifted in my chair to watch him.

He turned from the refrigerator and leaned against the door. "Ivy's death was hard on all of us, including your mother. I don't want to dig up those memories, at least not today. I'll explain everything to you, just not now. You should focus on the dance and having a wonderful night."

I nodded as the door leading from the garage opened. My mother stormed into the kitchen, her arms loaded with heavy grocery bags. "Oh, good," she gushed. "You're both here. Can I get some help unloading the Jeep?"

Neither my father nor I answered her, our eyes still locked on each other. His begged for understanding while I felt mine brimming with disappointment. I didn't want to wait to know who Ivy was and how she fit into our lives, especially after all the searching I had done the other night. Unfortunately, it looked like I didn't have a choice.

My mother set the bags down on the cluttered counter next to the coffee maker. When she turned around to face us, she seemed to realize we hadn't moved. Worry washed over her expression. "What's going on? What did

I miss?"

Breaking his eyes away from me, my father forced a smile and his expression softened as if our conversation had never happened. "Nothing, dear. Laken was just telling me how excited she is about the dance tonight. Isn't that right, Laken?"

Although I didn't like it one bit, I played along and smiled. "Yes. It's a big night and I can't wait to wear my new dress." I took a quick sip of my coffee before standing up. "I'll help with the groceries."

My smile fading, I slipped past my parents on the way to the garage. As much as I wanted to press my father for more information about Ivy and how we were related, I held back. His reaction to my questions concerned me, and I had the sinking feeling there was something more to the story that he didn't want to tell me. But I couldn't imagine what was so bad that he didn't want to talk about it in front of my mother.

Maybe she was a cousin who died tragically, or maybe Xander was right and she had a mental illness they've been hiding from me, I thought, heading through the garage to retrieve the groceries from the Jeep. Whatever it was, I had no choice but to heed my father's advice.

Tonight was the dance, and my thoughts and energies would be better spent focusing on what would surely be a magical night. I could wait at least one more day to learn about Ivy Jensen.

જીજી

At six fifty-five that evening, I stood in front of my dresser mirror, carefully applying dark lip gloss. Pressing my lips together, I studied my reflection. The burgundy dress hung from thin straps, hugging me from my chest to my hips. The satin material loosened around my legs, ending at the glittery high heels strapped to my feet, a split on the right side ending an inch above my knee. My hair was swept up in a twist, rhinestone earrings dangled in between a few strands of hair that framed my face, and my diamond necklace sparkled just above the dress neckline.

Turning away from the mirror, I leaned against the dresser, smiling at Dakota who sat a few feet away, watching me. "So what do you think?" I asked even though I knew he couldn't answer me. "Not too shabby for a girl who practically grew up roaming the mountains with her pet wolf, huh?" I laughed softly when I thought I saw him nod his head in agreement.

With a carefree smile, I grabbed the small purse that barely had enough room for my phone, keys, and lip gloss. Then I left the room, wobbling across the hardwood floor in my high heels. I kept a firm grip on the railing as I crept down the stairs, my weight balanced on my toes. The kitchen was empty when I reached the bottom, and I made my way to the coat closet in the hallway. When I opened it, my heart sank as I sorted through my options. Black leather jacket, no. Denim jacket, no. Fleece pullover, no. Flannel coat, definitely not. Nothing I owned would go with this fancy dress, and I would freeze if I didn't find something to cover my arms and shoulders. The temperatures were expected to dip into the thirties tonight.

I was about to shut the door in defeat when I noticed my mother's cream-colored wrap in the corner. It was perfect—warm, but dressy. I pulled it off the hanger and closed the door. Then I turned, my eyebrows raised, wondering where my parents were. They had been watching TV in the family room when I headed up to take my shower an hour ago and I knew they didn't want to miss seeing me leave for the dance.

With the wrap folded over my arm, I walked down the hall toward their bedroom. "Mom? Dad?" I called quietly.

When I reached the door to their room, I stopped, hearing voices beyond it. I raised my hand to knock, but held it inches from the door and listened instead.

"How in the world did she find out about Ivy?" my mother asked.

"It was the necklace. She stumbled upon a picture of a woman wearing it in a book at the library and then traced her to Ivy," my father replied.

Silence loomed as they paused. Finally, my mother said, "You have to tell her, Tom. You're her father."

"I know. I just always figured it would be easier than this."

"The longer you wait, the harder it will be. She has to know the truth."

"I realize that, Gwen. But I would have thought that you, of all people, would want to put it off as long as we could."

I felt a lump forming in my throat as tears filled my eyes. I fought to hold them back, knowing they would smear my make-up if they spilled down my cheeks. What were my parents talking about? What terrible secret were they hiding that they didn't want to tell me? And why did my mother insist that my father be the one to tell me? Lowering my hand, I continued listening.

"Of course, I'm not excited to tell her about Ivy," my mother said. "But Laken's a reasonable girl. She'll know that it doesn't change anything. We're still her family, and I still love her as if she was my own."

My heart skipping a beat, I felt dizzy, my knees growing weak, and I reached my hand out to the wall to catch my balance. What did she mean she loved me as if I was her own? Was I adopted? Who was Ivy Jensen and how did she fit into this picture?

"I know, and I'm sure you're right. But that doesn't make it any easier. She's not going to take this lightly. She probably won't trust us for a while," my father said. "I mean, imagine how it will feel for her."

"I've been worried about this since the first moment she was placed into my arms wrapped in a pink baby blanket. I'll never forget that day. I can't believe she's eighteen already."

"Believe it. And speaking of which, we should stop talking about this and get out there. We don't want to miss seeing her before the dance."

I opened my eyes wide and stared at the door. After what I'd overheard, I couldn't face them right now. I wiped at the tear rolling down my face, took a deep breath, and quietly rushed down the hall away from my parent's bedroom. *Please be here. Please, please, please,* I thought, hoping Noah was waiting for me in the drive-way so we could leave before I had to face my parents.

When I reached the entry hall, I flung the front door open and ran out of the house. I barely felt the cold air as I slammed the door behind me. Not bothering to lock up, I hurried down the sidewalk as fast as I could in my wob-bly high heels, the wrap still folded over my arm, not helping to ward off the cold. As I turned the corner, a pair of strong hands grabbed my upper arms and I skidded to a halt.

I looked up to see Noah's handsome face, his eyes studying me with concern and confusion. The headlights from his car shone behind him, a welcome beacon in the darkness, here to whisk me away from the secrets lurking in the house.

"Whoa," he said softly. "What's going on?"

I stared up at him silently, shaking my head. My heart

hammering in my chest, I worried that the tears I held at bay would spill out as soon as I spoke.

"What's wrong? Where are your parents?"

"Inside. Can we please just leave?" I whispered, feeling moisture in my eyes and silently begging him not to ask any more questions.

Noah glanced at the house and then back at me. "Yes, of course. Here, let me help you."

He turned to wrap his arm around my bare shoulders, walking me through the headlight beams to the passenger side of his car. He opened the door and offered his hand to me. I accepted, comforted by the warm feel of his fingers curled around mine while I eased into the seat. I swung my legs into the car, blushing faintly as the slit bared my right leg. On any other night, I would have been mortified, but tonight I was grateful for something to distract me from what I'd just overheard.

"Thank you," I murmured as he shut the door and hurried around to the driver's side. The engine hummed, its purring comforting me a little.

Noah slid into the seat beside me, gazing at me with worry in his eyes. "Are you sure you want to leave without saying goodbye to your parents? I feel like I'm driving a getaway car on the lam."

I shifted the wrap on my lap as I reached for my seat belt. "Yes, I'm sure. I'll tell you everything after we get out of here."

He sighed, and I could tell he didn't like leaving without bidding my parents a proper goodnight. But he nodded silently, clicked his seat belt into place, and backed out of the driveway.

I settled against the seat, relaxing a little. My racing heart even started to slow. When Noah pulled away from the house, I resisted the urge to look back as he drove down the dark road. By now, my parents surely knew I'd left without saying good night. Perhaps they were wondering if I had overheard them. I took a deep breath, trying to push their words out of my mind. But all I could hear was my mother saying "I still love her as if she was my own," over and over.

Chapter 7

Silence filled the car for the five minutes it took to get to school. The trees were left behind when we entered town, the buildings dark behind the dim streetlamps. I fought to keep my composure every second of the drive. Each time I took a deep breath, preparing to tell Noah what had happened just before he arrived to pick me up, tears clouded my eyes. I wasn't ready to talk about it without crying. I clutched my purse, feeling my phone inside it vibrate several times. I was sure my parents were trying to reach me, so I ignored it. By the time Noah pulled into the school parking lot, it had stopped and my pulse had slowed to a normal rate.

Tall street lamps lit up the corners of the parking lot. Boys in dark suits and girls in shimmering dresses scurried around the cars on their way to the dance. Noah carefully dodged the students as he drove through the lot and parked under a tree facing away from the school. He shifted into park, shut off the engine and lights, then turned to me, the soft glow from the distant lamps the only light in the car. Nervous, I looked at him, meeting his concerned brown eyes.

"So," he started gently. "Before we head inside, will you tell me what's going on?"

Not breaking my eyes away from him, I nodded. "Yes," I managed to say, my voice threatening to crack into sobs. I paused, taking a deep breath, determined to keep my composure. "Before you got to the house, I was looking for my parents to say good night. I know they wanted to see us leave." I stopped again, needing a moment to contain the emotions rising up inside me. As soon as I was sure I could hold my tears at bay, I continued. "They were in their room, and I overheard them talking. It seems that I'm—I'm adopted."

"What?" Noah gasped in disbelief, his eyes searching my expression for an explanation. "How do you know that? Are you sure?"

"Actually, no, I'm not completely sure. They were talking about some secret they needed to tell me. But then my mom said she loved me as if I was her own." A tear escaped one of my eyes and I wiped at it, hoping it wouldn't leave a black streak of make-up down my cheek. "I don't know what else that could mean."

"Oh, Laken. I don't know what to say. Are you okay?" He reached over to touch my shoulder, his gesture comforting me, if only for a moment.

"No, I don't think I am. The worst part is that I've been looking forward to tonight for weeks, and now it's ruined." I sniffed, drawing in a deep breath and swallowing the lump in my throat. Shuddering, I fought to pull myself together. As hard as it was, I couldn't let the secret my parents had harbored all these years prevent me from enjoying the dance. If not for me, I needed to hold it together for Noah.

"No, it's not," he disagreed firmly. "I'm going to

make sure tonight is everything you want it to be. I won't let this ruin it."

He lifted his hand from my shoulder, tracing the tear down my cheek with his fingertip.

I looked up at him gratefully. "Thank you," I whispered.

After a moment of silence, he asked, "What else did they say?"

"Not much. They were kind of cryptic. All I know is that it has to do with that woman, Ivy Jensen. This morning, my father admitted I'm related to her, but he didn't say how. So after what my mom said, I'm guessing she could be my birth mother."

"Wow. That's pretty heavy. And all just before the dance. The timing sucks."

I rolled my eyes as a small smile peeked out on my face like the first ray of sunshine cutting through dark clouds after a storm. "You're telling me."

"Look, I know it's going to be hard not to think about this tonight, but I want you to enjoy the dance. This really doesn't change anything. I'm sure your parents love you just the same, and you're still the most beautiful girl I've ever met. I don't care who your parents are."

I felt a blush race across my cheeks and hoped he wouldn't notice it in the dark shadows. "You're way too kind."

"Nope. Just honest. Has anyone ever told you that you have the most amazing green eyes?"

My smile broadened as I looked down shyly. "Okay, now you're embarrassing me."

"I'm serious. And now, maybe you'll find out who you got them from."

I mulled over his comment, realizing he was right. Both of my parents had brown eyes and I'd always wondered how I ended up with green ones. "Maybe," I said thoughtfully, lifting my dry eyes up to meet his again.

Noah grinned at me. "So you're okay now?"

"Yes."

"Good. Because this wasn't exactly how I hoped tonight would begin."

"Oh yeah? What were you hoping for?"

"That once we said good night to your parents and I walked you to my car where they couldn't see or hear us, I would do this." He ran his fingers along my jaw to my chin. Cupping it in the palm of his hand, he leaned across the middle of the car and kissed me.

The warm touch of his lips melted away my anxiety and apprehension. Suddenly, all that mattered was being with him tonight.

After his kiss which seemed to end all too soon, he leaned his forehead against mine. My heart pounding, I prayed he couldn't hear it. "I have something for you," he said in a low voice, his breath tickling my nose.

"Hmm," I murmured. "What's that?"

He shifted back into his seat. "A corsage," he said matter-of-factly, reaching behind his seat to retrieve a small container. The plastic creaked in protest when he opened it to present a cream-colored rose. He lifted the flower and delicately pinned it on my dress below my left shoulder, working slowly, careful not to prick me with the pin. When he finished, he straightened up, admiring his handiwork with satisfaction. "There. That looks nice."

I met his gaze, enjoying the moment as I tried not to think about my parents and the secret they were hiding. But my reprieve was short-lived. My purse vibrated again from where it rested on my lap, and I groaned inwardly. Noah raised his eyebrows at me, seeming to sense my uneasiness. Without a word, I pulled my phone out, not at all surprised to see "Mom" flash across the screen. I tilted the phone so Noah could read it, too.

"I better deal with this before she shows up here."

He nodded. "Yeah, I think you should."

Dropping my eyes to the phone, I read her text. *Are you OK? Please answer me. Are you at the dance?*

I typed a curt response. *I'm fine. Yes, we're at the dance.* With a frown, I sent the message to her.

Her reply came instantly, flashing across the screen before I could shove my phone back into my purse. *We missed seeing you leave tonight. We're worried about you.*

I resisted the urge to respond with a sarcastic comment asking how worried she could possibly be if she wasn't my real mother. Instead, I wrote, *Don't be. I said I'm fine.* After I sent it, I lifted my gaze up to Noah. "I almost don't know what to say to her."

"What do you want to say?"

"I want to ask her to tell me the truth about who I am and where I came from. I want to ask why she and my dad never told me about this. I want to know how they could raise me to believe truth and honesty are the most important things in any relationship when they weren't being honest with me."

Noah smiled compassionately. "That's a lot to put into a text."

"I know. That's why my questions will just have to wait until later," I said, realizing it was only a matter of time before I would have to confront my parents. The phone vibrated again in my hands, and I sighed in defeat. I wished my mom would stop with the messages and let me at least try to enjoy the dance. Reluctantly, I glanced down at the screen to read what I hoped would be her last text for the evening.

I hope you have a nice time tonight. And, Laken, we're sorry. Another tear rolled down my cheek as I read her words. At that moment, I was sure she and my father knew I had heard them talking. And her apology confirmed I was adopted.

"Laken?" Noah's voice broke my trance. "Do you want to tell me what she said?"

I looked at him, feeling moisture in my eyes, and held my phone up for him to read her message. "So it's true," I choked out.

Noah took a deep breath, concern flashing in his eyes. He looked like he was about to say something, but hesitated.

Refusing to let my emotions get the best of me, I willed away my tears and sobs. I had to be strong and prove to Noah that I could get through this without turning into a needy drama queen. Knowing exactly what I had to do, I pushed the power button on the side of my phone, watching the screen turn black. "There. No more of this tonight." I forced myself to smile as I dropped the phone into my purse. Then I wiped away my last stray tear and looked at him, hoping to convince him I could put this behind me, at least for the dance. "Shall we go in?"

He smiled, appearing relieved, although a dark shadow still lurked in the depths of his eyes. I suspected he wasn't convinced I was okay, but at least he followed my lead. "I thought you'd never ask."

Noah stepped out of the car as a cold draft rushed in, and I shivered, waiting for him to reach my side. When my door opened, he extended his hand to me. I gratefully accepted it, a glow warming me as soon as his fingers wrapped around mine. Clinging to his hand for support, I rose to my feet with my purse and the wrap in my other hand. Goose bumps raced along my arms in the bitter cold while he closed the door behind me.

Before we headed across the parking lot, Noah released me and lifted the wrap from my arm, gently draping it over my shoulders. "Have I told you how beautiful you look tonight in your dress?"

"I don't know," I replied with a giddy smile. After all, he had said I was beautiful just a few minutes ago, but I didn't think he'd been referring to tonight. "But I know I haven't told you how handsome you look tonight." It was true. He filled out the dark jacket and crisp white shirt quite nicely, the shades of brown in his tie matching his eyes. "I don't think I've seen you in anything except jeans until tonight."

"I think you're right," he said with a smile before turning and extending his elbow to me. "Shall we?"

I beamed, wondering once again how I had captured the attention of the new town heartthrob. "We shall." Shifting the wrap, I hooked my arm through his and we walked across the parking lot side by side.

Only a few straggling latecomers passed us on our way to the school. We slowed when we reached the steps, and I tightened my grip on his arm to keep my balance. At the top, he whisked me into the school, the doors slamming shut behind us. Bright fluorescent light greeted us in the long hall lined with green lockers between numbered classroom doors. "Ah, high school," Noah said with a reminiscent smile. "I don't miss this one bit."

"Hey," I teased, tugging his arm.

"I mean the school part. Tonight is actually nice. I get to be the cool older guy," he said, a sparkle lighting up his eyes. "Now lead the way because I have no idea where we're going."

"The dance is in the gym."

I led him down the hallway, our arms still linked together. My shoes clicked against the tile floor, but the music drowned out their sound when we turned the next corner. The gymnasium doors were propped open at the end of the hall where a few students in suits and dresses milled about, paying no attention to me and Noah before we entered the dance.

Loud music pulsed through the crowded gymnasium that had been transformed into a magical dance hall. Twinkling string lights decorated the perimeter and a disco ball rotated from the ceiling. Couples danced in the center while others gathered around the walls and bleachers, their steady hum of chatter competing with the music. Noah and I wandered through the crowd, occasionally bumping into other students as I searched for Brooke and Ethan. We found them beside the bleachers, watching the dance floor as if waiting for the perfect moment to join in. Brooke wore her short black dress and almost reached Ethan's chin in her high heels. Rhinestone hair clips pulled her red locks behind her ears, exposing matching earrings.

Brooke's eyes lit up the moment she saw us. "Hey! What took you two so long?" she asked, rushing over and pulling me into a hug. Ethan stayed close behind her, looking quite dapper in his dark suit, tie, and pressed white shirt. As Brooke backed away from me, her brilliant smile collapsed. "Oh my god. What's wrong?" Concern swept across her expression, as if she could read my mind.

"Nothing," I lied. "I'm just suddenly very hot in this wrap." Of course I would tell Brooke about being adopted, but not now and not until I had all the facts. I started to take off my wrap, but Noah swooped in behind me to lift it off my shoulders. His fingertips left a trail of goose bumps in their wake as he grazed my skin, and I flashed him a smile. "Thank you," I said before returning my attention to Brooke and Ethan. "You two look great. Have you been here long?"

"Yes. We've been waiting for you guys." The sparkle returned to Brooke's eyes as she spoke, while beside her,

Ethan greeted Noah with a friendly handshake. "You look gorgeous," she whispered, leaning toward me. "So does your date. You're going to be the envy of every girl here." As Brooke pulled back, she turned her gaze to Noah. "I don't believe we've met. I'm Brooke."

"Nice to meet you." Noah extended his hand to her, but she ignored it. Instead, she threw her arms around him.

"Oh, come here. I've heard so much about you, I feel like I already know you."

"Brooke," I groaned, rolling my eyes. She was almost as embarrassing as my parents could be.

Noah gave her a genuine smile when she released him. "Likewise," he replied.

She returned to Ethan's side, clasping his hand in hers. "Okay, Ethan made me wait until you guys got here to drag him out onto the dance floor. So, Laken, leave your things here on the bleachers." She gestured to an empty spot next to her coat. "And follow us." Excitement glowing in her eyes, Brooke led Ethan by the hand through the swaying crowd.

Noah handed the wrap to me. I folded it around my purse and placed it next to Brooke's coat. Empty-handed, I turned back to him with a smile.

"She has a lot of energy," he commented.

I nodded, scanning the dimly-lit gym for Brooke's red hair. "Yes, she does. But she's a great friend. I can tell her anything."

Without any warning, Noah grabbed my wrist, and my breath caught when he pulled me close to him. Speckled lights from the disco ball danced across his face. "What have you told her about us?" he asked curiously, a sexy smile curving his lips.

I leaned toward him to whisper in his ear. "Only what I want her to know." When I stepped back, I reached for his hand and pulled him through the crowd to join Brooke and Ethan.

When we caught up to them, Noah kept a firm grip on my hand, twirling me under his arm before pulling me close to him. I balanced on my toes, worried I'd fall if I dropped my weight onto my high heels. The longer we danced, the more I found myself drawn to him, and I smiled every time he caught me looking at him, which was quite often.

After several songs, a flash of red caught my attention from across the gym. Marlena, wearing a glimmering crimson gown, waltzed through the crowd with Xander following close behind, her hand in his. His black hair reached the collar at the base of his neck, matching his pressed jacket and pants.

As soon as they reached a tiny open space on the dance floor, Marlena twirled around, her blonde hair swishing against her bare shoulders. In a fluid movement, she landed against Xander and wrapped her arms around his shoulders. He slipped an arm around her thin waist, sliding his other hand below the small of her back. I scowled as jealousy ripped through me, wondering where the chaperones were. Touching below the waist was explicitly prohibited during school dances, and I desperately wished someone would intervene. But knowing Xander, it probably wouldn't do any good. He'd just do it again as soon as they looked the other way.

Noah noticed my frown and pulled me close. I assumed he thought my dark expression resulted from the earlier incident at home. He had no idea I struggled to ignore my growing feelings for Xander, and I had promised myself he never would. "You look upset again," he said in my ear, talking over the loud music.

I mustered up a smile to reassure him. "Sorry. It kind of sneaks up on me."

He nodded, seeming to understand. "I'm sure it's hard to completely forget what you heard tonight."

As I glanced up at him, the music slowed. Noah tightened his hold on me, pulling me against him while I wound my arms up around his shoulders and behind his neck. With a contented sigh, I rested my cheek against his jacket, the slow music relaxing me. I breathed in his spicy aftershave and enjoyed feeling his strong arms around me. My eyes falling shut for a moment, I felt as though we were the only two in the room. When I opened them just before the song ended, the last thing I expected to see were Xander's familiar yet unsettling blue eyes.

He danced with Marlena about ten feet away, watching me as he held her close. His chin grazed her shoulder, his hand rubbing her lower back.

Facing away from me, she was completely oblivious that someone other than herself had captured his attention.

My nerves rattled, I whipped my gaze away from Xander's stare and looked up at Noah. Without a single word, he brushed a gentle kiss against my mouth. His lips lingered on mine for a few seconds, as if he couldn't decide whether to lift away or deepen the kiss. But the moment ended when the music faded and the DJ's voice crackled over the loudspeaker.

"Good evening, Lincoln High!" he raved, sending the students into loud applause and cat whistles. "Welcome to homecoming. I hope everyone is having a fantastic time tonight." As he rambled on with his monologue that blasted above the cheers, Noah took my hand and led me through the crowd.

When we reached the empty space by the bleachers, I broke away from him. "Bathroom," I mouthed, and he smiled in acknowledgement.

"Hurry back," he said, a teasing look in his eyes. "I'm

going to get flashbacks of my own high school dances if you leave me here alone."

I gently touched his upper arm, our eyes meeting for a moment. "I won't be long."

Then I turned and hurried along the bleachers to the door. Most of the other students clustered in the center of the gym, listening to the DJ's speech while they waited for the music to resume. A few of them still lingered around the doorway both inside and outside the gym. I passed by, paying them no attention as I headed down the hall toward the nearest bathroom. I walked gingerly in my heels, my footsteps growing louder the farther away I got from the noise.

As soon as I reached the bathroom, I pulled the door open and slipped inside, relieved to find myself alone. I leaned my hands on the edge of a sink and peered into the mirror, making sure my earlier tears hadn't left black smudges under my eyes. Although Brooke would have told me if they had, she may not have been able to see them in the dark gym.

Under the bright fluorescent light, I inspected my make-up, pleasantly surprised to see everything still in place. *Whew,* I thought. *Now if I can just hold it together for the rest of the night.*

Before I could turn around, the bathroom door whipped open, and I instantly looked down at the sink. I turned on the water and washed my hands, hoping to avoid whoever had just walked in, especially if it was Marlena or one of her friends. But when I shut off the faucet and raised my eyes, my heart nearly leaped out of my chest. The last thing I expected was to see Xander in the mirror standing behind me.

I spun around to face him, forgetting my hands were still wet while my jaw dropped open in shock. But this was Xander. Nothing he did should surprise me anymore.

"What are you doing in here?" I demanded, skipping any semblance of a courteous greeting. "This is the girls' bathroom."

Xander smiled casually as he reached for a paper towel from the dispenser on the wall and handed it to me. I took it from him, my gaze never leaving him while I dried my hands.

"So? I wanted to see you alone and this seemed like the only chance I would get."

I finished drying my hands, but held onto the damp paper towel, nervously crushing it between my fingers. "Whatever you want to say to me, you can say in front of Noah."

"I wasn't talking about *your* date."

"Oh. Marlena."

"Exactly. The last thing I want to do is add fuel to her fire."

I forced a sarcastic smile. "Gee, thanks. You know, the best way to do that might be not following me into the girls' bathroom."

"Only if she finds out about it. I was careful to make sure no one saw me come in here. And I won't tell if you won't."

I wasn't quite sure how to respond to that. After a moment of silence, I asked, "What's so important that you had to barge in here?"

"I'm curious to know why, on a night like tonight, you look like someone just died," he replied.

"Why does it matter to you?" I shot back, wishing he wasn't so good at reading my emotions.

He smiled knowingly. "You've been asking me why I care for weeks. Do you honestly think you're going to get an answer that's any different than what I've already told you?" I took a deep breath, glaring at him. Of course, I wouldn't get a straight answer, but I would keep asking him until I did. "So who died?" he asked bluntly.

"Ivy Jensen," I blurted out before I realized what I was saying.

"Who?"

"Ivy Jensen. I told you about her yesterday. She is, or was, the last descendant of the woman wearing my necklace in that book."

"Oh yeah, her. So what's the problem? It's not like you knew her."

"No, but apparently, I'm related to her."

Xander's eyebrows shot up with immediate interest. "I knew it. So who is she?"

I shrugged, breaking my eyes away from his to stare beyond him at the bathroom stalls. "I'm not exactly sure."

"Okay then, what's your guess on how you're related?"

I looked back at him, meeting his steady gaze. "She might be my biological mother. I overheard my parents talking tonight before Noah picked me up and, apparently, my mother isn't my real mother."

I couldn't help wondering why I was telling him about this when I had lied to Brooke earlier. For some reason, I found it difficult to lie to him. Perhaps it was because he had rescued me from being stranded in the rain and had been with me when I'd found the photograph of the woman wearing my necklace. Either way, I felt like kicking myself. He was the last person I wanted to confide in.

"That's some pretty heavy stuff to deal with before a dance that's supposed to be fun," he said, seeming to actually care.

"Tell me about it," I groaned.

"Well, considering the news, you seem to be holding up well."

"I'm not so sure about that. I was a wreck when we

got here, but Noah's been very supportive and helpful."

A dark shadow raced across Xander's expression when I mentioned Noah. "About that—"

"Oh, no," I interrupted. "You're not going to start in on him again. You have no room to criticize my date when you have to corner me in the girls' bathroom just to talk to me where Marlena won't see us."

He took a deep breath and started to say something, but stopped when the door flew open and Brooke rushed into the bathroom. She halted when she saw Xander, her jaw dropping. I almost laughed at the shock registering in her eyes, realizing she wasn't as accustomed to his brazen ways as I was. After all, Xander following me into the girls' bathroom was just Xander being Xander.

As soon as she seemed to compose herself, Brooke shifted her gaze to me. "I hope I'm not interrupting anything here. Laken, Noah asked me to make sure you were okay."

I took a deep breath, wanting nothing more than to return to him. "I'm fine. And we're finished here. Xander was just leaving, weren't you?" I glared at him, hoping he would get the message.

"Yes, I should probably get back to my date," Xander said flatly. He headed toward the door, but stopped and turned around before leaving. "By the way, you both look beautiful tonight." Although he referenced both of us, he stared directly at me. "Laken, I'll see you Monday at school and we can set up a time to work on our History project next week."

"Great," I muttered, watching him disappear through the doorway.

"You weren't really talking about your History project in here, were you?" Brooke asked incredulously.

I offered her a faint smile. "Sort of. I found something when we went to the library a few days ago that may have something to do with my family. He was just wondering if I had asked my parents about it yet."

"Really? What is it?"

"It's a long story. And I promise to tell you about it soon, but right now, we should probably get back to the guys."

"Okay. Fair enough." She smiled brilliantly, the hurt and concern in her eyes from moments ago now gone. "Whew. For a second there, I thought you were going to say something happened between you and Xander. Because if that was the case, not only would you be risking your life since Marlena will kill you if you so much as touch him, but you'd also be hurting Noah who happens to be the best thing that has ever happened to you."

"You're right. He is by far the best date I've ever had at a school dance."

"Exactly. So come on. Let's not keep him waiting."

She grabbed my hand, and I tossed the crumpled paper towel in the garbage can as she whisked me out of the bathroom.

Noah was waiting for me where I had left him by the bleachers. For the next few hours, we danced in the shadows of the dimly lit gym, the other students around us a blur in the background. Fighting to push Xander out of my thoughts, I hoped I wouldn't see him again tonight. I didn't need any more reminders of the feelings he conjured up in me. Feelings that scared me and made me wonder if I would ruin the good thing I had with Noah. Noah was the one I wanted and, as long as he held me in his arms, I could forget Xander and everything else that had happened tonight. There would be plenty of time to deal with all of that much later, after the dance which seemed far more like a dream than reality.

Chapter 8

When the dance ended at eleven o'clock, Noah and I bid good night to Brooke and Ethan as we left the school. After they disappeared across the parking lot, Noah and I hurried to his car. Only a few other students remained since many had left early for parties or just to be alone. In fact, I hadn't seen Xander in a few hours, and I shuddered at the thought of him alone with Marlena.

I shivered in the cold, the wrap pulled tightly around my shoulders no match for the frigid air nipping at my arms. Noah and I headed through the dark lot, the light from the perimeter lamps barely enough to see the rows of cars we slipped between. Halfway across the lot, I fell behind him, limping a little from a blister on my heel. But I managed to catch up and as soon as we were seated in the car, Noah started the engine before turning to me. "You look cold. It's going to take a minute for this thing to warm up."

Facing him, I leaned my cheek against the headrest. "You could warm me up."

He raised his eyebrows and grinned. "Is that an invitation?"

"Maybe," I replied with a sigh.

"You better decide quickly if it's not because I'm about to accept." Without waiting for me to respond, he leaned across the console and kissed me.

I tingled from his touch, parting my lips slightly to taste him. But instead of deepening the kiss, he pulled away, leaving me to wonder what I'd done wrong.

"What is it?" I asked.

Noah reached for a knob on the dashboard and turned it. "You're shivering. I'm just turning up the heat for you."

My shivering wasn't just from being cold, but I didn't tell him that. "Thanks. I didn't realize how cold it would get tonight when I picked out this dress."

"For what it's worth, you look very beautiful in it. So I'm glad you didn't worry about the weather when you picked it out."

I raised my eyebrows with a smile.

He leaned toward me, a sexy look in his dark eyes. "Well, you should know you've captured my imagination in that dress tonight."

"Good." I loved hearing him say things like that, even if I wasn't sure what to do about it.

But the moment passed when Noah changed the subject. "Okay, ready?"

My smile faded at once. I was sure my parents would be waiting up to talk when I got home. "Yes, I'm ready to go," I said slowly. "But not home to my parents. Please take me anywhere but home. I don't think I can deal with them right now."

Noah sighed. "You can't run from them forever. Eventually, you're going to have to hear them out."

"I know. But it's late, and we just had a wonderful night. I don't want to ruin it. I'll be ready for that tomorrow, but right now, it's the last thing I want to think about."

"Don't you think they've already gone to bed?"

I shook my head.

"Yeah, you're right. They've probably been on pins and needles all night worrying about this. Not to mention I'm sure they're still hoping to see you all dressed up since they missed you before the dance."

"Well, as far as I'm concerned, they can worry all night. I don't want to see them. So where can we go?"

Noah studied me, a thoughtful expression on his face. "I have no idea. Are there any twenty-four hour diners in this town?"

"No."

He paused for a moment, and I watched him, expecting him to come up with an idea. "What about my place?" he finally suggested, his voice hesitant.

"That would be great," I replied before he could change his mind.

At least it would be quiet, away from the other students we had just spent hours with, and away from my parents and any chance of the uncomfortable conversation I desperately wanted to avoid tonight. It would also be private, just the two of us. Butterflies danced in my stomach as I thought about seeing where he lived, where he ate, where he slept. The thought of being alone with him at his place excited me and scared me at the same time.

"You sure?" he asked, as if he wasn't.

I wasn't about to let him change my mind. Anything was better than facing my parents tonight. "Yes."

He let out a long sigh. "Okay. We'll go there, but just for an hour or so."

"Then what?" I asked. "The only way I can be sure that my parents won't have this conversation with me tonight is to not go home."

"Laken, that's crazy. You can't stay at my place all night," Noah said, shaking his head. "What about spending the night at Brooke's house? I could take you there."

My heart sank at his suggestion. Was he trying to get rid of me?

"I don't know what I'd say to her. I can't tell her about this yet. She knew something was wrong tonight and I lied because I didn't want her to worry. If she finds out about it now, she'll be crushed."

"What about Ethan?"

I shook my head. "Why can't I just stay at your place?"

He smiled faintly. "You're kidding, right? Do I need to remind you who your father is?"

"No. I know exactly who he is. But I also know I'm eighteen now. I'm old enough to stay out all night if I want to," I stated defiantly.

"You might be eighteen, but you still live with your parents. This isn't about age because you're right, you are old enough to make your own decisions. But you can't stay out all night without letting them know where you are. It isn't right."

"Neither is not telling me I'm adopted," I muttered. As much as I hated to admit it, he had a good point. If I didn't want to go home tonight, I had to make sure everyone, including Noah, approved of the way I handled the situation. "Fine. Can we just go to your place for now and figure it out later?"

"Okay, I'll make you a deal. I'll call your dad once we get there. If he says you can stay the night, then I'll take the couch." He paused before adding under his breath, "And a couple shots of whiskey."

I mulled over his offer, although I didn't have a better alternative. He was doing me a favor, so I had to play by his rules. Besides, he was right. If I didn't let my parents know where I was, my father would have a search party out looking for me by dawn. "Deal," I answered, wondering what I was getting myself into.

With a smile, Noah nodded. Then he backed the car away from the curb and drove out of the lot. I settled into my seat, securing my seat belt as I searched for something to say, the air between us becoming too quiet.

Noah broke the silence after turning onto the dark road that led to town. "My place is pretty small. I hope you're not expecting something fancy."

"I don't care about that. As long as you're there, that's all that matters." I flashed him a faint smile as shadows danced across the windshield. Small or large, fancy or understated, I didn't care what his place was like. All I could think about was that we would be alone.

"It won't take us long to get there." At the next stop sign, he turned onto Main Street, passing by the dark antique shops, diners, and bed and breakfast inns lining the sidewalks. About halfway through town, he pulled into an alley, leaving the street lamps behind.

A few seconds later, he eased the car into a tiny parking area behind the buildings and shut off the engine. "This is it. My apartment is over the North Country General Store." He turned off the headlights, sending the world outside into pitch black. "Wait here. I'll help you get out. This is a gravel lot, and I'm sure it won't be easy to walk in those shoes." He jumped out of the car, ran around the front and opened my door, reaching down for me.

My purse in my left hand, I took his outstretched arm with my right one. As he helped me rise to my feet, I awkwardly shifted my dress to pull the skirt down over my legs. Bitter cold air stung my face, but I ignored it, knowing a warm apartment waited. I clung to Noah for support and, once he shut the door, he released my hand to wrap his arm around my shoulder. His body pressed close to mine, he led me across the gravel to a wooden staircase. I barely managed to hobble up the steps with one arm locked around his waist and my other hand grasping the railing.

"Are you okay?" Noah asked.

Wincing, I stepped down on my left foot, the one with the blister. "Not really. These shoes are killing me."

"Ouch. Well, we're almost there. You can take them off as soon as we get inside."

I nodded appreciatively as I made it up the last few steps to a small landing in front of a door. In the darkness, Noah unlocked it and ushered me inside. He let go of me to pull the door shut before flipping on a light. As he had explained earlier, the apartment was small with sparse furnishings. The living room contents consisted of a couch, two end tables, a coffee table and an old box television set perched on a stand.

The bare cream-colored walls reminded me of a blank painter's canvas. Not one picture or wall hanging decorated them. The hardwood floor bore deep scratches in the dull finish, and the kitchen area contained a refrigerator, stove, oven, and dishwasher—all of which were a dull green color, reminiscent of the 'seventies. A small white microwave sat next to the stove, and a few dishes cluttered the remaining countertop space. A folding table with two chairs had been set up in the corner next to a window looking out into the black night. A laptop was on the table, its power cord hanging off the edge.

While I studied the apartment, Noah walked over to the thermostat on the wall. "A deputy's salary in this town isn't much. I keep the heat pretty low when I know I'll be out for a while. It'll warm up soon," he explained as he adjusted it.

"Makes sense." I had noticed a slight chill inside and kept my wrap in place around my shoulders. As Noah rushed about the apartment, I stood in the living room, not quite sure what to do.

"Sorry about the mess. I wasn't expecting company tonight." He picked up a shirt that had been strewn across the couch and carried it into another room.

After he disappeared, I slipped my feet out of my shoes, gaining instant relief from the painful blister. As I nudged them against the wall with my foot, Noah emerged from the back room, his jacket and tie missing and his white shirt unbuttoned at the top. He caught my eye and smiled. I hoped he didn't sense my uneasiness at being in his apartment alone with him. After all, I'd never dated a guy who had his own place.

He quickly noticed my shoes on the floor. "I bet it feels good to get those off."

I smiled and nodded. "Yeah. It does."

"Well, you don't have to stand by the door all night. Come on in and make yourself comfortable. Are you warming up?"

I slowly walked across the apartment to the couch and sat down next to the armrest. "Yes, I can feel the heat kicking in."

"Can I get you something to drink? How about a Sprite?"

"That would be great."

"Coming right up." Noah headed across the room and poured two glasses of Sprite. When he returned, he handed one to me.

"Thank you," I said, taking the glass and sipping the soda while he sat down next to me.

"So, is this pretty weird for you? Being here, that is."

"How'd you guess?" I asked with a guilty smile, briefly meeting his brown eyes before looking away.

"I could just tell. You seem nervous."

"Great. So it shows?"

"A little. But don't worry about it. It's only me, remember? You can relax."

I sighed. "I know. I just never thought I wouldn't want to go home like this. I've never been so upset with my parents before. I don't even know if I want to go home in the morning. If it wasn't for Dakota, I'd have nothing to go back to."

"Laken, don't say that. You're going to have to give your parents the benefit of the doubt. I'm sure there's a very good explanation for all this. If there's one thing I know about your dad, it's that he loves you more than anything."

"If he loves me so much, why didn't he tell me about this years ago?"

"I don't know. You're going to have to ask him that." Noah took a sip of his drink before placing it on the coffee table. Turning to me, he leaned his elbows on his knees. "Speaking of your dad, I need to call him before it gets too late. Unless you want to do the honors."

I shook my head emphatically. "No way. It's all yours."

"I figured you'd say that." With a comforting smile, Noah tapped my leg before returning to the kitchen counter where he'd left his phone. As he picked it up, I tugged my dress down over my leg still tingling from his touch.

When I looked up, Noah was leaning against the counter with the phone pressed against his ear. He watched me with a steady gaze while listening to the other end. After a minute, he raised his eyebrows. "Good evening, sir. I hope I didn't wake you." He smiled, appearing relieved. "Glad to hear it." He paused. "Yes, it was very nice. Thank you." He fell silent again, his gaze resting on me. "Yes, sir, she did. It's been kind of a hard night for her. She insisted on not going home right after the dance, so we're at my place. I told her I'd have to take her home unless it's okay with you if she stays here for the night. The decision is yours." As Noah watched me, I rolled my eyes, wishing I could hear my father's answer.

I shook my head in protest, convinced my father was insisting I come home immediately.

"I see, sir. Yes, I understand." Noah smiled broadly, his eyes lighting up. "No, sir. I'll take the couch. She'll be safe here with me." He paused again, and my heart raced as I quirked my eyebrows, not sure I'd heard him correctly. "Okay. Yes, I'm sure you do. And, yes, she is. I'll give her the message." After one last pause, he said, "Thank you for trusting me. It means a lot. Good night, sir." Noah hung up the call and placed his phone back on the counter. "You got your wish."

I opened my eyes wide in disbelief. "You're kidding. He's letting me stay out all night?"

"He's letting you stay here. I wouldn't say that's out. Just think of this as a second home." Noah crossed the room and sat on the coffee table directly in front of me. He hunched over, resting his elbows on his knees. "He asked if you overheard him and your mom talking, and I told him the truth. He's really upset you had to find out that way, especially right before a dance. He asked me to tell you that it doesn't change anything. That he and your mom still love you very much."

"It may not change anything for either of them be-cause they've known all along. But it changes everything for me. The life I thought I had, the parents I thought were mine. It's all been a lie this whole time."

Noah ran his fingers through his hair. "He knows you're confused and that you're bound to have feelings like that. But he wants you to know you can still come home tonight if you change your mind. He said your mom is in bed and he's turning in. If you go home, they won't be waiting up for you."

"Well, I'm not changing my mind. I don't want to go home. Nothing you just told me makes this any better," I said, tears welling up in my eyes. I blinked a few times to keep them from spilling down my cheeks and took a deep breath to steady my voice. "Can we not talk about this anymore?"

"Sure. Why don't I find something a little more comfortable for you to sleep in? You must be exhausted."

At the thought of changing for bed, heat flushed through me, a welcome distraction from my parents. I nodded weakly, practically holding my breath. When Noah stood and wandered across the apartment to the back door I assumed led to the bedroom, I let my breath out like a balloon being deflated. *I can do this,* I told myself. *I can stay here tonight. We're both adults, and I'm sure he's had female overnight guests before.* I frowned at my last thought, wondering what he usually did with his female guests.

"Laken," Noah called from the doorway of the back room. "Can you come here?"

I took one last gulp of Sprite and placed the glass on the coffee table. The wrap still hanging around my shoulders, I walked across the room, the hardwood floor cold under my stocking-covered feet. Reaching the doorway, I leaned against the frame, peering into the bedroom.

A small lamp on the only nightstand cast a dim light across the room. The bed was nothing more than a queen-sized mattress set lifted off the floor by a box frame, a crumpled light brown comforter covering it. A flimsy white curtain hung over the window located above the bed. A chest of drawers was cluttered with keys, a wallet, and hairbrush, among other personal items. Just like the rest of the apartment, the walls were empty of pictures and any other decorations.

Noah stood next to the open closet on the side wall. "I'm afraid everything I have is going to be pretty big on you. How about something like this?" He pulled out a dark blue shirt and held it up. "Will this work?"

"That'll be perfect."

"And here's a hanger for your dress," he said, gesturing with one before returning it to the closet.

My eyes on him, I reluctantly approached, stopping close enough to reach for the flannel shirt. "Thank you," I said quietly.

"You're welcome." As he gave me the shirt, his hand grazed mine. I tingled from his touch, painfully aware that we were alone in his bedroom. He whipped away, as if reading my mind. "I'll give you some privacy to change," he said before dropping his gaze and heading to the doorway where he paused and turned back to me. Then he pointed to another door just outside the bedroom. "The bathroom is right there in case you need it."

"That's good to know, because yes, I will need it," I replied, trying to act as though I was completely comfortable spending the night in his bed.

He flashed a quick smile before leaving me alone. After he shut the door, I placed the shirt on the bed, removed the wrap from my shoulders, and shimmied out of my dress. I hung them both on the wire hanger and rolled my stockings down off my legs. Goose bumps prickled my skin in the cool air as I stashed the crumpled stockings in the corner. Then I slipped into the flannel shirt, not surprised that it reached halfway down my thighs and well past my wrists. But it was soft and warm and smelled like Noah. I rubbed my arms, finding it hard to believe I was borrowing his shirt in his apartment. After removing my jewelry, letting down my hair, and making a quick trip to the bathroom, I slid into the bed, suddenly realizing how tired I was.

I had just turned onto my side facing away from the lamp and closed my eyes when I heard a soft knock.

"Laken?" Noah asked from the other side of the door.

My eyes flew open as I bolted upright. "Yes. You can come in," I assured him. "I'm done."

He accepted my invitation, but paused in the doorway, a glass of amber liquid in his hand. A grin lit up his face. "Well, this is something I never expected to see. You in my bed."

I returned his smile, feeling the heat race across my cheeks. "Never?" I asked before I could stop myself.

"Maybe not never, but at least as long as you're still in high school and your father is still the sheriff and my boss."

"Yeah, then that pretty much means never," I confirmed, teasing.

He entered the room, setting his glass on the dresser before walking to the side of the bed where he sat down, facing me. "So is this okay? Are you comfortable?"

"Yes, everything is great. You've made me feel at home." I glanced across the room to the chest where he'd left his drink. "What are you drinking?"

"Something strong," he answered with a smile. "You know, I never expected tonight to end like this."

I nodded, my eyes locking with his. "I never expected it to begin the way it did, either. But thank you for everything. You've been so patient and supportive. I really appreciate it."

"It was nothing, really. Any guy would have done the same."

I shook my head, disagreeing with him. "I doubt that. If I'd gone to the dance with some kid from my class, he wouldn't have cared. You're different than high school boys. It's nice." I paused, inching closer to him and boldly lifting my hand to touch his shoulder, my eyes never leaving his.

"Laken," he muttered. "What are you doing?" He ducked his head, shifting his eyes to the comforter before raising them back to me. Heat simmered in their brown depths.

"What do you want me to do?" I whispered.

He didn't answer, but rather leaned toward me, claiming my mouth with a bruising kiss. My eyelids fell as I parted my lips, tasting the bitter liquor he'd been drinking when his tongue touched mine. He wrapped his arm behind me, pulling me close against his chest. I touched his shoulders, my fingers finding their way into his hair. He shuddered, pushing me onto my back and lowering himself on top of me. His body crushed my chest, wedging me between him and the bed.

His weight pressing against me, his kiss deepened. Fire sizzled through my veins, pitching my thoughts into a dizzy head-spin. But my excitement quickly disappeared, replaced with the growing alarm that I was asking for something I wasn't ready for. I stiffened as Noah lifted his lips from mine to trace a line of kisses down my neck. I held my breath, the tingling sensations shooting temptation through me.

"Noah, stop," I murmured weakly, hoping he had more strength than I did. "Please."

A long sigh escaped his lungs and he pulled away. "I'm sorry," he said, abruptly sitting up. He shook his head, glancing away. "I knew this wasn't a good idea."

He looked down at me as I lay against the pillow, my hair fanned out on each side of my face. Raising his eyebrows, he blurted out, "I need another drink."

With that, he shot up to his feet and retrieved his glass from the top of the chest of drawers.

"You don't have to apologize," I said, raising up to lean on my elbow.

"Yes, I do," he stated as he turned, his drink in one hand. He downed a sip, drawing in a sharp breath. "If not to you, at least to myself. When I promised your dad you'd be safe tonight, that wasn't exactly what I had in mind."

I swallowed nervously when his apologetic eyes met mine. "You know, if nothing at all happened here tonight, I'd think there's something wrong with me."

"There is nothing wrong with you. That's the problem." A faint smile tugged at the corners of his mouth as he took another gulp of his drink. "Now I'm going to grab a pillow for the couch and get out of here so you can get some sleep." He walked along the far side of the bed, and I turned to watch him grab the spare pillow with his free hand.

"What time do you need me to be up in the morning?" I asked.

"You can sleep as late as you like. I don't have to be anywhere tomorrow." Noah reached down to turn off the lamp, and darkness cloaked the room, the dim light sliding in from the living room casting a shadow over his face.

"My dad didn't say I had to be home by a certain time?"

"No. I think all he cares about is that you're ready to talk to him and your mom when you get back," he said, his voice growing faint while he headed toward the doorway.

"What if I'm not ready to talk?"

"You can't run forever," he reminded me.

"I know," I murmured before rolling over onto my other side and pulling the covers up to my neck. "In case I forget to tell you tomorrow, I had a great time at the dance tonight."

"Me, too. Well, get some sleep and I'll see you in the morning."

Then the door clicked shut and I closed my eyes.

The events of the evening raced through my thoughts, keeping me awake for what seemed like hours. I wasn't sure what bothered me more—my parents' voices echoing in my mind or visions of Xander holding Marlena close at the dance. In the end, the memory of Noah's kisses erased both of those nightmares, and I fell asleep thinking about him and wondering if this was what falling in love felt like.

Chapter 9

Despite the unfamiliar apartment and bed, I slept soundly and awoke the next morning feeling rested. When I first opened my eyes, memories of the night before starting with my parents' hushed conversation in their bedroom and ending with Noah's amazing kisses came flooding back to me. As much as I wanted to linger in the warm bed that smelled like him, I forced myself to get up. Somehow, I would get through today and the dreaded talk I would inevitably have with my parents about my adoption.

Sunlight peeked in from around the edges of the flimsy curtain, casting a soft glow across the room. I sat up, realizing the only thing I had to change into this morning was my dress from last night. I frowned, but my spirits lifted when I heard dishes clanking beyond the bedroom door. I thought I smelled coffee brewing as I slipped out from under the covers, craving a hot cup of it before I had to deal with reality.

My bare feet touched the wooden floor, and I cringed

at the cold surface. A chill in the air sent goose bumps racing up my bare legs as I hurried across the room to the door and slowly opened it. I hesitated in the doorway, jumping when Noah appeared, a grin on his face and a mug of steaming coffee in his hand. Freshly showered and shaven, he wore a gray T-shirt and blue jeans, making me feel a bit self-conscious as I ran a hand through my hair.

He greeted me with a smile. "Good morning. How did you sleep?"

"Really well," I admitted. "How was the couch?"

He cringed subtly. "Honestly, a little stiff. But I'm sure the whiskey didn't help, either."

"What time is it?"

"Almost ten o'clock."

"What?" I gasped. "I can't believe I slept this late. My father didn't call, did he? I know he didn't tell you when I needed to be home, but I'm sure they expected me hours ago." Shaking my head, I forgot all about my tangled hair. Not only was I worried about my parents' reaction when I arrived home late, but I dreaded putting my dress back on for the ride home. That was going to feel really weird—riding through town in last night's dress. I hoped no one would see me.

"I don't think you have anything to worry about. Your dad dropped by about an hour ago to bring you a change of clothes and a few other things. See?" Noah gestured toward the coffee table.

I looked across the apartment, smiling at the sight of my overnight bag. "Wow. That was really cool of him. I was just thinking how uncomfortable it would be to put my dress back on this morning."

"And now you don't have to. I'm guessing there's a toothbrush in there, too."

Surprised at my father's gesture, I shot past Noah to

retrieve the bag. Then I carried it back to the bedroom, stopping outside the bathroom door a few feet away from where Noah still stood. "If you don't mind, I'm going to get cleaned up."

"No, of course not," he said. "Take your time. I'll be in the kitchen. How do you like your coffee?"

"Loaded with creamer. Hazelnut if you have it," I answered before squeezing into the tiny bathroom with my overnight bag, not sure if he responded when I shut the door behind me.

Ten minutes later, I emerged from the bathroom in jeans, a black sweatshirt, and a pair of sneakers, my teeth freshly brushed and my hair combed into smooth waves. I would have loved to have taken a shower, but I didn't want to impose on Noah any longer than I had to. That would just have to wait until I got home.

Back in the bedroom, I placed the shirt Noah had loaned me for the night on his bed. Then I scooped up my jewelry and hair clips from the cluttered top of the chest of drawers and tucked them into the side pocket of my overnight bag. After zipping all of the compartments, I carried it back to the coffee table.

"Feel better?" Noah asked as I crossed the room to join him. He immediately stood, leaving his coffee on the table, and headed over to the kitchen counter. "I waited until you were done to get your coffee so it wouldn't get cold. Are you hungry? I can make us some breakfast."

"No, thanks. I'm not much of a breakfast person. I'll get some lunch later when I get home."

Noah turned to face me after he finished pouring coffee into a black mug. "Are you sure? I've got some cereal and there might be a few frozen waffles in the freezer, but they're kind of old."

"I'll pass."

"Yeah, that's probably a smart move. Now, if I'd

known you were going to spend the night, I would have made sure I had everything to make you blueberry pancakes for breakfast. I make the best blueberry pancakes," he announced before opening the refrigerator and splashing some creamer into my coffee.

"I'll keep that in mind," I said as he tucked the creamer into a shelf on the refrigerator door and shut it. "Maybe I can get a rain check?" I added, raising my eyebrows.

A smug look crept onto Noah's face when he returned to the table with my coffee. He set it down in front of me and sat in the other chair. "Are you trying to get me fired, or just killed?" he teased with a smile.

Returning his smile, I sipped the hot coffee. We lingered at the table for about twenty minutes, talking about the dance, Dakota, and the week ahead, everything except the conversation with my parents I wanted to put off as long as I could.

After we finished our coffee, Noah insisted it was time for me to get home. When we pulled into my driveway, I sat motionless, staring at the white farmhouse surrounded by yellow, orange, and red trees crawling up the mountains behind it. *Home sweet home,* I thought. *Or at least it was.* Stalling, I fidgeted with the plastic covering my dress that I held in my lap.

Noah seemed to sense my hesitation and turned to face me as the car engine purred softly. "Do you want me to walk you to the door?"

"No," I said, shaking my head as I stared at the only home I'd ever known. Slowly, I tore my eyes away from it and looked at him. "But thank you for offering."

"You sure you don't need some help with your things?" Noah asked when I made no move to open the door.

"I'm sure." I took a deep breath. "I guess I'd better go in and get this over with."

He offered me a reassuring smile. "It may not be as bad as you expect. Call me later. I want to hear how it went, if you're ready to talk about it, that is."

I nodded. "I will. But you can call or text me anytime. No matter what happens, hearing from you will cheer me up."

"Got it."

I reached for the door handle, my hand lingering on it when he spoke again. "Is it too soon to ask if you're free next Saturday night?" he asked.

I felt a wide smile light up my face. "No, it's not. And yes, I'm free. We don't have any plans."

"You do now. Maybe I'll make you dinner at my place, now that you've seen my apartment."

"That sounds great." My heart fluttered with excitement. It was one thing to have had a wonderful time at the dance, but it was even better to have another date with him to look forward to.

As I turned away and opened the door, I heard Noah's voice. "Wait, Laken, there's one more thing."

I looked back at him without a word, my eyes questioning.

"I just wanted to do this." He leaned across the console to kiss me, his touch gentle and as light as a feather. I let my eyelids fall closed for the brief moment his lips were upon mine, opening them when he pulled away. A sly grin lingered on his face. "Hmm. Maybe I'll stop by sometime during the week. I don't think I want to wait another week to do that again."

"I like the way you think," I said quietly.

"Well, you'd better get going before I take you back to my place."

I raised my eyebrows, my gaze hovering on him while his kisses from last night on his bed flashed through my thoughts. "Is that a threat or a promise?"

"You're bad," he accused, teasing. "And sometimes so not what I expected."

"I try." I paused, taking another deep breath. Then I tore my eyes away from him to look back at the house. "Okay, I'd better go. I'll call you later."

I pushed the car door open and climbed out with the dress and wrap folded over one arm and my overnight bag hanging from my shoulder. Noah flashed me one last smile before I shut the door and circled around the front of the sedan on my way to the sidewalk.

I heard Noah's car back out of the driveway and pull away as I let myself into the house. Trudging through the front door, I was greeted by an overwhelming silence. When I walked into the kitchen, neither my mother nor my father appeared. Even Dakota was nowhere to be seen. Instead, I found a note scribbled on the back of a torn envelope on the table. *We went out for brunch. We'll be home around noon. Love, Mom and Dad.*

I sighed thoughtfully as I stood in the quiet kitchen. Part of me was relieved that I didn't have to face my parents right away, but another part of me itched to get it over with. Trying not to think about it, I returned my mother's wrap to the coat closet, then carried my dress and overnight bag upstairs to my room. After hanging my dress in the closet, I unpacked my things before heading straight to the bathroom for a hot shower.

છબછ

Twenty minutes later as I combed the tangles out of my wet hair after showering, my stomach growled. I hadn't eaten since the night before, and it was catching up with me. Dressed in jeans and a gray sweatshirt, I descended the stairs to the kitchen and went straight to the refrigerator, my sights set on the egg salad I had made yesterday. After pulling it out with lettuce and a loaf of wheat bread, I dropped two pieces of bread into the toaster and pushed the lever down. I was about to find something to drink when I heard the garage door open, and my heart skipped a beat. My parents were home. The time of reckoning had arrived.

As I leaned against the counter next to the toaster, the door to the garage opened and my father walked in alone. Dressed in jeans, a black button-down shirt, and a dark green jacket, he carried a folded newspaper. As soon as he noticed me, he stopped, a somber yet relieved expression washing over his face. "Laken," he said with a faint smile. "You're home."

I nodded. "Yeah," I replied quietly, not sure what else to say as an awkward silence hovered between us.

Not even a minute passed before the toast sprang up with a loud wiry pop. I jumped, wishing the tension between us would disappear as quickly as the toaster had popped. As I expected, my wish went unanswered. "Where's Mom?" I asked.

"I dropped her off at school. She's a little behind and thought she'd get more done there. One of us will have to pick her up in a few hours." My father scanned the counter. "Making lunch?"

"Um-hm," I answered, realizing my appetite had vanished the moment he had walked in.

"Maybe we can talk while you eat."

"Or maybe we can talk right now. I can eat later." I hadn't planned to be so demanding, it had just come out like that.

He frowned, seeming uncomfortable. "Of course," he replied, gesturing at the table. "Why don't we sit down?"

With a nod, I walked across the kitchen and sank into a chair. My father followed, dropping the newspaper on the table and hanging his coat on the back of the chair across from me before sitting down. He looked at me, his eyes full of sadness. "Laken, I know you heard us last night, and I'm really sorry if it ruined the dance for you."

"Dad, I don't care about the dance. I care about knowing who I am and who my real parents are."

"I know you may not believe me, but we never meant for you to find out this way. We had always planned to tell you, we just never found the right time. You really caught me off guard when you asked about Ivy."

"Why? You said I'm related to her. How am I related to her?"

My father studied me thoughtfully before answering. "She's your biological mother."

Sucking in a deep breath as tears welled up in my eyes, I swallowed the lump in my throat. "If she's my real mother, who is my real father?"

"I am," he stated.

I remembered my mother telling him that he had to tell me because he was my father. She had meant because he was my real father. "What?" I gasped. "But—how? What about Mom? How could you do that to her? And how could she be okay with this?"

"It's not what you think. I know it's hard for you to see that now, but your mother was really fine with the way everything happened." He paused, watching me for a moment before continuing. "Your mother, Ivy, and I all grew up here in Lincoln. We went to the same schools right up through graduation. Your mother was my best friend, kind of like what Ethan is to you. We were inseparable, but it was a friendship. There was nothing romantic going on between us because I had always liked Ivy. I think, back then, your mother wanted more, but she knew I couldn't give her anything more than friendship until I got over Ivy."

"Then how did you two end up married?"

"Well, it didn't happen overnight, that's for sure. Ivy and I started dating in our junior year of high school. Your mother and I drifted apart then, and she dated some other boys. We were still friends, of course, but not as close. After graduation, Ivy and I moved away together."

"Where did you go?"

"Wyoming. Yellowstone, actually." He smiled wistfully. "Your mother, I mean Ivy, always had a special love of wolves. She insisted on trekking more than halfway across the country to be part of the wolf reintroduction program in Yellowstone. I thought she was nuts. The people working on that program had a formal education in wildlife biology and wolf behavior. But she insisted she'd be able to help even though she didn't have any credentials. It turned out, she was right. She'd always had a special touch with animals. I even remember her taking in an orphaned bear cub one summer. So when we got out west, she started volunteering and, within a month, she was offered a job. I found work as a deputy for the sheriff in a nearby town and we lived out there for about three years before she got pregnant with you."

"Were you married?"

My father grinned with guilt. "No, we weren't. I wanted to get married, but Ivy was a free spirit. She didn't believe you needed marriage to have a deeply committed relationship."

"Where was Mom all this time?"

"She stayed here in New Hampshire to go to college. We kept in touch with letters, but they grew less frequent the longer Ivy and I stayed in Wyoming."

I sighed, digesting all of this as my father paused again. Finally, I asked, "Why did my mother, I mean Ivy, give me up? Didn't she want me?" I distinctly remembered my mother's comment last night about the first time she'd held me as a baby. She and my father also had countless pictures of the three of us since right after I was born, so I knew Ivy couldn't have kept me for very long, if even at all.

Tears glimmered in my father's eyes. "Of course, she wanted you. Ivy was diagnosed with stage four cancer right before you were born. Fortunately, it wasn't anything that would hurt you, but the doctors told her she only had a few months left to live. She decided right away that she needed to find a mother for you who would be there for years to come. She chose to give you up right away. I wanted her to spend her last days with you, but she insisted it was better her way." He choked out a smile. "She could be quite stubborn. There was no convincing her otherwise. She also worried that, if the doctors were wrong and she survived a few more years, you would eventually lose her after you got to know her and depend on her. She didn't want to put you through that."

"What about you? Didn't she want to spend her last days with you?"

"Yes, but she gave that up to do what was best for you."

"Wow. I can't even imagine what she went through to make those decisions. She sounds really amazing." I admired her strength to put those she loved first while facing death. "What happened after that? How did you and Mom get together?"

"That actually happened pretty fast. Your mother had just taken a teaching position in Boston. It was an awful inner city school and she hated it. The kids had no interest in learning and she would write me letters telling me how she cried herself to sleep every night. By then, I knew quite a few people in town, and they happened to be looking for an elementary school teacher. So she packed up and left Boston to move out to Wyoming with me. You were almost a month old by the time she arrived. She instantly fell in love with you and, despite my grief from losing Ivy, I fell in love with the way she cared for you as if you were her own. She doted on you hand and foot. I barely had a chance to hold you after work because she wouldn't let you out of her arms. She was just as nurturing and protective as any mother would be. So you brought us together, and we got married about a year later, right before moving back to New Hampshire."

"Why did you move back here?"

"We missed it. And we both knew it's a great place to raise a child. You have loved it, haven't you?"

"Yes," I said, nodding. "Did you and Mom ever think about having a child together?" I had never really felt a void in my life from not having a brother or a sister with all the animals I had to keep me company, so I'd never asked my parents why they hadn't had another child.

"We tried for a while, but it just never happened. And we've always been okay with that. I think both of us worried a little that if your mom had her own baby, he or she would get more of her attention. It was easier to accept things for what they were and treasure the one child we had been given. You."

I couldn't imagine my mother ever playing favorites, but I respected their decision. "Did your parents know Ivy was my real mother?"

"Yes. They knew when Gwen moved out west, and the timing wouldn't lie."

So even my grandparents had known all along. "What about the town?"

My father shook his head. "Nope. No one else knew. When we moved back, both your mother and I had been gone long enough that we claimed you were ours and no one questioned it." He paused, his warm brown eyes appearing sad and reminiscent. "We never looked back, and I hope you won't either."

I met his caring stare and shook my head. "No, I won't. I know you and Mom have always done what's best for me." I paused long enough to draw in a deep sigh. "Wow. This was not what I expected."

"What did you expect?"

I shrugged. "To find out I was adopted from strangers. That maybe my real parents were high school kids who got in trouble. This is way more complicated, but at least I wasn't an accident or abandoned by parents who didn't want me."

"Far from it." My father reached over to squeeze my hand that rested on the table. "Wait here. I have something for you." He let go of me and rose to his feet. After pushing his chair behind him, he hurried out of the kitchen and around the corner.

Within minutes, he reappeared holding a battered old shoebox. He returned to his seat and placed it on the table in front of me. "Go on," he said. "Open it."

Raising my eyebrows, I lifted the lid to find dozens of old faded photographs inside. A sealed envelope with my name scrawled across the front rested on top of them, and I held it up. "What's this?"

"That's a letter Ivy wrote to you. She asked me to give it to you once I told you about her."

"So she wanted you to tell me about her?"

He nodded. "Absolutely. She wouldn't have had it any other way. But I'm sure she never expected you'd beat me to it." He forced out a small smile and then continued. "You don't have to open that now. You can wait until you're ready."

I placed the envelope on the table and reached for one of the photographs. The first one I picked up made me smile. A young woman with green eyes and blonde hair spilling out of her white knit hat laughed while a gray wolf licked her cheek. Snowflakes dotted the photograph and a wintry white landscape blurred in the background. My breath caught in my chest, unexpected emotions tugging at my heart. We looked alike, so much so that I could have been looking in a mirror. I held the photograph up. "This is her? Ivy?"

"Yes. You look more and more like her every day."

I put the picture down and reached for another one showing a slightly younger Ivy surrounded by the bright green foliage of spring as she nursed a bear cub with a bottle. I flashed this one up for my father to see. "Where was this taken?"

"That was right here in New Hampshire during the spring of our junior year. She found an orphaned bear cub on one of her hikes into the mountains and brought him home. Her father wasn't too happy about it."

"What about her mother?"

"Her mother died when she was young, which was another reason she didn't want you to know her only to lose her in the end. She knew how painful that was from her own experience."

I placed the picture back in the box, almost afraid to keep looking at them. One thing was certain, Ivy seemed to have a special touch with wild animals just like I did. I wondered if she could communicate with them like I could, but I had to accept that I might never find out. "So she was good with animals?" I asked, hoping my father would tell me everything he knew about that side of her.

He smiled. "Yes, very. She had a way with them that I never understood. No one did, not me and not her father. You can thank her for Dakota. The only reason I gave you a chance with him was because I figured you might have inherited her unique talent. It seems I was right, at least where Dakota is concerned."

Now it all made perfect sense. A part of me had always thought convincing my parents to let me raise a wolf had been much too easy. But I had been so excited to get him that I figured I shouldn't question their reasons for letting me keep him. "Maybe you should have told me about her when we got Dakota."

"No," he said, shaking his head. "You were thirteen and you had enough in life to worry about."

"Yeah, you're probably right about that." I smiled faintly as I sifted through the box of old photographs, picking up a few more. After several minutes, I placed them all back in the box along with the envelope. "Can I keep this? I'd like to look through the pictures a little more."

"Yes. It's yours. I want you to have everything in it."

"Thanks, Dad." I reached for the box and backed up my chair, my lunch forgotten.

"Not so fast," my father said, appearing to notice my intended getaway.

I stood beside the table, the shoebox in my hands as I raised my eyebrows. "Yes?"

"Are we okay here? I mean, last night, you wouldn't even talk to your mom. You were pretty upset and I want to make sure everything is back to normal. We are still your parents and we love you just as much as we always have."

I smiled before answering honestly. "Well, I won't say it's like nothing ever happened. But I'm not upset, at least not anymore. I'm just going to need some time to get used to this. And I want to know more about—her." I raised the shoebox as I spoke my last word.

"I understand. But can you do me a favor and pick up your mom later this afternoon? It would mean a lot to her."

"Sure. I can do that."

"Great. The Patriots play at one and I don't want to have to leave during the game."

"Now the truth comes out. You have an ulterior motive."

"It's more like a coincidence. I really meant it when I said it will mean a lot to your mom."

"I know." I backed away from the table, intending to head upstairs to my room. But I stopped after two steps when my father spoke again.

"Wait. I have one more matter to discuss with you."

"What's that?"

"About last night. It was an exception, a one-time deal. I know how upset you were and, at the time, it seemed like a good idea to give you permission to stay over at Noah's. But I woke up this morning feeling like a very irresponsible father. I can't and won't let you stay out at Noah's all night again. That said, I want you to know I only allowed it because I know I can trust you and I can trust Noah."

I felt heat flush through my cheeks and hoped my father didn't notice. "I kind of figured all that."

"Good. I just wanted to set the record straight," he said, a teasing smile lighting up his face. "Of course, I also know better than to think not letting you stay over at Noah's will keep you two from doing whatever you want."

I gasped. "Dad!"

"Hey, you're eighteen now. I remember what it was like to be eighteen and in love." He paused, his smile fading as his voice resumed a serious tone. "Just be careful."

"Dad, first of all, you have nothing to worry about. And secondly, this is a little embarrassing, so can I please go up to my room now?"

"Yes. But what about your lunch?" He gestured to the toast still sticking up out of the toaster on the counter.

"I'll be back down in about fifteen minutes." With the box clutched tightly in my hands, I rushed around the table to the stairs, eager to escape to my room. I had just lifted my foot onto the bottom step when I heard my name and stopped for the third time.

"Laken?"

I rolled my eyes and sighed, not quite sure what to expect this time. "Yes?" I asked wearily without turning around.

"I love you very much. I just hope you know that."

"I do," I said. I had never once doubted his love. "I love you, too, Dad." Hoping we were done, I bounded up the stairs to my room, anxious to sort through the pictures of Ivy in privacy. I wasn't ready to read her letter, but I would put it in a safe place and save it for another time.

When I reached the top of the stairs, I hurried into my bedroom and along the edge of my bed to the nightstand where I flipped on the light. Then I sat on the purple comforter and swung my legs over the side, leaning back against the pillows. In the silence, I removed the shoebox lid and began studying the photographs one by one. I wanted to learn as much as I could about Ivy, but most importantly, I wanted to know more about her special way with animals. Ever since I had started talking to animals, I had wondered how I did it and where I'd gotten that ability. I had a feeling I was about to find out.

Chapter 10

I spent hours poring over the pictures of Ivy that afternoon. There were photographs of her with wolves, bear cubs, and even one of her bottle-feeding a moose calf with long wobbly legs. There were others of her with a younger version of my father out at dinner, dressed up for formal dances, and snow skiing, their eyes locked on each other in every photograph. I could tell they had been very much in love. Then there were pictures of her when she had been pregnant, her belly swollen with her unborn child—me.

Buried beneath the pictures, I found an old newspaper clipping. Forgetting the photographs, I carefully lifted it out of the box. Thin and yellowed from years in storage, the newspaper nearly ripped as I picked it up when the headline jumped out at me. *Woman Saves Family from Grizzly Attack.*

I couldn't tear my eyes away from it as I read the story about an unidentified woman who had helped a family hiking in Yellowstone one spring morning. They had stumbled into the path of a mother grizzly bear with two cubs, and the article explained that as the bear charged at the family, an unknown young woman stepped between them. The man had told reporters she stood fearlessly before the bear, staring at it. She had instructed him and his family to stand still and not to run while she held her hand out. The charging grizzly slowed to a walk and, as if in a trance, approached the woman and sniffed her hand. The woman had smiled without taking her eyes off the bear, speaking softly over her shoulder to the family. "Turn around and walk away slowly. Whatever you do, don't run. You're safe now."

The woman had never been identified. The park service had asked her to come forward and accept a reward offered by the family, but I didn't find any other articles in the box indicating she had. I read the newspaper clipping at least four times, imagining what it must have been like to face a huge grizzly bear. I had only known black bears who were dwarfed by their notoriously temperamental western relatives. I wondered if fear had ever entered Ivy's mind as the grizzly charged at her. The only thing I could be sure of was that she had been just like me. And knowing at least one other person out there could talk to animals somehow made me feel a little less different.

Later that afternoon, I picked up my mother at the elementary school as I had promised. Even though my thoughts lingered on what I now knew about Ivy, I made sure my mother knew I still loved her. After learning how and why she had adopted me, I simply couldn't stay mad.

"You know it doesn't change anything," she told me as I guided the Explorer through town on our way home.

The sidewalks were bustling with tourists carrying bags from local shops while they enjoyed the fall afternoon. The bright sun and blue skies were blinding, despite the chill in the air.

"I know," I said, glancing at her as I drove. "I was really upset last night, but when Dad explained everything, I felt a lot better. I can't explain it, but I'm okay now."

"Good." My mother smiled, her eyes brimming with tears. "Because it was killing me last night. I was so worried about you. Did you have a nice time at the dance with Noah?"

"Yes, in spite of everything, he was great. I don't know how I would have handled things without him." *Including Xander's visit to the girls' bathroom,* a voice snuck into my head. As soon as Xander flashed through my mind, I scolded myself. I hadn't thought about him all afternoon. Why now? Couldn't I get through one day without being tormented by him?

"I'm sorry you felt you had to stay out all night. Do you want to talk about that?" my mother asked gently.

I had a feeling she meant more than what I had found out about Ivy. She meant if I wanted to talk about anything that had happened with Noah. Even though nothing had happened, I still didn't want to talk about it with her. "No. I'm good," I replied casually.

"He's a very nice young man. You seem happy with him."

"I am." Again, my answer was short and to the point. It felt really weird talking to either of my parents about him, especially my father. At least this conversation wasn't as embarrassing as the one I'd had with him a few hours ago.

"Well, if there's anything you want to talk about, you know you can come to me, right? After all, you're getting older and I know things can get complicated. With boys, I mean."

"Mom," I started, rolling my eyes. "I'm fine. You don't have to worry about any of that stuff. I know I can come to you if I have any questions." I flashed her a reassuring smile, hoping this conversation would end soon.

As we reached the edge of town, I turned onto a side street, leaving the activity behind us.

"You know I still love you just as much as I always have," she said, sending the conversation back to one about my adoption, much to my relief.

"Yes."

"Good. Because you are my daughter. It never mattered to me that I didn't give birth to you. What mattered was that Ivy trusted me with you, and being given that trust meant more to me than anything. I've cherished you more than you could know, ever since the first day you were placed into my arms," she said while tears returned to her eyes.

"Mom, I understand," I said, feeling moisture fill my eyes. "I think you did a wonderful thing, and I think Ivy did a very selfless thing. It's still going to take a little getting used to, but I'm okay."

She sighed, wiping at her eyes. "You're an amazing girl, did you know that?"

"Mom," I groaned. This was now almost as embarrassing as my conversation about Noah with my father a little earlier. Almost, but not quite.

"No, I mean it. Sometimes I can't believe what a wonderful person you turned out to be. So responsible and mature. You've made your father and me very proud."

"Thanks, Mom," I said with a quick sniffle, then took a deep breath as I turned onto our street.

Thank goodness we were almost home. I wasn't sure how much more of this conversation I could handle.

Fortunately, my mother didn't say anything more. The rest of the drive was spent in a comfortable silence.

When we arrived home, my mother joined my father to catch the second half of the football game, giving me the chance to escape them both and head upstairs to my room.

That evening, I barely finished my homework assignments in between phone calls with Noah and Brooke. I felt like a broken record as I told each of them about my birth mother. In true Brooke fashion, after mildly scolding me for not telling her about Ivy sooner, she pitched into an endless stream of questions about my night with Noah. She was far more interested in what had happened between us at his apartment than rehashing a past I couldn't change. I finally had to cut her off so I could get back to my homework. But I did it gently, reminding myself how much I loved her for always making me feel like a normal teenager.

୧৵৩

My week had only just begun the next morning when Xander approached me at my locker. The crowded hallway buzzed with chatter, the other students gossiping about the weekend's homecoming events as I sorted through my books alone. I barely glanced at him when I saw him out of the corner of my eye, wondering what he wanted now.

"What did you find out about Ivy Jensen?" he asked, leaning against the locker next to mine. Curiosity burned deep in his clear blue eyes.

I shot him a glance as I continued organizing my books on the top shelf inside my locker. His tan had started to fade and his skin appeared pale against his black shirt. He watched me, seeming to expect an answer right away, but I avoided his gaze and finished sorting my books. Then I removed my jacket, revealing the purple shirt I wore with blue jeans and black boots. My hair hung loose and my diamond necklace rested above my shirt. "Exactly what I needed to know," I replied before hanging my jacket on the hook.

"And what is that?"

I huffed, shaking my head and flashing an angry look his way. "First of all, it's none of your business. And secondly, would it kill you to say good morning?"

He smiled coyly. "Good morning. There, happy now?"

"It kind of defeats the purpose when you say it only after I had to ask."

"But now that I did, are you going to answer me?"

"No," I said flatly, hoisting my book bag strap up over my shoulder. Then I slammed my locker door shut and backed away. "See you."

I spun on my heels, ready to escape into the crowded hallway. Chills raced down my spine, but I ignored them. Ever since Saturday night, Noah had dominated my thoughts. It was quite refreshing to be able to brush off Xander so easily. A smile curled my lips and, as much as I wanted to see the look on his face, I resisted the urge to turn around. I had only taken one step when a hand grabbed my shoulder, stopping me while my confident smile faded. As Xander had promised many times, he simply didn't give up.

"My father has done some research on your necklace. He wanted me to ask you to come over soon. How about lunch next Saturday?"

Taking a deep breath, I swallowed nervously and wished the goosebumps on my arm would go away. Then I slowly turned far enough to see him out of the corner of my eye. "I thought he was just going to find out what it's worth."

"I thought you said you were never going to sell it. Wouldn't you like to know where it came from? What its history is?"

I sighed thoughtfully, tempted by his offer, especially

after discovering who my birth mother was. I might learn more about her, and possibly myself. "Fine. But only if you promise not to show up on my doorstep at midnight or follow me into the girls' bathroom again."

"You never forget anything, do you?"

"Nope," I said, smiling.

"Okay," he relented. "But in return, maybe you can tell me what you know about Ivy."

"Why do you care?" I asked, shaking my head in confusion.

He leaned toward me, stopping when his lips were so close I could feel his breath whisper across my cheek. "Because I care about you, and I don't like to see you upset like you were at the dance."

"Well, I'm fine now. I had a long talk with my dad yesterday and, for the first time since I can remember, things actually make sense."

"I'm glad to hear that. And I can't wait for you to explain what you mean by that. You're being awfully cryptic this morning, you know."

"And it's driving you crazy, isn't it? Now you know how it feels." I paused, realizing how satisfying it felt to turn the tables on him. He'd been talking in circles around me ever since he'd arrived in town, and now it was my turn. "All right," I agreed. "I'm free this weekend. Just let me know when to come over."

"Great. We should probably also get some work done on our project."

"Okay, just as long as we don't go back to that library. I don't think I have the energy to deal with the librarian this week."

"Maybe for this week, but we only got through a few books last time," he said. "I think we owe it to ourselves to check out the rest of them at some point."

"Yeah, I know. It did seem like we barely got started

before she closed up." I paused, silence falling over us as my eyes locked with his, the students in the hall becoming a blur beyond his stare. A few seconds later, I snapped out of my trance, shifting my gaze to the floor. "If we're done here, I'm going to homeroom. See you."

Xander scanned the crowd of students behind me. "Yeah. I'll catch you later," he said, his voice sounding distracted before he rushed past me and down the hall.

I was about to head to homeroom, but my curiosity got the best of me. I turned to see Xander pulling Marlena into his arms while students veered around them. Her light hair shining under the fluorescent lights, she touched his face when he kissed her. Jealousy ripped through me as it always seemed to whenever I saw them together, and I frowned, my feet frozen in place and my eyes locked on the happy couple. When Xander lifted his lips from her, she smiled at him. He hugged her close, but his eyes wandered down the hall, landing on me.

Mortified that he had caught me staring at them, I quickly looked away. Then I pushed my way through the crowded hallway, bumping into the other students in my quest to leave Xander as far behind as possible.

❧❧❧

Xander insisted on giving me a ride to his house Saturday. I tried to explain that I was perfectly capable of driving myself, but my words fell on deaf ears. I was up in my room packing my book bag when I heard his truck pull into the driveway. Pausing, I watched Dakota leap up from his bed and scramble across the room. He charged through the bedroom doorway, his nails scraping the hardwood floor as he raced down the stairs, apparently eager to meet Xander at the front door. I shook my head, still wondering what had gotten into that wolf. After a few seconds, I finished packing up, zipped my book bag, and hoisted the strap over my shoulder. Holding it close to my hip, I stormed down the stairs.

The doorbell rang when I reached the bottom and rushed across the kitchen. As I hurried into the entry hall, my father emerged from the family room wearing jeans and a black sweatshirt, a folded magazine in his hand. "Noah?" he asked, his eyebrows raised.

I shook my head, my hair brushing against my cheeks. "Xander. I'm going over to his house to work on our History project today." I stopped just shy of the door. "Actually, can you get it? I need to get my coat."

"Sure. But what about Dakota?" My father gestured to Dakota who stood at the front door, his nose glued to the handle and his eyes locked on it as if he could will it to open.

I shrugged, heading for the coat closet. "He'll be fine. They've already met, and don't ask me why, but Dakota loves him."

"How did that happen?" my father grumbled.

"I don't know. It was really weird. Dakota jumped on him like he'd known him all his life," I explained absent-mindedly, remembering their first meeting just after midnight.

"I don't mean how does Dakota like him, I mean how did they meet. Laken, we had a deal. No one, and I mean no one, can find out about him," my father warned.

I spun around, forgetting about finding a jacket for the moment. "I know," I said. "I'm sorry. It was an accident, really. Xander won't tell anyone. He promised."

"Well let's just hope he keeps that promise. But you need to be more careful in the future."

"I will," I muttered, hoping the lecture was over as I turned, opened the coat closet, and reached for my denim jacket.

Behind me, my father answered the door, letting cold air into the house when he opened it.

"Xander," he said, greeting him. "Nice to see you again. I'm glad you came by because I didn't get a chance to thank you for pulling the Explorer out of the woods."

"Oh, that was no big deal. I was just glad I could help," Xander replied. Then, he said, "Hey there, Dakota."

I dropped my book bag to the floor and slipped into my jacket, flipping my hair out from under the collar. Picking my book bag up again, I whirled around to see Xander kneeling in front of Dakota, scratching the fur between his ears.

The two of them were at eye level, causing alarm to shoot through me. Staring a wolf in the eye like that was a good way to get attacked. Xander apparently didn't know that a wolf shouldn't be treated like an ordinary house dog.

In spite of Dakota's wagging tail, I called him over to me. "Dakota, come here."

Reluctantly, he turned away from Xander and trotted across the foyer. When he stopped beside me, I touched the top of his head. "Good boy," I whispered.

Xander rose to his feet. "That's quite a pet."

My father shot me a concerned look. "Yes, well, he was sort of a rescue and we couldn't turn our backs on him. But I can't take the credit. Laken trained him and she takes care of him." He paused, taking a deep breath as he looked at Xander. "Not too many people know about him. We'd appreciate it if you kept quiet about him. He's no threat to anyone, but there could still be consequences if certain people knew there was a wolf running around."

Xander nodded, seeming to understand. "Laken already explained that. I won't tell anyone about him."

"Thank you, son."

Silently instructing Dakota to stay where he was, I approached the doorway. "We should get going," I said, slipping past my father. I caught Xander's gaze, but looked away immediately. "We have a lot of work to do on our project."

"Will you be home for dinner?" my father asked.

"Actually, I'll be home before dinner, but I won't be staying. Noah's taking me out. Bye, Dad," I said before rushing outside.

My father smiled. "I should have known. Don't work too hard this afternoon."

When he shut the door behind us, I turned to Xander. It was only the second time I could remember seeing him in a white shirt. His shirt tails fell over his blue jeans and he appeared to not even notice the cool autumn air with his sleeves rolled up. I squinted in the bright sunlight, glimpsing the fiery red maple tree in our front lawn out of the corner of my eye. "Ready?" I asked.

"Of course. After you." He gestured for me to lead the way along the sidewalk. As I walked ahead of him, I heard him laugh softly. "You know, it's kind of funny to be keeping a cop's secret."

I planted my feet on the pavement, spinning around to face him so fast that he nearly ran into me. I glared at him. While he could be so infuriating, he was still devilishly handsome and my breath caught for a moment. Finally, I gritted out, "No, it's not funny at all. My father only took Dakota in because he thought he would be good for me. It turns out he was right. Some laws can be bent if it's for the right reason."

"You mean broken. And you don't have to convince me. All I meant was that with all the trouble I used to get into, it's a little ironic that a cop asked me for something." He grinned, raising his eyebrows at me. "So, another date with Noah? How's that going by the way?"

I groaned, turning to continue down the sidewalk and away from Xander's smirk. "Can we just cut the small talk and get going?" I asked over my shoulder.

I didn't bother to wait for his response before circling around the front of the truck to the passenger side. I pulled the door open, tossed my book bag onto the floor, and climbed up into the seat. As I shut the door, Xander appeared behind the wheel next to me, a grin still plastered across his face.

His smile faded as he studied me, but I stared straight ahead at the garage door, pretending not to notice. Finally, he said, "I'm sorry. I don't know how I do it, but somehow I always end up starting off on the wrong foot with you."

"At least you admit it," I muttered.

"Can we call a truce? My dad's really looking forward to seeing you again, and he won't be too happy with me if you're upset when we get there."

I sighed, noticing a hopeful look cross over his face. "Fine. I suppose we should at least try to get along until our History project is finished."

"I couldn't agree more." His eyes beaming with satisfaction, he turned the ignition key.

As I clicked my seat belt into place and rested my head against the leather seat, he backed the truck out of the driveway.

Fifteen minutes of silence later, Xander turned the truck into his driveway under the canopy of gold, orange, and red leaves. Dappled sunlight filtered down from between the branches overhead, reflecting on the pavement, and the forest glowed with autumn colors in every direction. After passing through the gate, we drove for another minute through the woods before pulling up to the log home he and his father shared. He parked in front of the garage doors and shut off the engine.

Even though I'd been here once before, the sheer size of the house still took my breath away. Until now, I had never known anyone who had so much money. It impressed me, but more than that, I wondered what they thought of me, a poor small-town girl.

I unfastened my seat belt and hopped out of the truck. After reaching for my book bag, I hoisted it over my shoulder and pushed the door shut. By the time I turned around, Xander loomed in front of me, his white shirt nearly blinding me from where he stood in a stray ray of sunlight. Even the shark tooth hanging from the black rope around his neck glinted in the sun.

He smiled. "I was going to offer to carry your bag for you."

"I've got it," I answered, shrugging indifferently.

"Suit yourself." He turned to walk toward the house and I followed. As we marched up the steps to the front porch, I noticed cornstalks tied to the log pillars and a pumpkin on each side of the front door. "My dad suddenly got the urge to decorate for fall. We didn't get seasons like this in LA," Xander explained, practically reading my mind.

"It looks nice," I commented, stopping behind him while he twisted a key in the lock.

He opened the door and moved to the side, leaning against the wall. "Ladies first," he said, waving toward the doorway.

After hurrying past him, I stopped in the entry hall, glancing at the photograph of Xander surfing before my eyes were drawn to the towering stone fireplace in the two-story living room. The house captured my attention again, and I didn't even hear Xander follow me inside until he was right behind me.

"Can I take your bag and your coat?" he asked, touching my shoulder.

I whipped around to face him, frustrated by my rebellious heart that took off at his slightest touch. Nodding as he dropped his hand, I slid the strap off my shoulder and gave him my book bag before slipping out of my jacket and handing it to him next.

"Thank you."

After he took my things, I wandered through the living room to the kitchen. When I turned the corner, Xander's father greeted me from where he chopped broccoli on a cutting board at the island. He brought the knife down with a sharp thud, sending chunks rolling off to the side. Lifting his brown eyes, he smiled warmly. "Laken, hello. It's nice to see you again, dear."

He placed the knife on the granite countertop, rubbed his hands with a towel, and rushed around the island to pull me into a hug.

My arms hung awkwardly by my side as I smiled. "You, too. Thank you for having me over today."

After letting go, he stepped back. "You're quite welcome. I'm just sorry we haven't done this sooner. I've been so focused on a necklace I've been working on that I couldn't believe it when we flipped the calendar to October the other day. Anyway, I finally found time to do some research on your necklace. But before we get into that, please, help yourself." He gestured to the salad fixings spread across the island. "Xander told me you're a vegetarian. I hope this will do for lunch."

My stomach rumbled as I scanned the bowls of lettuce, hard-boiled eggs, tomatoes, carrots, and other toppings. "It's perfect."

"That's my dad. He always has the right idea," Xander said as he sauntered into the kitchen and lingered behind me. I didn't need to turn around to know he stood inches away.

"Don't worry. One day, you'll be just like me." Caleb grinned at him before turning his attention back to me. "Laken, would you like some iced tea to drink?"

"That would be great."

"I'll get it. Go ahead and get started. The plates are already out."

As he headed for the stainless steel refrigerator, I started to move toward the island. But I stopped when Xander lifted my hair, grazing his fingers along the back of my neck. I gasped softly, my heart jumping from his touch once again.

Instinctively, I reached up to grasp his hands. "What are you—"

"Relax," he whispered. He circled his hands out from under my hair and around in front of me, his fingers pinching each end of my necklace. When he lifted it over me, I turned to face him, watching him curiously, suspiciously. "I was just getting your necklace for my dad."

I frowned, my eyes meeting his. "A little warning next time, please," I muttered.

He raised his eyebrows before circling the island until he reached his father on the other side. "Here, Dad. I'll take that. You take this." He and his father exchanged my necklace for a glass of iced tea.

"Ah, it's even more beautiful than I remember," Caleb said before looking at me. "As are you, my dear. Come join me at the table once you have something to eat."

I nodded and made my way around the island. Loading up a plate, I remembered the last time I had been in this kitchen wearing my sweaty exercise clothes. I was much more comfortable today in clean jeans with my hair brushed and a little make-up on.

Xander and I joined his father at the table beside the

windows overlooking the mountains. Caleb hadn't bothered to make himself a plate and ignored the view, staring at the diamond pendant dangling from his hand instead.

"Dad, aren't you going to eat with us?" Xander asked.

Snapping out of his trance, his father lifted his eyes. "Not right now. I'll get some later. But you two enjoy."

I sipped the tea before taking a bite of lettuce dripping with Italian dressing while his father gazed across the table at us.

"Laken, your necklace has quite a history. I traced it back to two hundred and ten BC."

My jaw fell open. "BC? As in Before Christ?"

"Exactly."

"But it looks so new. Wouldn't it be rusted or tarnished by now?" I asked.

"Not if it's a magic necklace," Xander chimed in between bites of his salad, a knowing look on his face.

I rolled my eyes at him. "Quiet. Let your dad talk. I believe he's the expert," I said before looking back at Caleb for answers.

"He may not be that far from the truth," Caleb said slowly. He looked across the table, catching my gaze with his deliberate stare. "According to what I read, this necklace was made by an ancient jeweler for his true love. But the story also said that a sorcerer cast a spell on it, giving the owner of it a special gift. A power."

I forgot about my salad as Xander's father captivated me. Although the story sounded more like a fairy tale than something real, I couldn't help asking, "What kind of power?"

"I don't know. The story didn't say. But it did say that the necklace was handed down to a little girl, and that it was supposed to be handed down to her daughter. If it stayed in the family since then, that would make you her descendant."

After a moment of silence, I broke away from his stare, smiling nervously. "Wow. That wasn't exactly what I expected."

"Laken," Caleb said solemnly. "Have you ever done something and wondered how you did it? Something you could never tell anyone about?"

My smile collapsed and I wondered if he knew about me. Not sure what to say, I looked down at my salad.

"You don't need to answer that. Just think about it." He extended his hand across the table to me, my necklace dangling from his fingers.

I looked up, meeting his kind eyes as I took the necklace from him and reached up behind my neck to fasten it under my hair.

"There's one more thing," he said.

"Dad, do you really think this is the time?" Xander asked.

"Yes. She needs to know."

"Know what?" I looked from Caleb to Xander and back to Caleb. I wasn't sure I wanted to hear the rest, but not knowing would probably drive me crazy.

"According to the story, anyone who came to possess this necklace would meet an untimely death. The only way to break the curse is for her to find her soul mate."

As Caleb paused, fear settled upon me. An image of Ivy's vibrant smile flashed through my thoughts. She had died very young, so could this curse actually be true? "Who is her soul mate? And how would she find him?" I asked, painfully aware that both Xander and Caleb watched me, the intensity in their eyes flustering me.

"I wish I knew. The story ended there," Caleb answered.

Xander broke out into a disbelieving chuckle. "And it's just a story. Don't take it so seriously."

"Easy for you to say," I said with a deep sigh, trying to

calm my nerves. "You're not the one who's cursed."

"Hmm. I guess you're right. You'd better get started on your bucket list." His teasing smile faded when Caleb shot him a warning look.

An awkward silence fell over the three of us before Xander broke it. "Maybe we should have chosen your necklace for our History project."

"Nice try, but Mr. Jacobs would never have accepted it. The topic was supposed to be about New England history, remember? Besides, this doesn't sound real to me."

"Of course not," Caleb said. "It will take time for you to understand it."

I stared at him, suddenly realizing he believed in this curse that I wanted to dismiss as a centuries-old fable. And I would have, easily, had it not been for my ability to talk to wild animals and the knowledge that my real mother, the necklace's previous owner, had died young. *Don't be silly,* I told myself. *Xander's right. It's just a story. And everything else is coincidental. There's nothing that can prove what he's telling you is real.* Even though my reasoning sounded logical, I couldn't help wondering why Caleb seemed so convinced it was true. After all, he didn't know what I could do or that my birth mother had died young, and I wasn't about to tell him. Or did he know more than he was letting on?

I finally looked back at my salad, aimlessly poking my fork at a few pieces of lettuce. "And to think all I expected to find out was how much it's worth," I said, mustering up a smile.

Losing interest in my food, I put the fork down and lifted my fingers to the pendant.

"Its real value is in its history. It's a very special piece. I hope you realize that. Sometimes, you can't put a price on something like that," Caleb said.

"I know." Looking over at Xander, I changed the subject. "So when are we going to get started on our History project?"

"As soon as you finish your lunch."

Caleb smiled, scooting his chair out behind him as he stood. "I think it's time I fixed myself a plate."

While he headed across the kitchen to the island, Xander smiled at me as if to silently apologize for his father's storytelling. I nodded, appreciating his concern as I picked up my fork. Even though I'd lost my appetite, I doubted he would let me up from the table until I finished my salad. Eager to forget what his father had just told me, I took a bite.

Our study session couldn't begin soon enough.

Chapter 11

After we finished lunch, I helped Xander clear the dishes from the table before following him out of the kitchen. He stopped briefly near the entry hall to pick up my book bag, then he led me up the stairs and down the hallway. The thick beige carpet sank beneath my feet, a soft change from the hardwood floor I was used to at home.

Halfway down the hall, we turned through a timber-framed doorway into his bedroom. A queen-sized bed made up with a blue plaid comforter rested against the far wall under two windows. Curtains matching the bedding parted at the center, curling over to each side where a tie-back secured them. A desk sat across from the bed and built-in bookshelves lined one side of the room. Ocean landscapes and surfing posters hung randomly on the gray walls, and a tall, yellow surfboard stood upright in a back corner. The décor seemed far more fitting for a beach house in California or Hawaii.

Xander dropped my book bag beside his desk and

turned on the computer and monitor. I wandered around him, studying the books and trophies on his bookshelves. The books varied in topics from surfing to gemstones to travel, but the trophies were all from surfing. They lined the two middle shelves, several adorned with a metallic gold surfer riding the top of a crashing wave. Each trophy identified the place and year of the competition. Laguna Beach 2011, North Shore, Hawaii 2012, Santa Monica, 2014, and the list went on and on.

"Did you win all of these?" I asked.

"Pretty much," Xander replied flippantly. I sensed him approach behind me and knew he was inches away when he spoke again. "But I didn't bring you over here to show you my trophies. We need to get started, or you're going to be here all night. While I'd love nothing more than for you to stay the night, somehow, I don't think that's what you had in mind."

He was right. We had to get to work so I could arrive home in time to get ready for my date with Noah. I spun around, planning to retrieve my book bag, but Xander blocked me. I leaned back, grasping the shelf near my hips to steady myself. Glancing up at his blue eyes, I swallowed nervously. "What?"

"Why didn't you tell my dad about Ivy?"

His father's story about the curse came flooding back into my thoughts, sending another wave of dread over me. I wished Xander would drop the subject because I just wanted to forget it. "I'm not sure I understand."

"Ivy. She's your real mother, isn't she?"

I nodded with a deep sigh.

"And she died. Right?"

I shrugged, dodging his stare. "She got sick. It happens," I said, trying to brush off his question.

"How old was she when she died?"

I redirected my gaze toward him, my eyes locking

with his. "I didn't even know her. I have no idea how old she was when she died."

"But she was young, right? She had just had you."

"I know where you're going with this and I really wish you wouldn't."

"You don't believe my dad, do you?"

I huffed. "No, of course not. Do you mean to tell me you do?"

Xander smiled softly. "Not necessarily, but I'm also not about to dismiss it entirely when we know your real mother died at a young age. It might be in your best interest to take this a little more seriously."

"Fine," I gritted out, my teeth clenched. "If it makes you happy, I'll give it some thought. Now can we please get started on our project? I'm sure you have a hot date with Marlena tonight."

He wrinkled his eyebrows in thought, and I suspected he was searching for the perfect smart-ass response. "That depends on you."

I looked up at him, my eyebrows raised.

"If you agree to go out with me, I'll drop her in a heartbeat."

"Don't you ever give up?" I asked, shaking my head. "Why would I agree to go out with you now when I've said no every other time?"

A sly smile lit up his face, and I knew I was in for trouble. He lifted his arms up, caging me against the bookshelf. "Because I have you trapped."

"Is that how you roped Marlena into going out with you?"

"No. She never let me trap her against a wall. I had to pin her against my bed instead. Like this." In a flash, he dropped his hands away from the bookshelf and slid an arm behind my waist. Then he lifted me off my feet and spun around to the bed where he dropped me onto my

back. I landed on the comforter and barely had a moment
to breathe before he lowered himself on top of me, pin-
ning me down. He hovered an inch above me, his eyes
locked with mine. I took a deep breath, hoping he
wouldn't notice how fast my heart was pounding. My
blood ran hot, the heat of his body making me feel
flushed. "Nice try. It may have worked on her, but it
doesn't work on me," I lied, fighting to ignore the butterflies in my stomach. Everything except his mesmerizing
eyes blurred around me.

"But we share something I'll never have with her," he
whispered before rolling off to the side and propping up
on his elbow. My relief from his touch was short-lived
when he moved his free arm up the middle of my abdomen and between my breasts until he reached the pendant. "The secret curse behind your necklace."

My breath caught when his fingers lit a fire beneath
my skin. I inhaled slowly. "Is it really a secret?"

"Well, I'm pretty sure that—" He paused, looking up
for a moment before returning his stare to me. "—that no
one else knows about it. So, yes, that would make it a secret."

"What if I don't believe it?"

"You have to," he said, matter-of-factly.

"No, I don't."

"Yes, you do, if you want to keep the secret you've
been hiding from everyone your whole life."

Silence filled the room as I stared at him, wanting to
ask him exactly what he knew and deny it all at the same
time. Finally, I broke my gaze away from his and stared
up at the ceiling fan. "I don't know what you're talking
about."

"Say what you want. But you know something's going
on. How else do you explain the wolves or the person in
the woods behind your house?" He lifted the pendant off

my chest and studied it. "You need to be careful. Some-one out there knows something."

Escaping the trance he had on me, I shot up, causing him to lose his grip on my necklace. "What are you say-ing? That someone wants to steal a cursed necklace from me?"

"I'm just saying you need to watch your back. You can't deny how the pieces are fitting together. And I want to help you, but it would be a lot easier if you told me what you're hiding."

My nerves on edge from what he was insinuating, I shook my head, trying to erase the frightful image of the wolves and stranger from my thoughts. "I'm not hiding anything," I declared as I rolled off the bed and stood be-side it. "Now are we going to talk in circles about things that don't exist, or are we going to get started on the as-signment we came up here to work on?"

With a groan, Xander rose to a sitting position and scooted toward the foot of the bed before lowering his feet to the carpet. "You sure know how to take the fun out of things. I was really enjoying your company on my bed. When can we do that again?"

"You're impossible!" I marched over to the desk and grabbed my book bag. "If we're not going to work on this project, then maybe you should just take me home," I muttered, hoisting my book bag strap over my shoulder.

"Calm down," he said, standing up from the bed. "I have every intention of getting our work done. But I need to get another chair. Have a seat and I'll be right back." As he left the room, I dropped my book bag to the floor and sank into the only chair at his desk.

I pulled my History notebook and a pen out of my bag and placed them on the desk. While waiting, I stared at the picture of Xander on his computer screen, his black wet suit glistening in the sun as he surfed a white-capped wave. But that wasn't enough to distract me from what he and his father had told me today. Could the curse be real? Even if it was, that didn't explain why a stranger was stalking me. What could this person possibly want from me? It all had to be connected. My ability to talk to animals, the necklace, the curse. But how?

The thud of wood knocking against the doorframe startled me out of my thoughts. I jerked my head around to see Xander angling a wooden chair through the doorway.

"Here we go," he said, dropping the chair beside mine. "Now we can get to work." He sat down and turned his attention to me. "Where should we start?"

I thought for a moment, wanting to ask him more about the curse and if he suspected the stranger in the woods had something to do with it. But after a long pause, I chickened out, deciding I just wanted to forget about all of it. "I think we need to work on an outline and establish some goals for the next few weeks so we don't get behind."

Xander smiled. "Good idea." He reached beside the computer for his notebook and opened it up. From that moment, we focused on our project. Neither one of us brought up the necklace or the curse again, although they never strayed far from my mind.

Somehow I managed to get through the afternoon by reminding myself that my problems were nothing compared to what the slaves went through all those years ago to escape a life of torture and captivity.

※※※

That evening, Noah and I went out with Brooke and Ethan for a quiet dinner at the pizza shop. It seemed ironic that I would have dinner there when I'd been asked to work the lunch shift the next day. Business had picked up since the tourists had returned to town to see the fall colors and Mike had asked me to work the next few weekends.

Doubling with Brooke and Ethan was a first for me and Noah, but I welcomed the chance for them to get to know each other. Brooke asked Noah countless questions about where he was from and how he had ended up in our town. I could barely get a word in edgewise, but I enjoyed listening to them. It helped to distract my thoughts away from Xander, his father's story about my necklace, and the idea that I was cursed to die young like my birth mother. Part of me wanted to tell them about the curse so they could reassure me that things like that didn't happen in real life. But I held back, wishing I could just forget about it.

It was only ten o'clock when Noah pulled into my driveway after our evening out. He shut off the engine and headlights, pitching the car into blackness. As soon as my eyes adjusted to the moonlight coming in through the windows, I unfastened my seat belt and leaned an elbow on the console between us.

"Thank you for another great evening," I said with a smile, my hair falling over my shoulder.

"Did you really have a nice time?" he asked skeptically, seeming unsure.

"Of course," I answered, a bit surprised he would think otherwise. Flashing him a genuine smile, I studied his soft brown eyes. He was so handsome tonight in a white button-down shirt that contrasted with his brown hair and eyes. Or was it that he reminded me of Xander who had also worn white earlier today? "Why do you ask?"

"You seemed quiet tonight, that's all."

"I was letting Brooke grill you on your life history," I

said, grinning. After all, it had been Brooke's idea to come out with us tonight, and I had expected her to lead the conversation. "It was nice for the four of us to go out. They're my best friends, so it means a lot to me that they like you."

"You mean approve of me," he teased.

"Well, that, too," I admitted. "Of course, they like you and approve of you. They're happy for me."

"Okay. As long as nothing has changed between us," he said, gazing at me as if he still wasn't convinced.

My heart lurching, I longed to put his worries to rest and reached up with my free hand to touch his neck. "Nothing has changed. Why would you think that?"

"Because of last weekend. I'm sure spending the night at my apartment was a little awkward for you. Something just seemed off with you tonight."

I sighed, shifting my eyes away from him as memories from the afternoon at Xander's flashed through my thoughts. Not only did Caleb's story about the curse bother me, but I also couldn't stop thinking about Xander. The image of him hovering above me, his clear blue eyes staring down at me, had become permanently etched in my mind. Those moments had been exciting, and even intimate, despite the fact that nothing had happened. I worried that someday, I wouldn't be able to resist him any longer. And where would that leave things with Noah?

"I think I'm just a little tired. I haven't been sleeping well since I found out about Ivy. Not to mention my teachers are really starting to pile on the homework. It's been a bit of a challenge to keep up."

"Then it's a good thing I brought you home early tonight. I was going to ask if you wanted to go back to my place and watch a movie, but I'm glad I didn't. If you're tired, I want you to get your rest."

I glanced at him with a soft smile. "Maybe next week?"

He nodded silently, his eyes locked with mine. Then he leaned across the console and kissed me before pulling away far too soon. "Come on. I'll walk you to the house. Wait here," he said before jumping out of the car and hurrying around the front to open my door.

I stood up and stepped aside to let Noah shut it behind me, the cold October air sending a chill through me. Noah wrapped an arm around my shoulders, warming me a little, and side by side, we shuffled down the sidewalk through the shadows to the front door where the outside light glowed.

When we stopped, Noah released my shoulders and I shivered. "Brr," I said, rubbing my bare hands together. "I'm glad it wasn't this cold last weekend for the dance, although it was pretty close. I heard we're expecting a hard freeze tonight."

"Then you better get inside and warm up. Do you have your keys?"

"Yes." I unzipped my purse, and grabbed them, the clattering sound cutting through the night when I held them up. "Right here."

"Good. Now go on in. I'll call you tomorrow."

I separated my house key from the others, ready to slide it into the lock. But I hesitated, looking up at Noah, not sure why he seemed anxious to send me inside. "That's it? You're not trying to ditch me, are you?"

"Yes," he answered, matter-of-factly. "For two reasons. One, it's damn cold out here. And two, it appears from the lights on in your house that your parents are up and I don't want to linger too long."

"Okay. I was just checking." Disappointment nagging me, I wondered if that meant there would be no hot, sexy goodnight kiss. I glanced up at him, smiling when he leaned down to kiss me. But unlike some of his kisses last week, this one was quick and soft, barely what I would even call a kiss.

"Good night," he whispered, lifting his lips away from mine.

"Good night," I repeated before turning to the door and sliding the key into the lock. I heard him start to walk away as I unlocked the deadbolt with a click, but before I could reach for the handle, his footsteps grew louder behind me.

"Oh, screw it," he muttered from directly behind me, curling his arm around my waist and twirling me around to face him. The key was left sticking out of the lock as I wrapped my arms around his shoulders, my small purse still in one hand. Without another word, he pulled me close and lowered his mouth to mine with a fierce, crushing kiss.

After a few moments, he lifted his head away from me, gazing down at me. His eyes smoldered, and my heart skipped a beat as I realized he still wanted me. "I couldn't walk away without giving you a real kiss goodnight. Even if your parents are up."

Or if it means being seen by Xander, I added silently. I couldn't resist scanning the darkness, wondering if he hid in the nearby shadows. Well, if he was watching and saw us kissing, good! It would serve him right, especially when I had to put up with his and Marlena's public displays of affection nearly every day at school. Focusing my attention back on Noah, I nodded with a smile. "Good. Because you had me worried there for a moment."

"You have nothing to worry about. You are very beautiful and very sexy. You have no idea what went through my mind last week when you spent the night," he whispered, letting go of me before stepping back.

"Really? I'd love to hear more about that," I said, feeling heat flush through my cheeks and instantly hoping he couldn't see me blushing in the darkness.

Noah shook his head. "Another time, okay?"

I sighed. "Okay. I'll talk to you soon?"

"Absolutely."

I turned back to the door, pulling my key out as I opened it. Slipping into the warm house, I smelled cinnamon leftover from my mother's baking, but it wasn't enough to take my mind off Noah. I spun around in the doorway and peered out into the darkness, prepared to wave to Noah, but he had already disappeared down the sidewalk. His car engine humming, he backed out of the driveway and drove away, leaving me alone. The cold air nipping at me, I shut the door, twisted the dead bolt into place, and headed toward the kitchen, a smile plastered across my face.

As I hung my jacket in the hall coat closet, my mother called out from my parents' bedroom. "Laken, is that you?"

"Yes, Mom," I called on my way down the hallway before stopping outside their door. "I'm pretty tired, so I'm going up to bed. I'll see you in the morning."

"Okay, Laken. Good night."

"Good night," I replied, then retreated back to the kitchen, ready to escape to my room for the night.

As soon as I rushed up the stairs and down the hall, Dakota greeted me at my bedroom doorway. After giving him a friendly scratch between the ears, I changed into red flannel pajamas. Then I washed my face, brushed my teeth, and climbed into bed. Darkness cloaked the room when I reached over to turn off the light before resting my cheek against the pillow and pulling the comforter up to my neck.

Memories of the evening with Noah filled my mind, and I felt my smile linger until I drifted off to sleep.

❧❧❧

When I opened my eyes, alarm rattled me as I looked up at Xander from where I lay on his bed, the gray walls and ocean prints of his bedroom surrounding us. I felt as if I'd never left. He wore the same white button-down shirt he had worn earlier, the shark tooth necklace hanging from his tanned neck. With a sexy smile, he lowered his body on top of me, stopping when his lips were less than an inch away from mine.

I tried to breathe, but time seemed to stand still, choking me. After what felt like forever, he dipped his mouth toward mine and I closed my eyes, waiting for the touch of his lips.

Then suddenly, my eyes flew open and I shot up, finding myself alone in the darkness of my own bedroom. My pulse pounding at a runaway pace, I took a deep breath, determined to compose myself now that I knew it was only a dream. A very bad dream.

My heartbeat slowing, my eyes adjusted to the dark shadows barely visible from the faint moonlight. I scanned the room, comforted by the familiar surroundings until my gaze landed on Dakota. Curled up on his bed, he held his head up high, staring intently at me, his ears pointed toward me.

"Oh, no," I whispered. "Don't even tell me you saw my dream."

He let out a soft whine and swiped his eyes with his paw.

"Well, forget it. It's never going to happen. Now go back to sleep," I said with a huff before plopping back down on my pillow and turning away from him. I hoped he believed me, because I knew I hadn't convinced myself. I didn't know where that dream had come from, but I prayed Xander wouldn't haunt my dreams again as I tossed and turned for what seemed like forever before falling back to sleep.

Chapter 12

My shift at the pizza shop the next day helped take my mind off things, at least for a little while. I threw myself into my job, serving countless pizzas to hungry tourists. They were all strangers to me and, for the day, I cherished my anonymity. No one knew I was the girl who had rescued a little boy. No one knew that I could talk to wild animals, that a stranger was after me, that I had just learned who my birth mother was, and that I was supposedly cursed to die young.

Monday came all too quickly, but my classes also helped me set my worries aside. I knew I couldn't run forever from all that troubled me, but I would for as long as possible. School made me feel safe, except for one person. Xander. Not only did he remind me of the curse, but now all I could think about when I saw him was my dream. I tried very hard to avoid him all week and, aside from a few encounters here and there, he actually left me alone. When I saw him with Marlena, I turned away from the sight of them holding hands, walking arm in arm, or kissing. Occasionally, my eyes met his from across the hall, and I quickly looked away, pretending to find my books or something on my phone far more interesting. On the bright side, Noah called every night and texted me every day, giving my thoughts a reprieve from Xander and my dream.

Thursday afternoon as I waited for the bell to ring after turning in my French exam, my phone buzzed from inside my book bag. I glanced nervously around the classroom, hoping no one, especially our high-strung French teacher, Ms. Lyndt, had noticed. But she appeared preoccupied, sitting at the front desk, only occasionally looking up from grading papers to scan the students still working on the exam. Dark blonde curls fell over her forehead, brushing against her glasses each time she bent her head back down.

Relieved that she hadn't heard my phone, I reached for it, wondering who was calling or texting me while I was in class. Noah knew when I was free between classes and at lunch, and he was very careful to call or text only at those times. Curious, I slid my phone onto my lap under the desk. Scanning the quiet classroom one more time to make sure no one was watching, I sighed with relief. My classmates paid me no attention, hunching over their desks, some furiously writing, others pausing in thought.

I slumped down in my seat and swiped my phone to see that Noah had sent me a text. *Call me. Need your help ASAP!*

Alarm shot through me, my nerves on edge. What was that all about? My heart picking up speed, I looked back at the teacher to see her head bent over the exams she was grading. Then I glanced at my watch, realizing the bell wouldn't ring for another ten minutes. I couldn't wait that long to find out what he needed.

With a deep breath, I rose to my feet and slipped my

phone into the back pocket of my jeans. I tiptoed up the aisle, trying not to bump the elbows of those students still working on the test I had already finished. When I reached the teacher's desk, I stood over her for a moment before she realized I was there.

Ms. Lyndt reviewed a paper, whispering feverishly to herself in French. I raised my eyebrows, wondering if I should knock on the desk to let her know I was waiting for her attention. Fortunately, she looked up at me barely a minute later, and her whispering stopped. "*Oui?*" she asked, gazing up at me from behind her glasses, a heart pendant attached to a gold chain dangling over her brown turtleneck.

"Can I use the hall pass, please?" I asked quietly.

She narrowed her brown eyes at me before answering with a question. "Did you finish your exam and turn it in?"

"Yes, ma'am."

Her stern expression softened. "Very well, then. You are one of my best students." She reached into a side drawer and pulled out a thin piece of wood with "Hall Pass" painted across one side in black. She held it out to me slowly, but I grabbed it quickly, urgently.

"Thank you," I whispered before rushing out the class-room door. As I hurried down the empty hall to the bath-room, my tall boots echoing on the floor, I whipped my phone out of my back pocket. Resisting the urge to stop in the middle of the hallway to call Noah, I waited until I reached the girls' bathroom. Once inside, I breathed a sigh of relief to find it empty. Each of the three bathroom stall doors hung open, and sunlight peeked in through the foggy window, dimly lighting the small room.

Leaning against one of the stalls, I dialed Noah's number while my gaze landed on my reflection in the mirror over a sink across the bathroom.

My hair hung in two braids, one over each shoulder, the black bands around the ends sticking out against my blonde hair and cream-colored sweater. My gold hoop earring clicked against the phone as the seconds ticked by and I counted four rings before Noah answered.

"Laken, that was really fast. I figured you were in class and I wasn't sure when you'd be able to call me," he said, his voice calm, not at all urgent like his text.

"I finished my French test early and was just waiting for the bell to ring, so I was able to get away. Besides, your message scared me. What's going on?"

He paused before explaining, "I'm over at the Owens's place just north of town. Do you know it?"

"Yes." The Owens owned one of the few farms in the area, raising cattle and harvesting apples. I had never met them because they kept to themselves, but just about everyone in town knew where their farm was.

"How soon can you get here?"

"What? Why? What's going on?"

"A moose got caught up in a barbed wire fence on the edge of their property. It's tangled up pretty badly."

My heart sank at the thought of an animal suffering and in pain. "How bad is it?" I asked gravely. I wasn't sure I wanted an answer, but I had to know if anything could be done to save it. "Could it have a broken leg? Because if it does, even if we get it untangled, it won't have a chance."

"I don't know. I can't get very close without it thrashing around. All I can tell you is there's a lot of blood."

"I'm sure there is." I paused, not quite sure what to do. "Have you talked to my dad?"

"Not since we got the call. He sent me out here to put it out of its misery. He said he's put down his fair share of animals, mostly from getting hit by cars, and that I need to learn to do it, too."

"That sounds like something he would say." I paused, thinking. "What about calling a vet?"

"Even if your father would allow that, and he already said he can't hire a vet for a moose with the taxpayers' money, I don't know what a vet could do without getting close to it. Unless the vets around here carry tranquilizer guns."

"Yeah, I don't know either." That left me with two choices. Either tell Noah to put the poor moose out of its misery or rush over there to see if I could calm it long enough to cut it free. And even then, the animal's chance of surviving would be a long shot if it had a broken leg or any other life-threatening injuries. In the end, I couldn't turn my back on it. "Okay. I'll be there as soon as I can."

"What about the rest of your classes?"

"Don't worry about that. I think I just started to feel nauseous and I need to go home." I glanced across the bathroom at my reflection in the mirror, hoping the principal would buy it.

"Thanks. But can you please hurry? I'm afraid the longer he's tangled up, the worse he'll injure himself."

"He?" I asked with a groan. A full grown male moose could weigh over eighteen hundred pounds and their antlers could span five to six feet across. But the worst part was that during the fall mating season, they were often edgy and anxious. "You never mentioned it was a bull. How big is he?"

"Compared to what? He's big, that's all I can tell you."

"All right, never mind. I'll have to see him for myself. I'll be there as soon as I can." I hung up the call and took a deep breath, wondering what I'd gotten myself into. After returning my phone to the back pocket of my jeans, I stepped up to the bathroom sink and washed my hands. *I hope I can do this. But even if I can't, I have to at least try. I may be that poor animal's only hope.*

As I dried my hands with a paper towel, questions crept into my mind. Why had Noah called me? What made him think I could help with an injured moose? Did he know my secret?

Of course, he doesn't know, I scolded myself. *Don't be ridiculous. He's obviously very upset about this and trusts you a lot. Even if you can't save the moose, Noah probably needs a little support if he has to shoot it.* On that thought, I tossed the wadded up paper towel in the trash and flew out the bathroom door. I ran back down the hallway, out of breath when I reached my French classroom.

The bell rang seconds after I returned the hall pass to Ms. Lyndt and took my seat. As some of the other students scrambled to finish their exams, I grabbed my book bag and pushed my way out of the crowded room. The quiet from a minute ago was gone. Voices, footsteps, and the rustling of papers and books filled the air while I weaved between the students, rushing to the principal's office to sign out.

Fortunately, I only had two classes before the day ended, so I wouldn't miss much. However, one of them was History and Xander was bound to wonder where I was when I didn't show up. Shaking my head, I hustled through the crowd, wondering how my thoughts always seemed to revert back to him. Well, when he asked, I would give him the same story I was about to give the front office, that I was feeling sick to my stomach. After all, it wasn't a complete lie since the thought of a bleeding, tangled up moose really *had* turned my stomach.

I must have looked nauseous when I stopped in the principal's office because they allowed me to sign out for the day with no questions asked. The secretary, wearing a yellow, orange, and red leaf-printed vest over her white turtleneck simply said, "I hope you feel better, Laken." Genuine concern shone in her gentle brown eyes and sympathetic smile.

"Thank you," I replied before darting out of the office with the hope that she hadn't seen through my lie.

ↄ৵ↄ

I arrived at the Owens's farm fifteen minutes later and slowly guided the Explorer down the long gravel driveway lined with red maple trees on both sides. A white clapboard farmhouse with dark green shutters and a wrap-around porch loomed at the end of the driveway, tall golden trees towering behind it. A dusty brown pickup truck had been parked near the porch steps. The lawn, still green from the summer sun and frequent rain, sloped upward from the house with boulders and trees scattered through it. To one side, rows of apple trees lined the hillside. On the other side, a red barn cut into the mountain, surrounded by a wooden four-board fence. Black and red cattle milled about, chewing hay and sipping water out of a huge trough.

I pulled up next to Noah's car, the Lincoln Police Department shield on the front door. Leaning against it, he waited alone, a fleece-lined denim jacket over his light blue button-down deputy shirt and fog billowing out of his mouth with every breath he let out.

I shifted into park, shut off the engine, and stepped out of the truck, hugging my jacket around me in the frigid air. The sweet scent of a wood-burning fire blew across the yard, but I barely noticed it. All I could think about was the moose.

I rushed toward Noah, my eyes meeting his, and I recognized the worry in his expression. Maybe it was even worse than I had imagined. "Noah?"

He walked toward me, his footsteps echoing on the gravel stones before he met me halfway between the cars. "Thank God, you're here. I can't do this alone."

I looked around, but the only signs of life were the cattle up on the hillside. "Where are the Owens?"

"They're inside. They're pretty distraught over this. They told me they've lived here for forty years and never had a problem like this. Mrs. Owens said it's pretty common to see moose walking through their yard just about any day of the year. She's particularly upset."

I glanced up at the barn and fencing. "I don't see any barbed wire. That board fence looks pretty secure."

"It is. They said they started replacing their fence last year. They were going to finish it this year, but then had a few unexpected bills and had to put off the back section for a while. That's where the moose is. Up there." He pointed at the hill and I followed his finger with my eyes. I couldn't see the moose from here, and I was relieved for that. I wanted to examine him by myself without Noah or the Owens watching.

With a deep sigh, I buried my freezing hands in my pockets and focused on everything but the cold. "Okay. Wait here. I'm going to go check it out." I started walking up the hill, only to hear Noah jogging behind me to catch up. I stopped immediately and turned.

"I'm coming with you," he said.

"No, you're not," I said, shaking my head. "I need to do this alone."

"Laken, you can't possibly handle an animal this size on your own," he protested, genuine worry in his voice. "I can't let you get hurt."

Meeting the fearful look in his eyes, I swallowed while reaching for his hand. "I'm not going to get hurt, and I know you know that. You wouldn't have called me if you thought I'd be in any danger. So trust me."

He started to say something else, but stopped when I squeezed his hand. "Please," I begged.

"Okay," he relented. "But if you're not back in ten minutes, I'm coming up there."

"Fair enough." I released him, spun around and continued up the hill. After hiking the short distance to the wooden fence, I followed it away from the barn until I reached a section of grass on the other side. Grateful that I wouldn't have to traipse through the mud in my tall boots, I climbed up the boards and jumped down into the pasture. The cattle barely looked up from the metal hay-feeder they congregated around as I headed away from them inside their enclosure.

The pasture crested over a ridge and then sloped downhill on the other side. I continued until I reached a stream trickling through the narrow dip in the field. Without a moment's hesitation, I jumped to the other side before trudging up the next hill, no end to the pasture in sight. At the top, the terrain leveled off, and I finally saw the moose at the edge of the field, trees rising up beyond him. As Noah had described, he lay on his side, his long legs sprawled out in front of him. I could barely see the wire fence, but I could tell right away that he was trapped.

As soon as he saw me, the moose tried to rise, but he snagged the wires, pulling them tighter around his enormous chest. I stopped and breathed slowly, studying him. He was young, not quite as thick and bulky as the bull moose who had chased the wolves away the night I ran off the road in the rain. His antlers jutted out roughly a foot on each side, sharp points along the edges. They weren't nearly as large as those of a mature male, but they were equally as dangerous.

"Shhh," I whispered, meeting his fearful brown eyes. "I'm only here to help." I took a hesitant step forward, continuing to talk softly. "I won't hurt you. But you have to be still or you're going to hurt yourself more." My words seemed to sink in because the moose stopped struggling, his eyes appearing relaxed and his chest heaving with a sigh.

I approached him, sadness overwhelming me as I studied the long gashes all over his neck, chest, and legs. His wounds dripped with blood, some so deep they exposed flesh and muscle. A wire ensnared one of his antlers and another cut into his face just above his nostrils. His pain-filled eyes seemed to beg me to help him.

A tear rolled down my cheek when I stooped beside him, carefully inspecting his legs all the way down to his split hooves. As far as I could tell, the wires only cut through fur, skin and muscle, and his bones appeared intact. I reached out to gently stroke the coarse fur on his neck, careful to avoid the wires.

"I'm going to get you out of this, I promise. But you have to be patient. I'll be right back." I needed wire cutters, and in my haste to find the moose, I hadn't thought to bring them with me. I gazed into his eyes, the relaxed look in them giving me hope that he would stay still while I left to get the cutters.

I rose to my feet and backtracked across the meadow, slowing to balance myself down the hill. By the time I crossed the stream at the bottom, Noah was walking toward me. I stopped as he approached, noticing the wire cutters in his hands.

"I thought you were going to wait for me by the cars," I said when he stopped in front of me.

He held out the wire cutters, the handles facing me. "And I realized you might need these." They were a little longer than a pair of scissors, but the rubber handles were thick, the curved blades wide and short.

I took them from him. "You must have read my mind."

"So what do you think? Is he going to make it?"

"Well, I'm no vet, but his wounds look superficial to me. He might be a little sore for a while, but I think he'll be okay if I can cut him free."

"How are you going to get close enough to do that? I barely got within twenty feet of him before he freaked out."

My gaze shifted to the grass by my feet that had been worn thin from the grazing cattle. After a few seconds, I looked up at him. "Please don't ask me that," I whispered, meeting his curious eyes.

He nodded. "Just promise me you'll be careful. Those wires looked pretty tight. If you get your hand caught under one and he starts to panic, you're liable to lose a finger."

"I already thought of that. I'll be careful, I promise." I flashed a weak smile before turning and crossing the stream. Reaching the other side, I spun around. "Wait here. Don't come any closer, okay? I can't risk him being scared of you." Without waiting for Noah to agree, I whipped around and started up the hill. I didn't need to hear his response. He wouldn't come any closer if he wanted me to be safe, and I knew he understood that.

At the top, I returned to the moose's side. He calmly watched me out of the corner of his eye as I stooped beside him, scanning the maze of wires and wondering where to begin. Each strand consisted of two stiff wires twisted together with spikes poking out every six inches or so. I reached out to stroke his neck, accidentally startling him. He flinched from my touch and jerked up, pulling the wires even tighter. "Whoa, big boy," I whispered softly, pressing my hand against him, hoping to steady him.

He tried to lift his head, but his nose and antlers were trapped. I gazed into his eyes, willing him to trust me. "I'm going to cut you free, big guy. Stay still and everything's going to be fine. I promise."

I opened the cutters and slid the bottom blade under a taught wire. Then I clamped my fingers around the handles, squeezing them. I expected the wire to snap, but the blades stopped with it lodged between them. I bit down on my bottom lip as I tried using both hands. With my eyes closed, I squeezed as hard as I could, but nothing happened. The rubber handles pushed into my palms, nearly cutting off the circulation to my fingers.

I opened my eyes and inhaled, squeezing one more time. But again, they didn't budge. The wire was too thick and I wasn't strong enough to cut through it.

The moose looked at me as I pulled the blades out from around the wire in defeat. A cold autumn breeze blew, rustling the branches overhead, and red maple leaves showered down upon the ground from a nearby tree. I barely noticed, frowning when I realized what I had to do. With the wire cutters in my hand, I rocked backward to sit on the ground by the moose's head. Stroking his neck, I felt something sticky and wet, and I pulled my hand away to see blood covering my fingers.

"Okay, here's the deal," I said softly, wiping my hand on a dry patch of his fur. "I'm not strong enough to cut the wires. I have to get help. When I come back, I won't be alone. Please don't be afraid. My friend just wants to help you, so you can trust him." I offered a faint smile, hoping my plan would work. I had spent nearly all my time with animals alone, so I wasn't sure how the moose would react when I brought Noah back with me.

The only other time I had communicated with a large animal around someone else was when I had asked the black bear to approach Xander while we were hiking.

Since that had worked, maybe this would too.

Without wasting another second, I rose and jogged across the field before flying back down the hill to where Noah waited on the other side of the stream.

As soon as he saw me, he tilted his head and raised his eyebrows. "Wow. That was fast. Are you done?" he asked when I stopped in front of the stream, my shoulders falling forward as I caught my balance, the wire cutters still in my hands.

"No," I gasped, out of breath. My stomach filled with dread from what I was about to ask him to do. Surely he would think I was crazy when I asked him to cut the wires, but I had no other choice. "I can't do it. I'm not strong enough. I need your help."

Noah stared blankly at me, confusion in his eyes. "What? But how? I don't think you understand. I won't be able to get close enough to him."

"I'll take care of that. Trust me."

"How is that possible?"

I stared at him, silently begging him to not ask any more questions. "It doesn't matter how. He's calm now, and I can keep him calm while you cut the wires. Will you help? Please?"

"Of course," Noah replied with a reassuring smile as he hurried across the stream.

"Thanks," I said, my thoughts churning. He was about to see me work a miracle, but I couldn't dwell on that. All that mattered was helping the moose, even if it meant showing Noah the one talent I had that I'd hidden from everyone else. "Well, come on. Let's hurry up. The longer he's trapped, the worse it will be."

Noah and I headed back up the hill together. When we crested over the top and walked across the level section of the pasture, Noah stopped about twenty feet away from the moose. "Laken, are you sure about this?"

"Yes. It's okay. I'll show you." I approached the moose and knelt by his face. Gently stroking his cheek, I looked into his eyes, silently reminding him not to be afraid. The moose heaved a big sigh, a painful look washing over his face when the wires tightened around his chest. "Okay, Noah," I called softly. "You can come over."

Noah slowly crossed the field, his eyes darting from the huge moose to me, astonishment and awe in his expression. He dropped to his knees next to the animal, sweeping his gaze across the moose as if he hadn't seen him at all until now. "Laken, this is amazing. How did you do this?"

I shook my head. "I don't know," I answered honestly. "But it doesn't matter. The important thing is that he's calm. Can you cut the wires?"

Noah nodded and, without another word, he slid the blades around a tight wire, squeezed the handles and cut it. One side of the wire snapped up and he reached out to catch it, preventing it from flinging upward. He tossed a surprised smile my way before moving on to another one.

Noah started with the wires that circled the moose's body and then moved to those tangled around his legs. I stayed by the moose's head, stroking him and silently telling him not to be afraid, that he would be free soon enough.

Aside from an occasional breeze rustling through the nearby branches, the only other sound was the sharp snap of the wire with each cut.

After a few minutes, Noah scooted over to me on his knees. "I think I got everything except his head." He leaned over the moose and cut a wire wrapped around an antler. "One more." Noah knelt above the moose's face and cringed. "Ouch. Poor guy. That looks pretty painful," he said, studying the bloody gash just above his nostrils.

"That one looks really tight. It might hurt even more when I cut it."

With a quick thought, I warned the moose that this last one could be more painful than the rest. Then I backed up slightly to give Noah some room. "Easy, buddy," he murmured, carefully slipping the blade under the wire. As soon as he had a good grip on it, he squeezed the handles. The wire snapped in two, releasing the moose's face. Instantly, he jerked his head up and Noah launched backward just in time to avoid being gored by an antler.

The moose seemed to realize he was free and lifted his head as if ready to spring to his feet at any moment. Noah scrambled farther away, but I reached over to stroke the moose's cheek. "Easy," I whispered. "Not too fast. We can't be sure we got all the wires." I stood and backed up slowly as the moose put his hooves squarely on the ground and pulled himself to his feet.

Once upright, he stood still, his eyes appearing tired yet relieved. I approached him, smiling when I stopped in front of him and he nudged my hands with his nose. I reached up to stroke his neck, not surprised to find that he towered above me at nearly six feet tall.

"Can you keep him still for a moment?" Noah asked from a few feet away.

"I can try. Why?"

"He still has a wire around his hind leg that I missed."

"Okay."

"He won't kick me, will he?"

"No," I said before silently conveying to the moose what Noah was about to do. Once I was sure the moose understood, I nodded at Noah. "Go for it."

I stayed by the moose's head as Noah walked around his hind end to his back leg on the far side. Then I heard a loud snap.

"I think that's it," Noah said, returning to my side.

"Wow, that is one big animal," he mused in awe. "You look tiny next to him."

I wondered what Noah would think if I told him this wasn't the biggest moose I had run into, but I kept that to myself. "You were a very good patient," I told the moose. "You're free to go. Just stay off the roads. We didn't save you so that we could scrape you off the pavement some-day." I stepped back, clearing the way for the moose to head back into the forest.

Noah stood beside me, admiring the moose who lin-gered for a moment. "He's pretty bloody. Do you think he'll be okay?"

"Yeah, I think so. There really isn't much more we can do at this point. He'll heal, I hope."

The moose turned to look at us, and I interpreted his gesture as a silent thank you. *You're welcome,* I thought with a sigh. Then he sauntered away, lifting his front legs over the fence that had entangled him moments ago be-fore disappearing into the woods.

Noah and I were left alone, staring at the downed barbed wire fence. After a few seconds, Noah turned to me and glanced at my shirt.

"What?" I gasped, looking down at my chest to see blood from the moose's face streaked across my cream-colored sweater. "Oh," I said with a sigh.

"I think your shirt may be ruined. Sorry."

I shrugged. "That's okay. It's a small price to pay for saving him." I scanned the forest for any sign of the moose, but he was gone. Then I looked back at Noah as I swiped at a loose strand of hair blowing across my face. "We did it."

Noah caught my eye, reaching up to gently rub his thumb over my cheek. "You just got blood on your face."

I opened my palms, noticing that both of them were smeared with blood. "Wow. I'm a mess."

"You sure are. Come on. I need to return these wire cutters to the Owens and I'm sure they'll let you use their bathroom to wash up."

He wrapped an arm around my shoulders and started leading me back to the house. Walking beside him, I wondered what he must be thinking. At least he wasn't hammering me with questions about how I had calmed the moose, but I expected he'd ask soon enough. I needed to be prepared with answers, but right now, I had no idea how I would explain it to him.

All I knew was that it was finally time to share my secret with someone.

Chapter 13

Noah and I retraced our path up and down the hills until we reached the barn. We skirted around the herd of black and red cattle, dodging the mud and cow piles on our way to the fence. Noah helped me climb over it before following, the wire cutters still in his hand.

Once on the other side, we walked toward the house, cutting across the front lawn to the far side by the pick-up truck where we headed up the steps to the front porch, our shoes thudding against the wooden planks until we reached the door. Noah cast a reassuring glance my way as he knocked lightly. Barking immediately erupted inside the house, and we heard voices hushing the dog.

As soon as the barking faded, the door was opened by a woman with kind brown eyes and silver-streaked hair pulled back from her face, her tanned skin wrinkled, presumably from years spent outside under the sun. She wore a white turtleneck tucked into loose, high-waisted jeans, and her expression flashed with concern. "Deputy. Come in, both of you. It's awfully cold out there." She moved aside and ushered us into the warm house. "I didn't realize you weren't alone," she said to Noah as she shut the door behind us.

"I needed a little help," Noah explained. "Mrs. Owens, this is Laken Sumner, Sheriff Sumner's daughter. Laken, this is Margaret Owens."

"Hi," I said shyly, briefly meeting her gaze before looking away.

"It's nice to meet you, dear," she replied, holding her hand out to me.

I started to reach out to her, but stopped when I saw the blood smeared on my hand and remembered what a mess I was. "I'm sorry. I must look like I just walked out of a butcher shop," I said, pulling my arm back to my side.

Mrs. Owens drew in a sharp breath at the sight of my hands before scanning my shirt and my face. "That's not your blood, I hope."

"No, ma'am. It's from the moose."

She frowned with a heavy sigh, glancing back at Noah. "What happened to him? I never heard a gunshot. Did you have to—" Her voice trailed off.

Noah smiled, appearing relieved. "No. We were able to cut him free. I'm just returning your wire cutters and Laken was hoping she could wash up before driving home."

She looked at him, her expression curious. "How?"

Noah glanced at me. "It's a long story. Let's just say it definitely took the two of us."

I held my breath, hoping she would accept his explanation, as weak as it was.

"I'm sure it did. Well, however you did it, thank you. I'm just grateful we don't have a dead moose up there to bury." She shifted her attention to me. "Now, Laken, I'm sorry I haven't shown you to the bathroom yet. Please, come with me." She turned, gesturing for me to follow her down the hallway.

The scratched wooden floor creaked beneath my weight as I fell in behind Mrs. Owens. Black and white photographs of prized cattle with ribbons dangling from their halters adorned the wood-paneled walls, capturing my attention and slowing me down. By the time I caught up to Mrs. Owens at the end of the hall, she held open a door.

"Here you go. Take your time."

"Thank you," I said before slipping into the bathroom, barely making eye contact with her. While she shut the door behind me, I looked in the mirror, cringing at the blood and dirt smudged across my face.

I scrubbed my hands in the sink, the filthy reddish-brown water pooling against the white porcelain before disappearing down the drain. Then I used a damp paper towel to wipe the marks off my face. When I finished, blood still streaked my shirt, but I would have to wait until I got home to change out of it.

As I emerged from the bathroom, an unfamiliar male voice came from the entry hall. I returned to Noah's side to find that he and Mrs. Owens had been joined by her husband, a tall, wiry man with tufts of gray hair behind his ears and a few thin strands combed over his bald head. A flannel shirt the green color of pine fell loosely over the waist of his worn blue jeans. His gray eyes studied me, and I partially hid behind Noah, as if he could shield me from the questions I expected Mr. Owens to ask.

Noah draped an arm around my shoulders. "Mr. Owens, this is the sheriff's daughter and a very good friend of mine, Laken. Laken, this is Jack Owens."

"It's nice to meet you, Laken," Mr. Owens said. "I was putting the dog away when Margaret let you in. Noah was just explaining that the two of you were able to save the moose. Nice work, although it looks like you may have ruined your shirt."

I nodded. "We're just glad we could help," I said quietly, glancing up at Noah.

Noah's gaze caught mine, and he smiled before shifting his attention back to the Owens. "Yes, but unfortunately what was good for the moose was very bad for your fence. There's a pretty big gap where we had to cut through it, so you'll probably need to keep your herd down by the barn until you can secure it."

"Thanks for letting us know. I'll head up there first thing in the morning," Mr. Owens replied. "They'll be safe enough tonight. We've had to put them in the barn every night lately, ever since we lost one a few weeks ago."

"How did that happen?" Noah asked as I looked up at Mr. Owens, alarmed.

"We're not sure. She disappeared one night without a trace. It was a few days before we found her, at least what was left of her. The dog actually found her remains in the woods. There wasn't much, mostly just bones and hide."

I sucked in a deep breath as Noah asked, "What do you think happened?"

"We have no idea. She was the oldest of the herd, so the only thing we can think of is that a predator got her since they usually go for the weakest animals. Whatever it was, it somehow dragged her under the fence. It was either really strong or there were a lot of them," Mrs. Owens explained.

"Did you report this?" Noah asked.

Mrs. Owens shrugged. "Didn't seem like it would do any good. It's not like we'd get her back. We just assumed it was an animal, or animals."

"I guess you're right. There isn't much the sheriff can

do about a wild animal finding a meal. I take it this only happened once?" Noah asked.

"Yes, thank goodness," Mr. Owens answered. "I mean, it's crazy. We've never had our cattle taken like this in over forty years. Might have been a rabid bear. That's all we could think of. I mean, it's not like we have mountain lions or wolves around here."

Noah's eyes locked with mine at the mention of wolves. "Well, I'm sorry to hear about that," he said.

"Thank you," Mr. Owens said. "She was a good cow. Produced a healthy calf for us every year for the last ten years. And speaking of this, it's getting late now. We should head up to the barn and put the herd in for the night."

"Yes, it's that time." Mrs. Owens extended her hand to Noah. "Thanks again for your help today, Deputy. We didn't know who else to call."

Noah shook her hand then reached for the one her husband offered. "No problem. But I can't take all the credit. I couldn't have done it without Laken's help. It was definitely a two-person job."

A curious haze shadowed Mr. Owens' expression as he let go of Noah and looked at me. "About that. How did you—"

I breathed deeply, nervously biting my lip while glancing down at the floor. Before he could finish his question, Mrs. Owens touched his arm. "The only thing that matters is that they took care of it. Now I'm sure these two young folks need to be on their way and we really need to finish with our chores."

Relief washed over me when Mr. Owens didn't push for an answer. "I suppose you're right," he mused.

We bid a quick goodbye to them and stepped outside. The temperatures were falling as the sun dropped toward the horizon, casting shadows in the twilight. I rushed ahead of Noah, hurrying down the porch steps and to my car as the Owens followed us out before cutting across the lawn on their way to the barn. Noah jogged to catch up to me, his footsteps growing louder on the gravel when he reached the driveway.

"Laken, wait up," he called out as I approached the Explorer.

I turned, leaning against the cold SUV when he stopped inches away from me. I shoved my hands into my pockets, closing my fingers around the keys in my right pocket. Avoiding his gaze, I watched a red maple leaf scurry across the gravel in the breeze. I may have escaped the Owens's curiosity, but I knew I wouldn't escape Noah's questions.

"I want to get home before my mom starts to worry. I'm sure the school called to tell her I went home sick." I lifted my eyes to his, hoping he wouldn't ask how I had calmed the moose up on the hill. I didn't get my wish.

"Yeah, you're probably right. But, Laken, we need to talk about what just happened up there." He glanced up at the mountain before looking back at me.

I sighed with defeat. "Okay. Can you come over tonight around seven-thirty? There's something I want to show you." The newspaper article and photographs of Ivy in the shoebox flashed through my thoughts. I found comfort in knowing I wasn't the only one who could talk to animals. Even though she had died, perhaps if Noah knew about her, he wouldn't think my talent was too strange.

He nodded, his eyes locking with mine before I pulled the keys out of my pocket and spun around. As I reached for the door handle, Noah inched closer, reaching his arm around me and curling his fingers over my hand. Without a word, I turned back to him. Our eyes locked, and he dipped his head, grazing his lips over mine. His kiss was soft and gentle, but most importantly, it reassured me that nothing he had seen in the last hour had changed how he felt about me.

After a few moments, he pulled away and backed up, smiling softly. "See you soon," was all he said before disappearing around the front of the Explorer on his way to the police cruiser.

✑✑✑

When I returned home, I changed into a black shirt and clean jeans. Fortunately, neither my parents nor Dakota were home to see or, in Dakota's case, smell my bloody clothes. My parents certainly would have wanted to know exactly what happened. Since my father knew about the moose, he probably would have guessed where I'd been before I even told him. Arriving home to an empty house was, therefore, a huge relief. After dressing and brushing my hair out of the braids, I spent the remainder of the afternoon on my homework.

At six-thirty, I headed downstairs to take a break only to hear Dakota scratching at the back door. As soon as I let him in, he charged up to my room, probably tired from a long day in the woods. I was about to follow him when I heard the garage door open and, minutes later, my mother walked in. Instead of returning upstairs, I stayed with her, and together we prepared spaghetti and salad for dinner.

She asked how I was feeling, a question I brushed off by answering that I was much better. I added the lame excuse that I must have eaten something at lunch that hadn't agreed with me. Thankfully, she accepted my explanation without asking anything more.

I ate a quick dinner with my parents before rushing upstairs to touch up my make-up and spritz a dash of perfume on my wrist. Time was ticking away and Noah would be here any minute.

Without waiting for the doorbell to ring, I ran down the stairs at seven-thirty. If I knew Noah, he was probably walking up our sidewalk at that very moment. As if on cue, a knock sounded on the front door and I rushed into the entry hall, biting back a wide smile.

Before I reached the door, my father appeared from the family room off to the side. Looking tired, he stopped when he saw me.

"Don't worry, Dad. I got it."

He glanced at his watch. "Who are you expecting on a school night?"

"It's just Noah. And he won't stay long, I promise." I hurried to the door and opened it, smiling at Noah who now wore dark blue jeans, a gray shirt and a black leather jacket. "Hi," I said. "Come on in." I stood to the side, giving him plenty of room to come in out of the cold.

"Hi, there," he said with a grin that quickly faded when he noticed my father. "Good evening, sir."

"What brings you over here tonight, Noah?" my father asked as I shut the door.

I wondered how many questions we would have to answer before we could escape up to my room. "Dad," I groaned. "He's just here for a short visit. Does he have to have a reason?"

My father took a deep breath. "I suppose not. Is your homework done, Laken?"

"Dad," I said with a heavy sigh. "My grades have always been stellar. I've got it under control." I met his tired eyes, silently begging him to let us go.

"So where are the two of you headed?"

"Upstairs to my room," I answered. "Is that okay?"

"Do I have a choice?" my father asked with a teasing smile. "Yes, of course, it's fine."

"Thank you, sir," Noah said. "Don't worry. I won't keep Laken from her homework for long."

I caught his eye, nodding my head toward the kitchen. Without a word, I started to walk away, hearing Noah's footsteps close behind me.

"One more thing, Laken," my dad called. I stopped without turning around. "Keep the door open."

Mortified, I felt a blush roll across my face. "Got it," I said before disappearing into the kitchen.

"Sir, you have nothing to worry about. We're just going to talk," Noah assured him.

"I'm not worried, Noah," I heard my dad say. "I know I can trust you two."

"Thank you, sir."

By that point, I had reached the kitchen table. I stopped to wait for Noah who lingered in the entry hall, clearly more focused on my father than on me.

"Come on," I mouthed to him.

He nodded, finally following me as my father returned to the family room. When Noah reached the kitchen, I continued around the corner and led the way up the stairs.

Dakota met us in the doorway to my room, blocking it. My father must not have realized Dakota was home, otherwise he would have insisted Noah stay downstairs. I hadn't yet revealed to him that Noah knew about Dakota and, after the way he had reacted when he learned Xander knew, I wasn't about to if I could help it. I stopped, sensing Noah inches behind me. "Not you, too, Dakota," I groaned, scowling at him. "Can you please go to your bed?"

Dakota huffed, scanning both of us with his honey-colored eyes before retreating to his bed, his nails clicking against the wood floor. I walked a few feet into my room and turned to Noah. "Okay, that was embarrassing. First my dad, then Dakota."

"I take it your dad's not used to you having guys up in your room," Noah said, grinning as he stepped closer to me.

"Sure, he is, if you count Ethan."

"Okay, not counting Ethan."

My smile fading, I wasn't sure what he was getting at. "Yes, I know. My social life has been totally lame up until now. I've never really had a boyfriend before."

"That's okay. Actually, it's better than okay. I love knowing I'm the first guy to steal your heart."

With a sexy smile, he lifted both hands to the sides of my face, tilting my jaw up as he kissed my lips. His touch was as soft as a feather, and his mouth teased mine. I reached my arms up over his shoulders, wanting to pull him closer, but he stayed back, leaving some space between our bodies. After a few minutes, Noah pulled farther away. I opened my eyes as he muttered, "Hmm, that was nice. I don't want to stop, but your dad, who is also my boss, is right downstairs."

I stared into his brown eyes. "Really?" I asked, my voice dazed. "You still like me that way?"

"Of course. Why would you even ask that?"

"I don't know," I said nervously. "I just kind of worried that you might have changed your mind after what you saw today." I glanced down at the floor and then back up at him.

"Are you kidding? You were amazing today. I don't know anyone else who could have done what you did, calming that huge moose. It was as if he'd known you his whole life. If anything, I like you even more now."

"You don't think I'm weird?"

"Weird? Laken, no, definitely not. Special is more like it."

My heart glowing, I realized he meant every word by the look in his eyes. "I've always felt...different." I almost said "like a freak," but changed my mind at the last minute. "I think it's why I don't have a lot of friends. I've always felt more comfortable around animals than I have around people."

"Maybe you should give people a chance. They might surprise you."

"You've surprised me," I admitted.

"I hope that's a good thing."

"Of course it is," I responded with a grin, meeting his gaze and noticing a smile tugging at his lips.

"So what is it you wanted to show me?" he asked.

I gestured to the bed. "Have a seat. I'll get it."

He crossed the room with a few steps and sat down as I approached the dresser, opened the top drawer and retrieved the old shoebox. Plucking off the lid, I set it on the dresser before turning to face him. Then I walked over to the bed and handed the box to him.

"Here," I said.

"What's this?" he asked, studying its contents for a moment before placing it on his lap while I sat sideways next to him. He lifted a photograph, his eyes glued to it. It was the first one I had pulled out when my father had given me the box, the one with a gray wolf licking Ivy as the snow fell. "Is this her? Your birth mother?"

I nodded. "Yes."

"You look like her. You have her eyes."

"I know."

"She was beautiful." He paused, looking up from the photograph to gaze at me. "Like you."

I blushed at his flattery, grateful when he returned his attention to the picture. "So she loved wolves, too?" he asked.

"Apparently. My dad told me she had a special bond with them. She helped with a wolf program out west. That's where that picture was taken. It's also the reason my dad let me keep Dakota. He remembered how the wolves had taken to her and figured it might be the same with me and Dakota."

"Ah," Noah mused, raising his eyebrows. "That makes a lot more sense now. I have to admit, I was a little surprised when I first found out the sheriff allowed his daughter to keep a wolf as a pet." As his words drew to a close, he shuffled through the rest of the photographs, occasionally lifting one up to study it closer. After a few minutes, he stopped and looked at me. "It's really great that your dad kept all these pictures for you. You should know something about her."

I smiled. "It's actually been a huge relief to know about her."

"Why's that?"

I hesitated, twisting a finger in the hem of my shirt as I stood up and walked over to my desk. I turned and leaned against it, feeling a little better to put some space between us. "I—I think she could do what I can do."

Noah raised his eyebrows. "What's that?"

I took a deep breath, mustering my courage. "Oh, boy. This is really hard. I've never told anyone this."

"Not even your parents?"

"No, not even them."

"Well, I'm honored. But what can you do?" he asked.

"Talk to animals." My words rushed out on a breath I could no longer hold in and I studied his reaction, wondering if he believed me.

"Talk to animals?" he repeated, as if he didn't understand.

"Yes. Well, I guess a lot of people talk to animals. The difference with me is that they understand me, and I mean *really* understand me." I paused for a moment and when he didn't say anything, I had to ask, "You believe me, don't you?"

"After what I saw today? Yes. Besides, you have a very well-behaved wolf. And that suddenly makes sense."

"Whew." Lightheaded with relief, I grabbed the chair to steady myself. "I was so afraid to tell you. I thought you'd think I was crazy."

"That's not possible now that I've seen you in action. So tell me more. What kind of things do you tell them and how do you know they understand you?"

"It all started with a fawn in the backyard when I was almost seven. I'll never forget how it let me touch it when I told it not to be scared, that I wouldn't hurt it."

"I'll bet that was amazing."

"It was. And then its mother came out of the woods and let me pet her, too." Memories of that day flooded my thoughts, but I frowned at the image of my mother scolding me when she'd seen me so close to the deer.

"What are you thinking?"

My eyes had drifted away from his as I stared across the room, deep in thought, and I quickly glanced back at him. "I was remembering that day and how amazed I was when they weren't scared of me. But then my mom came outside and got a little upset when she saw what was happening. She was worried I could get hurt."

"I'm sure any mother would worry about that."

"I guess so. She made me promise never to get close to a wild animal again."

Noah smiled knowingly. "You didn't keep that promise, did you?"

"Nope. I broke it the first chance I got." I paused, grinning. "Well, actually, I didn't really break it because, when I made her that promise, I added, silently of course, that I would only do it if the animals wanted me to."

"You were a sneaky little devil at almost seven," he said with a chuckle. "I'm almost afraid to ask, but what other animals have you 'talked' to?"

"Pretty much all of the ones that live around here. Moose, deer, bears—"

"Bears?" he interrupted. "Isn't that dangerous?"

I shrugged. "Maybe. I never really gave it much thought. We only have black bears around here, and they're pretty easy going, at least with me."

"Have you ever touched one?"

I smiled slyly. "Yes. They're kind of like big dogs. Some of them love to be scratched around the ears."

"And what about dogs? Do they understand you, too?"

I shook my head. "No. It's strange. Only wild animals understand me. It's never worked on dogs, cats or any other domestic animal."

"Hmm, that's interesting. Do you know why that is?"

I laughed, shooting him a big smile. "You're kidding, right? I don't understand any of this. I don't know how I do it, why they hear me, trust me, and sometimes help me. So I have no idea why it works on some animals and not on others."

"Yeah, I guess that was a lame question."

"Now how weird do you think I am?"

"Stop asking crazy questions like that. You're not weird, just special." He paused thoughtfully. "You've always been very special. Ever since I met you after you rescued Ryder. Is that how you found him?"

I straightened the hem of my shirt and sat beside him on the bed. "Yes. I had a little help. I mean, we, me and Dakota, had a little help."

"From who? Or should I ask, from what?"

"Owls. And a bear. She found me right after I fell and hit my head. So I asked her to find Ryder and keep him warm."

Noah stared at me in amazement. "Did she?"

"Yes. By the time I found Ryder, she had curled up

around him. It was quite sweet, actually." I smiled, remembering the vision of her covering his tiny body in the clearing under the moonlight. "His mother told me he was talking about a bear the next day. I told her my stray dog kind of looked like one."

"Wow. I don't know what I would do if I came across a bear."

"Well, as long as you're with me, you'll be fine." I grinned at him, liking the idea of a future with him. "But if you want a good bear story, I have something for you to read." I reached for the shoebox on his lap, sifted through the pictures until I found the newspaper article about the family who had been spared a grizzly attack by an unknown woman, and carefully lifted it. "Here. Check this out."

"What's this?" He gently took the flimsy yellow newspaper from me, scanned the headline, and then looked at me, his eyebrows raised. "Your mother?"

I shrugged. "I presume so. They didn't know who she was. Go on, read it."

Noah dropped his gaze to the article, awe sneaking into his eyes while he read what had happened. After a few minutes, he took a deep breath, raising his eyes back up to me. "That's incredible. It must be amazing to know she had a special way with animals, too."

A lump forming in my throat, I stared into his soft brown eyes. "You have no idea what it means to me. Until now, I thought I was the only one animals understood." I shook my head, blinking back the tears threatening to fill my eyes. "I've lived with this secret for eleven years. I can't believe that in the last few weeks, I not only found out my birth mother had the same secret, but now I'm telling you everything. This is going to take some getting used to."

"Is that a good thing?"

"I'm not sure yet. That depends."

"On what?"

"You," I said simply, smiling at him. Then I sighed, studying him. "Can I ask you something?"

"Of course. Anything."

"Why did you call me today?"

"I didn't know what else to do. Your dad acted like it would be easy. Find the moose and put him out of his misery. But when I got there and I saw him, I couldn't do it. I needed someone to endorse it, I guess. I figured that if you came out and said nothing else could be done, then at least I could do it with a clean conscience."

"I'm sure you didn't expect to save him."

"No, I certainly didn't."

I sighed, looking away from him to stare at the floor as silence hung in the air between us.

"Hey," he said softly, grazing my jaw with his fingers until I lifted my face to look at him. "I'm glad things turned out the way they did. That moose got a second chance at life, and I now know more about you than anyone else. It's nice. I feel closer to you now."

I gasped as a horrible thought flashed into my mind. "You can't tell anyone. People around here can be kind of superstitious. I'd be branded a witch in no time."

"A witch?"

"Yes. You know, like the Salem witch trials. There are some old people around here who really believe in that."

He raised his eyebrows. "You're kidding."

"I wish I was."

"Well, I'm not one of them. And your secret is definitely safe with me," he reassured me. Then he dropped his hand away from my face, looking back down at the shoebox. Something seemed to catch his eye and he reached into the pictures. "What's this?" he asked, lifting an envelope out from under the photographs. It was the letter my mother had left for me still sealed away.

"My dad said Ivy wrote me a letter right after I was born. He said she wanted me to read it when I got older and found out she was my birth mother."

"You haven't opened it yet."

"I know. I'm not ready. Maybe soon, but not now."

Noah gently set it down on top of the pictures. "It might be good for you to read it."

"Perhaps. I mean, I want to, I'm just...scared."

"Of what?"

Another lump formed in my throat and I swallowed, hoping my voice would stay steady. "Of wishing that I could have gotten to know her. Of mourning the loss of someone I never knew. Does that make sense?"

Noah nodded, his eyes glistening with moisture. "Perfect sense." An awkward silence hovered between us for a moment. Finally, he handed the shoebox to me. "Here."

I took it from him. "Thanks." I stood and carried it back over to the dresser where I placed the lid on top of it and returned it to the drawer. After closing the drawer, I turned and leaned against the dresser. "This doesn't change anything between us, does it?"

"Yes," Noah stated, rising to his feet before walking across the room to stand in front of me. "It makes me like you even more. You are a fascinating girl, Laken." He leaned his hands on the dresser beside my hips, boxing me in. He was inches away, and my heart fluttered when he leaned down to whisper in my ear. "If your father wasn't downstairs right now, I'd have you on your back faster than you can blink."

Flustered, I gazed into his eyes, his breath on my neck sending shivers skating up and down my spine. "Really? I'd be lying if I said that thought hadn't crossed my mind," I told him, wishing my father wasn't home and probably counting the minutes until Noah left.

To my disappointment, Noah dropped his arms away from the dresser and stepped back. "Good. Keep that thought. But for now, we can't. It's a school night for you and a work night for me. I need to let you finish your homework."

"Okay," I agreed with a sigh. I knew he was right, I just didn't like it.

He inched toward the open doorway. "I'll see myself out, okay?"

"Sure."

"And I'll call you tomorrow. We'll do something Saturday night."

"I'll look forward to it." I smiled at the prospect of another night with him as he disappeared through the doorway, his footsteps fading until silence filled my bedroom. Then I sighed, wondering how I would ever be able to concentrate on my homework for the rest of the night.

Shaking my head, I tried to push him out of my thoughts while my gaze wandered to my desk, landing on the textbooks piled high next to my computer. Determined to finish my homework, I headed over to my chair.

When I reached the desk, my phone buzzed from where it sat next to the keyboard. I sat down and grabbed it, wondering if it was Brooke or Ethan.

I casually glanced at it, but my heart skipped a beat when I read the name flashing across the screen. Xander. Taking a deep breath, I read his text.

Missed u in History today. Hope everything is OK. See u in the morning. Sweet dreams.

His last two words conjured up the dream I'd had of him last weekend. I closed my eyes and sucked in a deep breath, wishing he would leave me alone. Or did I wish I could forget he existed? I wasn't sure. All I knew was that Noah and I had taken our relationship to a whole new level tonight when I had told him the one thing I'd never told anyone. And no one, not even Xander, could ruin it.

If only I believed that.

Chapter 14

The next morning, Xander didn't even give me two minutes to get to my locker. Instead, he cornered me in the parking lot with a smug grin on his face as soon as I stepped out of the Explorer. As I shut the door and turned, my eyes immediately locked with his cool blue stare.

He was back to black today in a black shirt, black jeans, and black leather jacket that caught the morning rays of sunshine within its folds. His breath blew out in a fog from the cold air that had coated the leaves, grass, and rooftops with a frosty glaze.

I huffed with frustration and shoved my hands into the pockets of my jacket, hugging it around my red sweater, a morning breeze pushing a few wisps of hair against my face.

The silence between us broke when Ethan shut the passenger door on the other side of the Explorer. "Hey, Laken," he called across the roof. "I'm going to meet Brooke. See you in homeroom?"

I turned far enough to see him out of the corner of my eye. "Sure. I'll be in soon."

He raised his eyebrows, his gaze darting toward Xander. "I can wait for you if you'd like."

I smiled reassuringly. "No, you don't have to. I'll be fine. Now go before Brooke hunts you down out here."

As Ethan took off, I turned back to Xander.

"Your friends don't like me, do they? They don't even want to leave you alone with me in the school parking lot? What have you told them?" Xander asked, stepping closer to me.

"Nothing except the truth. They've made their own conclusions."

"Maybe you should tell them I'm only trying to keep you safe."

"How do I know that? I still can't figure you out. Between you and your dad, I don't know what to think." I sighed, remembering his father's story about the ancient curse and wondering how much of it was actually true.

Xander acted as though he hadn't even heard me. "What happened to you yesterday? You missed History."

"I wasn't feeling well, so I went home a little early." A vivid image of the moose tangled up in the barbed wire flashed through my mind, and I could only hope he believed my lie.

"Then how come I didn't see your truck in the driveway when I drove by your house after school?"

I glared at him, although not at all surprised by this. It would have been far more out of character for him had he not tried to find me when I hadn't shown up for class. "Because I had to take care of something."

"And what was that?"

"Nothing that concerns you."

He smiled knowingly, frustrating me even more. "I figured you'd say that."

"So if you drove by my house and knew I didn't go home, why didn't you send out a search party?"

"It was tempting, but when I drove by again later and saw your truck, I knew you'd gotten home safely."

"You know, you're starting to creep me out again."

"Even after what my dad told you?"

"Especially after what he told me. It sounds like a fairy tale. Are you sure you two aren't watching too many Disney movies? Sounds a little like Beauty and the Beast to me. But what really freaks me out is that both of you seem to believe it."

"I'm surprised you don't believe it," Xander said seriously.

"Of course, I don't. Why would I?"

Xander's smile faded as he leaned toward me. Heat radiated from his body, warming me in the frigid morning air. "You know why," he whispered, his breath hot against my ear.

I fell into a trance, my nerves rattled by him once again. How could I let him get to me so easily?

When he raised his head and stepped back, his confident smile returned. "I'm glad to see you're feeling better. See you in class."

Without waiting for a response, he walked across the parking lot toward the school. I didn't catch my breath until he disappeared beyond the rows of cars and trucks.

With a deep breath, I pushed Xander, his father, and the curse out of my mind, refusing to believe in their nonsense. It was crazy to think that magic existed in real life, and I would not let Xander scare me into getting whatever he wanted from me.

Shivering from the cold, I spun around to get my book bag out of the back seat. After pitching it over my shoulder, I slammed the door.

Then, reminding myself that today was Friday and I

would see Noah tomorrow, I finally made my way to the school, determined to ignore Xander for the rest of the day.

¢⁄ɔɕ⁄ɔ

My weekend was a complete bust. I worked the lunch shift at the pizza shop both Saturday and Sunday, pocketing some much needed cash. Brooke asked me and Noah to join her and Ethan again Saturday for dinner and a movie. I reluctantly agreed, disappointed that Noah and I wouldn't be alone as I'd hoped. We didn't have more than a few minutes to talk in private on the ride to town and back to my house. Neither one of us mentioned the moose or the secret I had shared with him. A part of me was relieved, but a bigger part of me felt let down. I craved his acceptance, and I needed to hear again that it didn't change the way he felt about me.

Instead, he seemed distant when he dropped me off that night. He walked me to the door, kissing me with a quick peck before insisting I get a good night's rest for my lunch shift the next day. I tried not to let it bother me, telling myself he was right since I also had to squeeze in my homework. But after sharing with him the one thing I'd never told anyone, I had expected a little more than his quiet demeanor and the pathetic kiss that ended our night.

I started the following week with the dreaded feeling that Noah felt differently about me. He hadn't called on Sunday, and I'd resisted the urge to call him. I forced myself to be patient, to give him some space and time, reminding myself that he was probably working on his book. I would just have to wait until I saw him next to ask what was bothering him. The only problem was I had no idea when that would be.

I threw myself into my schoolwork that week. The

days were growing shorter, and darkness came earlier each day. The temperatures continued to drop, and frost covered the ground and rooftops in the morning. Wind howled every night, whipping the fading leaves from their branches. The transformation from fall to winter had begun.

I reluctantly agreed to return to the library with Xander on Thursday. As he drove along the winding road that afternoon, I quietly watched the late fall scenery. Gray clouds hovered low, skimming the tops of the mountains, the forest dark except for a patch of pine here and there now that the leaves were gone.

All I could think about on the drive was Noah. He still hadn't called all week, and I was beginning to wonder if it was over. Just the thought of never seeing him again brought tears to my eyes. I tried not to think about it, but I wasn't very successful.

"You're awfully quiet today," Xander said softly. "Cat got your tongue?"

I glanced at him with a frown, letting my sullen eyes do the talking.

"I can tell something is bothering you. Let me guess. Boyfriend trouble? Do you realize you've worn black for three days now?"

I huffed. How dare he critique my clothes? But I couldn't deny it. Black had matched my mood all week, and today was no exception. Between my sweater, skirt, tights, boots, and jacket, the only color other than black was a hint of purple woven into my skirt. My silver necklace sparkled against my chest, the diamonds shining like stars against a midnight sky. "You're one to talk. You wear black just about every day." Except today, he wore a gray shirt and blue jeans.

"Yeah, but it works for me. You're too nice for all that black."

"Really? Is there such a thing? Can someone be too nice for a particular color?" Amused that we were taking about something as trivial as clothes, I felt a small smile emerge on my face.

He laughed softly. "How did we get started on this?" He paused, his grin fading. "Oh, yeah, your boyfriend problems. I must have guessed right. So, there's trouble in paradise?"

My smile vanished as I snapped my gaze away from him to look out the window. "Maybe," I muttered.

Although Xander was the last person I wanted to talk to about this, it wouldn't hurt to get a guy's opinion. There was only one big problem. Even if I told him Noah hadn't called or texted since he'd dropped me off Saturday night, I wasn't about to tell him the secret I had shared with Noah last week. And if I couldn't tell him that, then I couldn't ask if he thought it had anything to do with Noah's sudden change of heart.

"We've got about twenty minutes until we get to the library if you want to talk about it," he prodded gently.

I half expected him to gloat, laugh arrogantly, or do something else equally condescending, but his voice held a hint of compassion.

I shrugged, staring out the windshield. "There isn't much to talk about. Everything was going great until Saturday."

"What happened on Saturday?"

"Nothing. That's the problem. And now I haven't heard from him since then." I sucked in a deep breath, finding the courage to ask, "Do you think I should call him?"

"Laken, I can't answer that. No matter what I say, I'll probably be wrong and I don't want you to blame me if it doesn't work out. But if you ask me, he's a fool."

I looked back at Xander, my eyebrows raised.

"If you were my girlfriend, I wouldn't leave you hanging for five days. I would let you know every day exactly how I felt."

"Why doesn't that surprise me? I'm sure Marlena appreciates that."

"Let's not drag her into this. We're talking about you." He paused for a moment. "Look, as much as I would love it if he disappeared from your life completely so I could help you forget about him, I have a feeling he'll be back. So don't worry. He's just a typical guy, noncommittal and spooked."

Or he's freaked out over what I told him last week, I thought. "I hope you're right," I muttered, forcing myself to smile appreciatively. After a few minutes of silence, I changed the subject. "What do you think we'll find in our research today?"

"Maybe a story about a witch who helped the slaves escape," Xander mused, a teasing sparkle in his eyes.

"Oh please," I groaned. "I can't handle any more craziness right now."

"Ah, yes, the curse. Don't tell me you're still upset about that."

Confused, I stared at him. "No, I was never upset. It's just weird the way you and your dad really believe it."

"I guess I can't fault you for that. There's a lot in our world you wouldn't believe," Xander said quietly, his eyes focused straight ahead.

"I'm sure there is. Los Angeles is probably as different as you can get from small town New Hampshire. You must feel like you moved to another planet," I said, dismissing his comment. I could have read a lot more into it between the ancient curse and how it might be related to the secret I had kept hidden for years. But thinking about this was exhausting.

All I wanted was to worry about my boyfriend problems and trudge through the History assignment like a normal teenager.

"It's good to see you understand something about me," Xander replied with a smirk.

I raised my eyebrows and returned my gaze to the passing trees. Was I really starting to understand him? What was the world coming to?

Xander and I arrived at the tiny library two hours before it would close. After passing the librarian, we escaped to the back table tucked in the corner behind the bookshelves, far from her suspicious eyes. We tossed our bags on the table and hung our coats on the rickety chairs before retrieving the books we had started reading the last time we were here.

When Xander expressed a morbid interest in the coroner's journal, I scoffed at him. "What do you think you'll find in that?" I asked as we sat down at the table.

"You never know," he replied slowly, opening the dark cover to reveal pages of handwritten script.

Shaking my head, I turned my attention to a book that told the story of a slave's journey to move his family to Canada. I had found it last time, but there hadn't been time to read it since I'd spent that afternoon reading about Josephine Kramer. I flipped through the brittle pages, studying the black and white illustrations of the family. The musty library smells seemed to disappear as the book captivated me. The father described a journey of pitfalls. Some nights, they were lucky enough to find a sympathetic northerner to open their doors to them, providing food, shelter, and warmth in basements and closets. But other nights, they were left to fend for themselves, battling frigid cold nights and snowstorms. When the children fell ill, there was no doctor to help them and no medicine to heal them. Food was often scarce, and they stayed alive by hunting squirrels and rabbits and stealing apples left in unsecured barns on orchard farms.

The trials and tribulations overcome by this family impressed me. I couldn't begin to imagine what they had endured on their way to the Canadian border. I slowly turned page after page, not wanting to miss a single word. In my fascination, I barely took any notes. About halfway through the book, the story became even more intense as bounty hunters from the south began to track them.

My heart nearly stopped when I read what happened after they passed through our town. A light dusting of snow covered the forest floor of leaves and fallen logs the night after they left a home and continued north. The family huddled around a fire, every blanket and coat they owned wrapped around the children as the sun dropped below the horizon. But the quiet evening was interrupted when two bearded men in confederate uniforms emerged from the woods, pointing their long muskets at the family, poised to shoot. The moment the father rose to his feet, a black bear charged out from between trees and hurled itself at the bounty hunters, tackling one as his gun fired, smoke billowing out from the weapon.

The second bounty hunter whipped around, aiming his musket at the bear, when another one lumbered out of the surrounding woods and pounced on him. The family watched in disbelief as the bears mauled the bounty hunters, relieved when the animals disappeared into the forest. The hunters had fallen to the ground, their lifeless bodies spilling blood onto the snow. The father recalled wondering if he should tell his family to run from the bears. But something told him to stay calm, to keep his wife and children by his side and not tempt the bears by giving them something to chase. He also noticed that one of the bears had looked at him before taking off into the woods, its eyes meeting his for a split second.

I couldn't believe what I was reading. Why had the

bears protected them? Why had they killed the bounty hunters and spared the family? It was as if they knew exactly what they were doing. Black bears weren't known for attacking people, either. There must have been a purpose for their actions.

I lifted my eyes from the book, staring at the wall across the table as I imagined the bears mauling the hunters.

"Holy shit. You've got to see this," Xander gushed in a whisper, breaking me out of my trance.

I turned my eyes toward him. "What?" I asked quietly, hoping the librarian wouldn't hear us.

"I know you thought this wouldn't have anything related to the Underground Railroad, but there's a section from the eighteen hundreds where they found several bounty hunters mauled to death by bears."

I wondered if there could be more than just the two I read about. "How many?"

"I've counted six so far." He gazed at me, a deep wonder in his eyes. "But that's not all. Get a load of this. There's something in here about Josephine Kramer. Isn't that the woman you read about the last time we were here? The woman wearing your necklace?"

"Yes. Why?" I asked, holding my breath as I waited for his answer.

"She died in eighteen thirty-three."

"So? What's interesting about that? Was she mauled to death too?" I exhaled deeply, curious to know why he found her death so fascinating, but also a little disappointed if that was all he could tell me about her.

"No. She was hung in the town streets. It says in here she was convicted of being a witch who cast spells on bears. People in town believed she told the bears to attack the bounty hunters. In fact, it also says all of the maulings occurred along a path the slaves followed that went right by her house. Several people knew she was a slave sympathizer and that her house was part of the Underground Railroad. And interestingly, only the bounty hunters were attacked, never the slaves. Isn't that odd?" He raised his eyebrows at me.

I looked away from him, staring up at the cobwebs woven across the corners of a small dusty window. "Why are you asking me? Yes, of course, it's a little odd."

"Because you're the one who told me black bears rarely attack people. That they try to avoid humans as much as possible."

I shrugged. "Yeah. So? Most people around here know that." I paused, desperate to change the subject. "Does it say anything else about her?"

"Only that she left behind a husband and a young daughter. She was only twenty-six when she died." He shot me a smug grin. "And you thought there wouldn't be anything on the Underground Railroad in the coroner's journal."

I rolled my eyes at him. "You got lucky," was all I said before looking back down at the pages in front of me.

Xander glanced at my book. "What are you reading? Anything interesting?"

"It's about a slave family who escaped through this area." I paused then added, "They were saved from bounty hunters by bears."

"Really?" Xander asked incredulously. "Can I check it out?"

"Sure." I pushed the book over to him as he shut the coroner's journal and slid it to the side. "It starts right here." I flipped back a few pages to an illustration of the family sitting around a campfire.

As Xander glued his eyes to the book, engrossed in the story, I sat still, staring ahead, lost in my thoughts. I couldn't believe Josephine had been branded a witch. But what bothered me the most was that if she had been a witch, what did that make me? She was my ancestor after all, and it seemed we had more in common than I could have imagined.

I frowned, my heavy thoughts weighing on me. The more I learned about Ivy, and now Josephine, the more questions I had. And the only person who knew my secret had disappeared. I desperately wanted to talk to Noah about all of this, but not until I knew why he hadn't called all week.

"Wow," Xander gasped, his voice barely louder than a whisper. "That is so cool."

"A woman was hung to her death in the street as people watched. Do you really think that's cool? The evidence was only circumstantial and she left behind a little girl. It's sad, not cool."

"I didn't mean about that. I meant how the bounty hunters were attacked. But there's more about Josephine than what I told you a few minutes ago."

I lifted my eyes, meeting his steady gaze. "What?"

"Apparently, witnesses testified that they had seen her talking to animals, feeding bears right out of her hands. It was rumored that the bears understood her," he said slowly, deliberately, as he watched me.

"That's crazy," I said, looking away from him and trying to seem surprised. But the fact was, he was telling me something I already knew.

"Is it?"

"Yes," I replied. "Don't tell me you believe all of that, too."

"Maybe I do."

"Well, then, you're as crazy as the old folks around here who believe in witches." I huffed, glancing at my watch. Five-thirty. "We only have a half hour left before the library closes. We'd better get our notes before we leave." I grabbed the book in front of Xander, pulling it back to me. Then I reached for my notebook and pen and started scribbling what I wanted to remember.

"Good idea." Xander reached for his own notebook. "How much of this should we use in our project?"

I stopped writing for a moment as I mulled over his question. "I don't know. Let's just take all the notes we can now and decide what to include later." The bounty hunter maulings would definitely bring our project to life. We were bound to get extra points when Mr. Jacobs saw how far we had gone in our quest to learn more about the Underground Railroad than what could be found online. The part I didn't want to mention was the trial and hanging of Josephine Kramer. After all, our topic didn't include witchcraft.

As I resumed taking notes, my mind swarmed with images of Josephine Kramer, first talking to black bears and then hanging from a noose in the town street while onlookers gaped at her lifeless body. I fought hard to push these unsettling visions out of my head. The connection to my own life was frightening. Just like Ivy, Josephine had a special way with animals and had died young. As much as I wanted to dismiss my suspicions, I was suddenly faced with more evidence that the curse Xander's father had uncovered was real.

I took a deep breath, desperately trying to shake the fear rising up inside me. The clock was ticking, and I needed to concentrate if I was going to write down the important parts in the little time we had left.

Chapter 15

Noah didn't call Thursday night or Friday. When the weekend arrived, I realized it would be my first Saturday night alone since school began. Brooke attempted to cheer me up, even offering to come over and hang out with me. I politely thanked her, but insisted she enjoy her night with Ethan and not worry about me.

The only thing I had to do this weekend, sadly enough, was homework. Mike had to let me go for the rest of the season since the tourists had disappeared as quickly as the fall leaves had been blown away. My only other option was to accept Xander's invitation to go out, but I scolded myself every time that thought crept into my mind. Surely there was a better way to get through this dry spell with Noah.

I wasn't ready to accept that he was gone from my life. Maybe he had just gotten so caught up with writing his book that he didn't want to get distracted until he finished. But even as I tried to justify it, I wondered why he couldn't give me a quick call to tell me about it. Didn't he think I would understand and give him the space he needed? As time went on, all I could figure was that he really had been freaked out by my gift of communicating with animals. How many other girls had he seen calming a huge moose? That had to be it. Until now, he had never acted so cold and distant.

By Saturday evening, my spirits had fallen to a new low. Fortunately, my parents were going out to a friend's birthday party which meant I wouldn't have to endure their attempts to cheer me up. Dakota's silent company was all I could handle. He had stayed by my side all day, nudging me every time I stared at my phone's lifeless black screen, tears streaming down my cheeks.

I didn't come out of my room until I heard my mother's SUV pull out of the garage. Relieved that the house was finally empty, I headed downstairs, Dakota following at my heels. He'd been cooped up inside all day and needed a quick bathroom break.

After grabbing my navy parka from the coat closet, I slipped it on over my black sweatshirt. I pulled a navy knit hat over my loose hair and slid my hands into a pair of gloves. As I wandered through the kitchen to the back door, Dakota waited patiently in front of it. Cold air swept into the house when I opened the door and Dakota raced past me into the darkness while I flipped on the outside light.

Taking a deep breath, I walked out to the edge of the patio and stopped. The trees surrounding the yard stretched up to a dark purple sky, their branches twisting up like black serpents. The full moon cast shadows onto the grass that swayed in the evening breeze. I briefly thought of the wolves and the man in the woods, suddenly wondering if I should be alone outside after dark. But I wasn't really alone. Dakota was with me.

I watched Dakota's silhouette as he roamed through the backyard, the cloud from my breath reflecting in the moonlight while I shoved my hands into my pockets. I usually didn't mind the cold, but tonight, I couldn't wait to return to the warm house and lock the door.

After a few moments, Dakota jerked his head up from where he'd been sniffing the grass and stared intently at the side of the house. I followed his gaze, expecting to see a rabbit or another animal. Instead, Noah walked around the corner, causing my heart to pick up speed. I felt the incredible urge to laugh and cry at the same time, and I hoped he wouldn't notice how flustered I was.

Wearing a fleece-lined denim jacket but no hat or gloves, he approached hesitantly, his steps slow and deliberate. After a moment, I tore my eyes away from him to look back at Dakota who watched Noah's every move.

"What are you doing here?" I asked in a quiet voice, my eyes never leaving Dakota.

Noah stopped in the grass a few feet beyond the edge of the patio where I stood. I felt his gaze on me as he spoke, but I refused to look at him. "I needed to see you. I'm sure you're upset with me, and you have every right to be."

I took a deep breath as he climbed up the patio steps.

Standing beside me, he continued. "Laken, look at me. Please."

Reluctantly, I shifted my gaze to him, noticing the shame in his eyes. Remaining silent, I waited to hear what he had to say.

"I'm sorry I didn't call this week. I had some things to take care of," he said.

"I just figured you were working on your book," I replied, trying to sound nonchalant, but the sadness in my voice gave me away. My eyes moist, I searched his expression for any sign of his true feelings. "If you don't want to see me anymore, all you have to do is tell me."

"That's just it. I don't want to break up with you. I want to keep seeing you. Things were really great between us. But I need a little time."

He paused as I stared at him with one unspoken question. Why?

"It's hard to explain. I can't talk about it right now," he said.

My heart dropped into the pit of my stomach and a lump formed in my throat. I swallowed back tears, worried they would spill from my eyes at any moment. "Why do I get the feeling you're hiding something from me?"

"It's only to protect you," was all he said.

"Then stop protecting me and just tell it like it is. I can handle it, whatever it is," I insisted as Dakota rushed over to the patio, bounded up the steps, and pushed his way in between me and Noah. He stood beside me facing Noah, his lip curled up, a low growl rumbling from deep within his throat.

"Dakota, stop. It's okay," I told him.

He glanced up at me, his growl subsiding. Then he turned his eyes back toward Noah, glaring at him.

Noah smiled faintly. "I actually feel a lot better now, knowing he can understand you."

"That doesn't mean he always does what I tell him to do." An awkward silence hovered between us and I shivered, craving the warmth inside the house. But I wasn't about to invite Noah in. Something was different between us. He was hiding something and I suddenly didn't feel comfortable around him. "So let me understand this. You showed up here tonight to apologize for leaving me hanging for a week, but you can't tell me what's going on? Or how long it's going to take you to get past it? Is that about right?"

Noah nodded, his sober eyes meeting mine. "I wish it didn't have to be like this."

"Then don't let it," I pleaded. "Rise above whatever it is and let's get back to the way things were."

"I wish it was that easy. There's something I have to fix first and, until I do, I have to stay away."

I studied him, shaking my head. Once again, I was reminded that he had started pulling away from me right after I had shared my secret with him. As much as I didn't want to believe it, I couldn't ignore the obvious. He must have decided I was too strange, too different. But if so, why was he here? Why the elaborate charade of pretending to want to be with me, but claiming he couldn't? "I think I get it," I said slowly. "It's because of what I told you after we rescued the moose."

"No, Laken, that's not it. Don't think that."

"Why not? I noticed something was different last Saturday night. You were withdrawn and distant. I would have chalked it up to Brooke's endless questions, but then you barely kissed me when you dropped me off." Tears returned to my eyes and I blinked furiously to hold them back. "Don't deny it. You've just confirmed what I suspected my whole life. That I'm a freak no one will want once they learn the truth about me." A tear rolled down my cheek and I reached up to wipe it away. "I always knew I shouldn't put any faith in people. They're far too complicated. Animals are easier. Much easier." I lowered my hand to touch Dakota's head. Knowing he stood beside me, that he would never judge me, made me feel a little better.

"Laken, stop talking like that. You couldn't be further from the truth. That has nothing to do with this."

"Then tell me what's going on," I challenged him.

He took a deep breath while I waited, wondering if he would tell me the truth. "Look, I'm involved in something I have no control over. I'm trying to sort it out and I need time to get through it. I'm going to make things right so we can be together again."

"Okay. Now you're scaring me. Are you in some kind of trouble?"

He averted his eyes and stared at the ground rather than answering me.

My heart skipped a beat with worry. "What about my dad? Can he help you with this?"

With a weak smile, Noah lifted his gaze to meet mine. "No, I'm not dragging him into this. Can you please just trust me and give me a little time?"

"I don't want to," I whispered as another tear rolled down my face.

"I know. I wouldn't expect you to."

"But I guess I can try." I longed to reach out for his hand, to feel him draw me into his arms, but I knew now wasn't the time for that. "Maybe for a few weeks. But not forever."

"No, of course not. A few weeks should be long enough. At least I sure hope it doesn't take any longer than that," he replied as uneasiness bordering on fear flashed across his face.

I decided not to ask him any more questions. "Halloween's almost here. I suppose this means I'll be going to the dance alone."

"Possibly. But I have to tell you, I hate dressing up in costumes."

His confession prompted me to smile faintly as I realized once again how much we had in common. "I'm not crazy about it myself."

"So are you okay now?"

"I wouldn't say I'm okay, but I'm going to trust you. Just promise me one thing."

"Anything."

"If you decide you don't want to see me anymore, then tell me. Please don't leave me hanging."

"I would have told you if that was the case. And I certainly wouldn't be here right now if I didn't still care about you," he said, his steady gaze leading me to believe he was speaking the truth.

I sighed softly. "I'm glad you came tonight. It means a lot that you wanted to tell me in person, even if you didn't tell me everything."

"I'm glad I came, too. But it's getting really cold out here, so I'm going to take off. You should get inside."

I nodded. "Don't be a stranger, okay? You can call just to say hi every so often."

"I'll try."

I frowned, wondering how a simple call required so much effort. But I brushed it off. "You're going to keep working for my dad, right?" I asked.

"Of course. That won't change." He turned, gesturing toward the door. "Now no more questions. You need to go. It's freezing out here."

"Yeah, you're right," I said quietly before heading toward the door. When I stopped at an arm's length from the handle, I turned. Dakota remained at the edge of the patio, his eyes glued to Noah. "Dakota," I called. "Come on. Time to go in."

He reluctantly tore his gaze away from Noah and trotted across the patio. I opened the door, letting him into the house. Following him, I stopped and turned in the doorway to look back at Noah one last time.

"Make sure you lock up," he reminded me.

"I always do."

"Well, have a nice night, okay, Laken?"

I swallowed back another lump in my throat, wondering how he thought I could possibly have a nice Saturday night without him. Nodding silently, I pushed the door, but before closing it completely, I watched Noah through the gap along the frame. He scanned the woods surrounding our yard before rushing down the patio steps and disappearing around the side of the house.

As soon as he was gone, I shut the door and clicked the deadbolt into place. Then I turned and leaned against the door, the tears I had been holding back bursting from my eyes. I slid down to the floor, propping my legs up against my abdomen and wrapping my arms around them. My forehead fell to my knees, and my sobs rang out through the silence. Whining, Dakota nudged my face with his cold wet nose, as though trying to comfort me.

Lifting my head, I met his worried amber eyes while he sat down on his haunches and rested his chin on my arm. "It's just you and me, now," I whispered. "Maybe that's how it should be."

Even though earlier, I'd had a glimmer of hope that Noah still cared about me, I now felt more alone than ever before. What if he never called again? What if it really was over and he just didn't know how to tell me?

My insecurities running rampant, more tears welled up in my eyes. The truth would be revealed in time, but until then, I could only wonder. Shuddering, I buried my face in Dakota's thick fur and cried until I had no more tears to shed.

ꙮ

"Josephine Kramer."

I hadn't even seen Xander sneak up behind me in the busy hallway as I hung my parka in my locker. Sighing, I wondered why he was thinking of her on a Monday morning. I spun around, my book bag on the floor forgotten. The students chattering in the hallway swarmed in the background as Xander's blue eyes captivated me.

"What?" I asked, confused.

"I said Josephine Kramer."

"Yes, I know. I heard you the first time. But do you have a point or do you just like to say the name of a woman who lived two hundred years ago?" I raised my eyebrows, noticing how his tight black T-shirt outlined his broad shoulders, the sleeve cutting off the top half of his tattoo.

"I have a question," he replied simply.

I waited for him to continue, but he remained silent, studying me. "So what is it?" I asked with a deep huff.

"Well, she was a witch, and we also know now that she's your ancestor." He paused, leaning in close to me and causing my nerves to tingle. "Maybe you're a witch, too."

"That's not a question," I retorted, frustrated with his suggestion even though it brought my senses back to reality.

"Do you always have to be so technical? My question is simple. Are you?"

"What?" I gasped, stepping back from him. "Of course not. Are you crazy? Don't tell me you believe in ancient curses *and* witchcraft."

Xander's composure didn't waver one bit. "Maybe you should believe in it. After all, your ancestor was hung for it."

"First of all, it's not like I ever knew her. And secondly, I don't believe she was a witch any more than I believe in that curse." I only wished I could be as certain as I made myself sound.

Doubts had been creeping into my thoughts lately, making me wonder. But I couldn't let Xander know a part of me was starting to buy into all this nonsense.

"Tell that to the bounty hunters she killed."

"She didn't kill them. Bears did."

"But she told the bears to do it, so she was pretty much responsible for their deaths."

I shook my head. Ripping my eyes away from him, I stared out into the hallway as students passed by. "Why are we talking about this?"

"Because it's fascinating. And you're related to her. How much of this should we put in our report?"

"None. Our report has to be factual. You asked me this last week, remember?"

Xander wrinkled his nose. "I did, didn't I?" With a sigh, he leaned against the neighboring locker. Even if we were done talking about Josephine Kramer, he obviously wasn't leaving any time soon. As he fell silent for a moment, his eyes scanned over me. "So, black again?" he asked, referring to the sweater I wore with jeans and black boots. "I like it. It makes your hair look really blonde."

"Gee, thanks," I said sarcastically, shifting my gaze back to him. "Look, I'd just like to get my books and not be late to homeroom. So maybe you can quit hovering and go find Marlena or something."

"I'll see her later," he replied. "She's getting a little annoying lately and now she's pissed because I'm going out of town next weekend."

"Where are you going?"

"Back to LA. My dad's driving out there this week and I'm flying out on Friday to meet him. I'll have just enough time to see some old friends and catch a few waves before we fly back on the red eye Sunday night."

"Your dad's driving all the way to California?" I asked incredulously. "How long will that take?"

"About a week."

"Why isn't he flying?"

"He's taking a jewelry set worth a couple hundred grand to his broker. He's not comfortable going through airport security with it. And it's not exactly something he's going to put in a FedEx package. He makes his deliveries in person. Always has and always will."

"Makes sense," I said, shrugging. "So I guess your dad is over the whole car-stealing incident if he's letting you go back to California."

Xander grinned. "I'm going to regret telling you about that, aren't I? But, yes, he said I paid my dues since I haven't seen the ocean in two months. And since I've refrained from hot-wiring any cars around here, he bought me a ticket. So did you and Noah patch things up?"

"That's none of your business," I shot out.

"Oh, boy," he groaned, reading into my knee-jerk reaction. "Say no more. I get it."

"There's nothing to get," I said, bending down to pick up my bag. I wedged it between my thigh and the side of my locker as I pulled out my French book. After adding it to the stack of books in my locker, I removed my Calculus book from the shelf and shoved it into my bag.

"Really? Then why are you being so defensive? Don't worry, I can read between the lines. I can tell you don't want to talk about it. But I was actually hoping you guys had worked things out so you'd have someone to hang out with while I'm gone."

I gazed at him suspiciously. "Why? I thought you wanted us to break up."

"I do," he replied with a grin that faded when he continued. "But not until after my trip. Because as long as you're with him, you should be safe."

"I thought you didn't trust him."

"I don't, but ever since I saw him with you at the dance, I got the impression that he's pretty protective of you. That said, I still don't like him. I could go on for hours about what's creepy about him."

"Oh, no," I protested, thinking about all the times I

had thought of Xander as creepy. "Here we go with this all over again. Could you just give it up?"

"Not until I know who was in the woods behind your house a few weeks ago. Have you seen anything else suspicious since then?"

I shook my head. "No. Other than the wolves when I ran off the road in the rain." *And the man,* I added to myself, realizing now more than ever that I could never tell Xander a man had been with the wolves that night in the rain. "But it's been a few weeks since that happened. Don't you think whoever it was would have done something by now if they were after me?"

"I don't know. I wish I could believe that, but I think he's playing with you. Lying low long enough to give you a false sense of security."

The hair on the back of my neck stood on edge. "So now you're trying to scare me? I liked having a false sense of security better. At least then I could sleep at night. If someone is after me, I don't want to know about it because I know I'm safe. Dakota won't let anything happen to me."

"Neither will I. When I get back, that is. But if you see anything suspicious this week, let me know and I won't go."

"Don't be ridiculous. My father's the sheriff. If anything else happens, I'll tell him and he won't let me out of his sight." I hated to admit it, but the memories of the person behind my house and with the wolves terrified me. Only I could never let Xander know how scared I was, especially since he believed I was cursed.

He studied me for a minute and I hoped I'd convinced him I would be fine for one measly weekend. Finally, he changed the subject. "If you and Noah aren't together anymore, will you go to the Halloween dance with me?"

"What about Marlena?"

"Agree to go with me and she's history. So what do you say?"

"Um, maybe," I said slowly before I could stop myself. *What are you doing? You can't go out with him!* I scolded myself. *Noah will be back. You're just going to have to be patient. And why would you even consider going out with Xander? He's arrogant, cocky, and sometimes creepy.* "I mean no," I corrected quickly.

Xander smiled. "I liked maybe better."

"Sorry, I don't know what came over me. The answer is definitely, without a doubt, no. Noah will be back in the picture soon, I just don't know when."

"What does that mean? Did he leave town?"

"No," I said with a sigh while I finished getting the books I needed and shut my locker. My book bag hanging from my shoulder, I leaned against the metal door.

"Are you guys are on a break?"

"Something like that," I murmured.

"Listen, Laken. I don't know how to tell you this, but guys ask for breaks when they get cold feet. He may not want to see you anymore, and he just doesn't know how to tell you."

I narrowed my eyes, hanging on to every ounce of my composure while swallowing the lump forming in my throat. "You don't even know him, so how can you say that?" I hissed. "I believe him when he says he'll be back."

"Yeah? Sorry to burst your bubble, but I think you're just naïve."

"Then it's a good thing I don't care what you think." I glared at him, hurt and frustrated by his accusation. Taking a deep breath, I shifted my book bag strap up a little higher on my shoulder, preparing to escape into the mob of students.

"Have fun on your trip and watch out for sharks," I

remarked, tearing my gaze away from his cold blue eyes. Then I brushed past him, running off into the crowded hallway before he had a chance to say another word.

Chapter 16

Friday morning, I arrived at school only to remember Xander had ditched classes to fly to California. At least I wouldn't have to watch him and Marlena flirting and kissing all day. When I reached my locker, I pulled off my parka, exposing the diamond pendant that dangled against my purple sweater.

I hung my jacket on the hook, stuffing the thick sleeves into the narrow compartment. Then I pulled off my hat and started to slide it onto the shelf when I noticed a white envelope leaning against my books. I grabbed it, stashing my hat in its place as I read my name on the front of it.

Ripping it open, I slid out a white card and lifted the cover. A handwritten note had been scrawled on the inside. *I'll be thinking of you while I'm away. Call me any time if the mood strikes. I'll see you next week.* It was signed *Xander*. Below his name he had added, *P.S. My invitation to the Halloween dance still stands if you change your mind.*

I rolled my eyes and groaned inwardly as I read his

message a few times. If Noah didn't come back to me soon, it would get much harder to resist Xander. I sighed, staring at the card and aimlessly running my finger along the edge.

A few seconds later, Brooke emerged from the crowded hallway, her gaze drawn to the card in my hand. "What's that?"

Without a word, I gave it to her, my eyebrows raised. She read what Xander had written, her curious expression transforming into a teasing smile as she took in each word.

When she looked up at me, her blue eyes twinkled as much as the silver earrings peeking out from behind her red hair. She handed the note back to me. "He just won't give up, will he?"

"Guess not," I mused, taking it from her.

"Still haven't heard from Noah?" she asked gently.

I shook my head. "No," I said with a disheartened sigh. "My weekend is looking pretty depressing. I don't know how I'm not going to go nuts. I wish I could at least work, but Mike doesn't need me when it's this slow."

"Let's have a girls' night Saturday," Brooke suggested. "It's been a while since we've done that."

"Yeah, it has. The last one was my birthday weekend."

"That's right. So let me take advantage of this. What do you say?"

I smiled, resisting the urge to accept her offer at once. Instead, I asked, "You don't have plans with Ethan?"

"Nothing I can't break to spend time with my other best friend. He'll understand."

Ethan approached just in time to hear Brooke. "Are you talking about me again?" he joked.

Brooke smiled at him as he draped an arm around her shoulders. "Sort of. I'm going to have to break our date for Saturday to have a girls' night with Laken."

"Oh, goody. Can I come too?" Ethan teased.

"Yes," I shot out. "Please. It will be just like it used to be with the three of us. As long as you both promise no mushy boyfriend girlfriend stuff. Saturday night, you're back to being just my best friends."

Ethan studied Brooke. "I think we can manage. Brooke, you in?"

"Of course. Should I bring a movie?"

"No, please, dear God, no," Ethan groaned. "If you're picking the movie, it will be some awful chick flick. Please don't torture me."

"Hey!" Brooke said in a mocking tone. "If you complain too much, I'm sure we can find another guy who'd jump at the chance to spend Saturday night with two pretty girls."

"Really? Name one."

Brooke sighed, narrowing her eyes. "Let me think—"

"I was only kidding," Ethan quipped. "Any chick flick is worth spending an evening with my two girls."

"No," I said. "No chick flicks. Ethan, you're in charge of picking the movie. Nothing even remotely romantic, okay?"

He smiled. "You know you can count on me. Cool, a night with my two best girls and a good beat-em up action flick." I could tell he was going through a long list of action movie titles in his head as he leaned down to kiss Brooke's cheek.

I laughed. "Okay, you two. That's what I mean," I scolded, waving my hand with the notecard at them. "No kissing or touching Saturday night."

Brooke pondered my request for a moment. "I'll agree to Saturday night, but not a minute sooner," she said, leaning into Ethan.

But Ethan's smile faded when he noticed the card in my hand. "What's this?" he asked.

I frowned, pulling it back toward me. I looked at Brooke, wondering if I should show it to Ethan. She gave a subtle nod in approval.

"A note from Xander," I told him. "Here, read it." I held it out to him.

Ethan slowly took it, but held it unopened for a moment. "You sure? I don't want to invade your privacy if you'd rather I didn't," he said honestly.

"It's really nothing. And I want you to read it. I could use a guy's opinion."

"Okay, if you insist," he replied before opening the card and reading Xander's note in a matter of seconds. As soon as he finished, he raised his brown eyes to me. "He asked you to go to the Halloween dance with him?"

"Yes. But I turned him down."

Ethan shrugged and handed the notecard back to me. I took it, wondering what he thought of Xander's gesture. "Well, you've got to give the guy credit for trying," Ethan said.

"Except you're forgetting he and Marlena are an item," Brooke piped up. "She'll kill Laken if she goes out with Xander. Hell, she'd probably kill Laken if she knew Xander asked her out."

A sinking feeling settled over me. Brooke was right. Maybe that curse was real after all, because if Xander didn't quit asking me out, Marlena would never let me see the light of another day.

"So there's your answer," Ethan concluded. "Besides, I like Noah a lot better. He's good for you. Xander seems like…well, he just seems like he'd only be trouble."

"Thank you," Brooke said. "And there you have it. Decision made." She smiled knowingly as if the case was closed. But her hope seemed to fade when I frowned, thinking of Noah. I agreed wholeheartedly with Ethan. Noah was good for me, when he was around. "Don't worry, Laken. He'll be back. It was pretty obvious how much he liked you," she offered gently, as if reading my mind.

"Thanks." I tried to smile, but I don't think much of one appeared. "Hey, we should get to homeroom before we're late."

"You're right," Ethan agreed. "I'm going to walk Brooke to her room. I'll meet you there, okay?"

I glanced at both of them, grateful for their friendship. "Of course."

"See you later," Brooke said. "And cheer up. At least it's Friday." With that, she and Ethan disappeared down the hall, leaving me alone in the crowded hallway.

After I turned back to my locker, I stared at the notecard, contemplating whether to leave it where I had found it on the shelf or slide it into my book bag where I could pull it out any time. As much as Xander's arrogance often infuriated me, I couldn't deny the spine-tingling shivers that surged through me every time he was near. And my dream still taunted me, even though I'd tried to erase the memory of it.

My mind made up, I tucked the notecard into my book bag before heading down the hallway to homeroom.

❦❦❦

Ethan and Brooke arrived on my doorstep the next evening bearing gifts of two pizzas, one veggie supreme and one pepperoni. They both also brought movies. Ethan's choice was the latest Fast and Furious installment while Brooke flashed a comedy she'd picked for the night. I wasted no time thinking over that decision. Fast car chases and action were what I needed.

My parents had gone out, so we took over the kitchen with the pizza and sodas. After dinner, we left the empty boxes on the table to be cleaned up later and moved into the family room where Brooke and Ethan plunked down on the couch together. I lingered in the doorway, smiling as I tapped the Fast and Furious DVD in my hand. Paying no attention to me, they kicked off their shoes and propped their feet up onto the coffee table. In that instant, I realized how much I loved knowing they felt at home here.

"No, don't get up, you two. I'll set up the movie," I teased with a grin, waving the DVD in the air. I crossed the room to the TV and put the disk in the player. As the screen came to life with light, I heard a faint scratch around the corner at the kitchen door. I turned, placing the DVD case on the coffee table. "You guys go ahead and start the movie. I need to take Dakota out."

"Can't you open the door and let him out?" Brooke asked, seeming confused since that was what I used to do before the other wolves had shown up. But I hadn't told her about them, at least not yet.

"Not tonight. He's been hanging around the house a lot lately, so he'll probably insist on coming right back in."

"Okay," she said with a smile, her hand reaching for Ethan's. "We'll wait for you. Take your time."

I raised my eyebrows, suspecting she'd enjoy a few minutes alone with Ethan. He didn't seem to mind one bit, either. "Thanks guys." Without another word, I hurried out of the family room and across the foyer to the coat closet. The movie previews began in the background as I grabbed my parka, hat, and gloves.

By the time I wandered into the kitchen all bundled up, Dakota eagerly paced across the room. He whined when he saw me, then trotted to the door and lifted a front paw against the wood.

"Easy boy," I said, a bit alarmed at his sudden anxiety. Either something was out there or he really had to go. But

I had just let him out two hours ago, so I wasn't convinced this was an emergency bathroom break. Apprehension sinking into the pit of my stomach, I approached the door, flipped on the outside light, and reached for the handle. "What is it?" I asked him, once again wishing I could understand his thoughts the way he could understand mine.

Instead, he let out a loud groan, his amber eyes intently focused on my hand which was poised to open the door.

"Okay, okay," I relented, finally opening it. As cold air shot into the house, Dakota stormed outside. He ran across the patio to the edge where he stopped short of the grass. I stepped out into the night, pulling the door shut behind me.

Shoving my gloved hands into my coat pockets, I cautiously crossed the patio, searching the yard and dark woods for any sign of movement. The frigid air nipped at my face, the bitter cold passing through my jeans as if they weren't even there. Longing to head back inside, I hoped Dakota would hurry up and finish whatever he insisted on doing out here.

For a moment, the only movement in the darkness was the fog escaping my lips and Dakota's nose. The tiny clouds of breath glowed in the soft light coming from the single bulb beside the door. Then Dakota let out a low rumble, lowering his head, the fur on his back ruffling up like a thick mohawk along his spine. His growl grew louder as he eased down the patio steps, staring straight ahead at the woods. He walked through the grass before coming to a stop in the middle of the yard.

Fear taking over me, I scanned the woods, but saw nothing. He must have picked up on a scent or a noise so subtle I couldn't smell or hear it. The wolves and the man from the rainy night flashed through my thoughts, and I wondered if they were back. Noah was the only one I felt comfortable turning to, and now he was gone. I couldn't tell Brooke and Ethan about this. I didn't want to draw them into anything that could be dangerous, so if a threat lurked out here, I was on my own.

"Dakota," I whispered, hurrying down the steps to the grass and walking toward him. He stood still, focusing straight ahead. He didn't turn to look back at me, nor did he flick an ear my way, but I knew he heard me. I stopped beside him, watching the forest, waiting for a sign. "What is it?"

My eyes adjusting to the darkness, I could see the trees within the shadows, their spider-like branches reaching up to the sky. But my attention was drawn away from them when I heard a faint rustling. Dead leaves scratched against each other from what sounded like something moving through them. "Dakota, please stay. Whatever you do, don't leave me," I begged quietly, but my words dropped away when he charged ahead to the woods.

I sucked in a deep breath as he disappeared. In his hurry to chase off whatever was out there, he'd left me alone, vulnerable and unprotected. I whirled around, prepared to hurry back to the house, but a man stood before me blocking my path to the patio steps.

With a gasp, I skidded to a halt, recognizing the stranger as the man who had helped Noah with the drunk boys at the bar on our first date. He stood over six feet tall, towering above me with his dark hair pulled back into a ponytail. Lines creased his face, and I guessed him to be in his late forties or early fifties. His black button-down shirt and matching overcoat blended into the darkness behind him.

Fear blasting through me, my heart hammered in my chest. I started to move to one side, but the man stepped with me, remaining directly in front of me. Looking up into his cold, dark eyes, I stopped, feeling like a deer trapped by a mountain lion.

Not sure what to do, I realized I had few options. I could try to run, or I could accept my fate, whatever that might be. But I didn't have a chance to decide before he spoke.

"Hello, Laken," he said, his deep voice loud enough to drown out my pounding heart. He smiled wickedly, his coal black eyes meeting mine.

I swallowed nervously. "Who are you? What are you doing here?"

"Please don't be alarmed, my dear. I'm not going to hurt you."

"Then why are you here?" As much as I wanted to believe him, why else would a stranger show up at night in my backyard? If his intentions were innocent, he would have knocked on the front door. I glanced behind me, desperately wishing Dakota would come back.

"He won't be back for a while. My wolves are taking him on a long chase so I can have a few words with you."

I turned back to him, standing tall and meeting his gaze dead on, trying to act as though I wasn't intimidated by him, even as my legs trembled in fear. "Your wolves?"

He chuckled softly. "Well, actually, I'm not sure. It may have only been the black one. She tends to wander off more than the others."

"So they're with you. That's...great. But you haven't told me who you are yet. You know my name, so it's only fair I know yours." I concentrated on every word, trying to keep my voice steady in spite of my panic.

"Laken, my dear, you're practically famous around here for rescuing that little boy. And I know you remember me."

"From the bar, yes. You helped with the drunk boys. Of course, I remember. It was nice of you to help that night, but that doesn't explain why you're here right now."

He continued smiling, as if amused by my confusion. Once again, I looked for an escape route, but I knew I wouldn't be able to outrun him.

"You didn't answer me. Who are you?" I asked.

"That's not important."

"Then tell me what you want. Or leave. Now."

"So many questions. You're awfully inquisitive. Isn't that exhausting?"

"If you're not going to tell me what you want, then get out of my way. My friends are waiting for me inside and they're bound to come out here looking for me if I'm gone too long."

"Ah yes, Brooke and Ethan." He smiled knowingly, his eyes filled with a dark evil that sent more panic shooting through me. If he knew Brooke and Ethan by name, what else did he know? And more importantly, what did he want? "I'm guessing the two of them aren't missing you that much. I have some time."

"Fine. Then perhaps you can cut to the chase and tell me what this is all about."

"You're very jumpy, my dear. You don't need to be so alarmed. I'm only here to thank you."

"For what?" I shot out, my eyes narrowing.

"For rescuing the little boy, of course. You were even faster than I had hoped."

My mouth dropped open in shock as I stared at him. "What?"

He clasped his black leather gloved hands together, satisfaction and amusement written all over his face. "You've been very helpful, Laken. Everything I planned is falling right into place."

"What does that mean? What do you know about Ryder? And what about the other guy?"

He shook his head. "It was a shame that he fell to his death, but he served his purpose. I thought the wolves would only scare him a little, but it's better that he's no longer around."

"So they really are your wolves?"

"If you mean the wolves you saw the night you ran off the road, then yes, sort of. I feed them enough to keep them coming back, so they put up with me. But I'm sure you know better than anyone that wolves don't make good pets. Take your wolf, for instance. He has a special bond with you, but does he really obey your every command?"

I sighed thoughtfully, wishing I could say yes. But the truth was, Dakota had a mind of his own.

"That's what I thought."

His voice brought my attention back to the matter at hand. "You never answered me about the guy who took Ryder. How did you know him?" I asked, remembering that he had received a big bank deposit right before Ryder had been taken.

"Nothing gets past you, does it? You didn't actually believe the boy's disappearance was random, did you? Didn't you think it was odd that it practically happened in your backyard?"

I stared blankly at him, not quite sure what to say.

After a moment of silence, he continued. "My, my, Laken, you're even more naïve than I first took you to be."

"But I don't understand. Why would you have an innocent child taken from his home?"

"He was bait. He meant nothing to me. It was just part of the plan. I knew if you found him, they would find you. It worked even faster than I expected," he explained, his sinister smile widening.

"Who would find me?"

"Caleb and his son."

My mind racing, I wondered how Xander and Caleb fit into all of this. "What do you want with them?"

"You don't need to worry about that, my dear. From what I can tell, Caleb's son has been more of an annoyance to you than anything else. Tell me, has he shown up on your doorstep at midnight again?"

"How did you know about that?" I asked, my heart jumping again. "Have you been watching me? Was that you in the woods that night?" I spoke quickly, my questions all running together.

"You are a curious one, aren't you?"

"Can you blame me when you know so much about me and my friends? Just answer one thing for me. How could you have been so sure I would find Ryder?"

"Because you're special, Laken. You know that."

"What do you mean?"

"You know exactly what I mean."

"But—how do you—"

"Because I knew about your mother. It's not every day a teenager shows up for a program like reintroducing wolves into the wilderness and gets a job without any specialized training, a PhD, or knowing someone on the inside. So I knew about you since before you were born."

"Did you know my mother?" I whispered, tears welling up in my eyes from both fear and sadness.

"I knew of her, but I never met her. I was younger then, and I didn't quite understand all of this. I missed my chance with her, and that's why I had to wait for you to grow up."

"Understand what?"

"Ancient history, Laken. Ancient history. Your friend

and his father have something I want. So I figured out a way to get it from them." He paused, smiling down at me.

I stepped back, hoping he meant it when he said he wouldn't hurt me. "Don't you think I'll tell Xander and his father about you?"

"Maybe. But it won't matter. They won't run now that they've finally found you."

"What if I run with them?"

"You wouldn't leave your wolf and your parents behind."

I shuddered, realizing he knew way too much about me. To think he had been watching me since I'd been born made me nauseous. "Speaking of my wolf, I hope he doesn't come home bleeding again."

"Oh, yes, I'm sorry about that. I'm sure they'll all learn to play nice in time."

The man pulled a watch hanging from a gold chain out of his inside coat pocket and glanced at it. "Well, this has been quite nice, Laken, but it's time for me to go. You should get back to your friends."

He returned the watch to his pocket and closed his coat. Then he raised a gloved hand to touch my chin, and I jerked my head away from him.

"Don't be frightened. I may be many things, but I am a man of my word. I told you I won't hurt you, and I meant it. It's them I want, not you." With an evil smile, he pulled his hand away before turning and walking across the yard, his black shadow disappearing into the darkness.

I watched him retreat, my heart still pounding out of control, my nerves rattled with fear. What did he want with Xander and his father? And why was I so important to them?

Trembling, I shifted my attention to the woods in the direction Dakota had taken off. I hoped he would return tonight, but there was no guarantee he would. Tearing my eyes away from the darkness, I ran through the grass, up the steps, and across the patio. Whipping the back door open, I rushed inside and slammed it behind me. After locking the dead bolt into place, I leaned against it as if my weight could keep the stranger out. *He's gone. You're safe now. Brooke and Ethan are in the next room and you can't tell them anything. Whatever is going on is way too dangerous to involve them. They can't know about any of this,* I told myself. *But what about Xander and Caleb? What am I going to do? Do I tell them about this stranger?* I shook my head. How could I even ask myself that? Of course, I had to warn them.

I wasn't sure how long I leaned against the door frozen in fear before Brooke appeared. "I thought I heard you come back in. Where's Dakota?" she asked curiously.

"He took off. He must be tired of raw chicken and saw a deer or something," I replied, trying to appear nonchalant while still quivering under my parka. The stranger's wicked smile and evil eyes flashed through my mind. It would be days, if not weeks, before I'd be able to shake the image of him from my head.

Brooke stared at me as if she was noticing me for the first time. "Laken, your face is so pale. Why do you look like you just saw a ghost?" she asked with grave concern.

I sighed, nervously averting my eyes. I hadn't figured out what to tell her and Ethan, but I'd better think fast. I certainly didn't want to scare them by explaining that a strange man had been lurking outside in the backyard. I shook my head, peeled my gloves off, and reached up to pull off my hat. "I'm just having flashbacks. It wasn't long ago that Noah was here one Saturday night when Dakota ran off just like he did tonight. I guess I miss him more than I expected. I wish he was here."

Brooke's frightened expression softened into one of sympathy and compassion. "Oh, Laken, I'm sorry. I wasn't thinking. It's going to take time for you to get past this. Which is why we're here. So come on, let's get the movie started. We're waiting for you."

I smiled faintly. "Thanks," I said with a sigh, longing to call Noah and tell him about what just happened. After all, he was the town deputy. And I felt much more comfortable telling him than I would telling my parents. They would no doubt feel as though they needed to babysit me, and I didn't want to worry them. "Speaking of Noah, I should give him a quick call."

"Laken," Brooke started in a disapproving voice. "I know you miss him, but the only way he's going to come back to you is if you give him the space and time he needs."

"I know. But I haven't called him all week."

"Did he call you?"

"No."

"Then wait. Let him be the first to reach out to you."

I knew Brooke only had the best intentions, but she didn't know about the man in the backyard. "I know you're looking out for me, but it's complicated. I know what I'm doing. Trust me."

Brooke sighed, and I could tell she wasn't convinced. But she gave up on trying to change my mind. "Okay. Ethan and I will wait to start the movie."

"You don't have to. I know I'm taking a little longer than I expected. I'm sorry."

Brooke grinned. "Take your time. I don't want to start the movie any sooner than I have to because you know how Ethan tunes out everyone around him once a good action movie starts. And if you talk to Noah, I want to hear every detail."

"I wouldn't expect anything less."

"Good." Brooke smiled, holding up her hands, her fingers crossed. "Good luck," she said before returning to the family room.

A long sigh of relief escaped from my lips as I realized Brooke didn't suspect a thing. Gathering my courage, I stepped away from the door, dropped my gloves and hat on the kitchen table, and rushed up the stairs to my room, my hiking boots echoing in the silence. At the top, I raced to my desk where I'd left my phone. The only light in my room came from the hallway, but I didn't want to waste time turning on the lamp beside my bed. Instead, I grabbed my phone and swiped the screen. It lit up at once and I scrolled through my contact log until I found Noah's number. Taking deep breaths to calm myself, I touched the screen to call him.

The other end rang several times. When his voice mail picked up, I sighed, debating whether or not to leave a message. The only problem was I had no idea what to say. As his greeting came to an end, I hung up the call, deciding to send him a text instead. Then I wouldn't feel obligated to start off with something like "Hi" or "How are you?" I could get to the point and, hopefully, he would read it immediately, no matter where he was.

My hands trembling, I typed a message, missing my intended letters several times due to my unsteady fingers. It took twice as long as it should have to compose the text as I made each correction slowly. Finally, after what seemed like forever, I finished typing. *Stranger in the backyard again. Please call ASAP.*

I stared at the message, my finger hovering over the send arrow. I hoped this would get his attention for what it was—an honest cry for help. Still shaking, I tapped the arrow and watched the status of my text change from *Draft* to *Sent*.

Chapter 17

Fighting back tears, I stared at my phone for a few moments, hoping it would light up with a call or text from Noah. But nothing happened, except for the silence and darkness growing more intense. Finally, I forced myself to stand. The longer I stayed upstairs, the more questions Brooke and Ethan would have when I returned.

With my phone in my hand, I hurried out of my bedroom and down the stairs. It turned out Brooke and Ethan hadn't really missed me. By the time I reached the family room, they were stretched out on the couch, deeply engrossed in a kiss as the movie menu music blared out from the speakers. An hour ago, finding them like this would have really bothered me. After all, tonight was supposed to be a friends only night, just like it had been before they started dating. Seeing them kissing would have only depressed me more. But after the man had confronted me in the backyard, romance was the furthest thing from my mind.

I leaned against the door frame, waiting patiently for

Brooke or Ethan to realize I was back. After a few seconds, I unzipped my parka, starting to feel overheated from wearing it inside. When they didn't hear the zipper, I cleared my throat.

Ethan jerked up at once, jumping to his feet in between the couch and the coffee table. Blushing furiously, he stared at me, his expression both embarrassed and curious. "Laken, sorry. We were just—" His voice trailed off when he seemed to notice the smile on my face.

I raised my eyebrows as Brooke slowly sat up on the couch. "It's okay. I'm not mad, even though you guys did promise me a girls' night with none of this."

Ethan's bright red cheeks simmered back to their normal coloring. "Where were you? We were starting to get worried."

"Yeah, right," I teased with as much of a grin as I could muster, considering the apprehension still lodged in the back of my mind. They might think I was mad, but I was actually grateful for a distraction to take my thoughts off the stranger.

"Why are you still wearing your coat?" Ethan asked.

I glanced from him to Brooke, taking in their curious expressions. I was about to explain that I just hadn't had a chance to take it off yet when a knock sounded at the front door. Numb with fear, I whipped around to stare at it, an image of the man flashing through my mind.

"Laken! Are you there?" Noah's muffled voice came from the other side.

"Noah!" Without another word to Ethan and Brooke, I raced across the entry hall, unlocked the dead bolt, and flung the door open. Lightheaded with relief, I suddenly felt safe.

Cold air swept through the house as Noah rushed in and pulled me into his arms. Even through my thick parka and his fleece-lined denim jacket, I felt his strong embrace. I leaned my cheek against his shoulder as he ran his hand along my back, his other one on my hair while he kissed the top of my head.

"Laken," he whispered. "Thank God, you're okay. I got here as soon as I could after I read your text."

I pulled back, tilting my head up to look into his familiar brown eyes. "I'm a little spooked, but I'm a lot better now that you're here. Thank you for coming."

Soft footsteps padded on the entry hall floor behind me, followed by Brooke clearing her throat. "What's going on guys?" she asked.

I shot Noah a quick apprehensive glance, shaking my head to let him know I hadn't told her anything yet. As Noah released me and closed the door behind him, I turned to face her, waiting until Ethan joined her to explain. "I didn't want to scare you guys, but there was a man in the backyard when I took Dakota out."

"A man?" Brooke gasped. "What did he want?"

I shrugged. "I don't know. He said he wouldn't hurt me. He was looking for something."

"What?" Brooke asked.

"I—I'm not sure," I lied.

Silence fell over us as Brooke and Ethan stared at me. Finally, Noah asked, "Where's Dakota?"

"He ran off after a wolf right before I saw the man."

"Wait a minute," Ethan muttered under his breath. "There's another wolf?"

I nodded slowly. "Yeah," I answered with a deep sigh. "I first saw it at the bonfire."

"The bonfire at Matthew's Pond right after school started? That was like two months ago. Laken, why didn't you tell us?" Brooke shot out, her blue eyes clouded with a mixture of concern and disappointment.

"There wasn't anything to tell. As long as it doesn't hurt anyone, it's free to roam the mountains just like Dakota does," I said, remembering Dakota's bloody neck two days after the party. But I didn't want to mention that to Brooke and Ethan. We had enough to worry about without dredging that up.

"That really doesn't matter right now," Noah said. "We can deal with the other wolf later. Laken, tell me what happened out there tonight."

Shifting my eyes away from Ethan and Brooke, I looked up at him. "Dakota took off and, when I started to head back to the house, the man was right there, in my way." I briefly glanced back at Ethan and Brooke, wondering what they must be thinking. At least I already knew someone was out there, but they had no idea anything was going on. We lived in a town where crime was something that only happened far away in big cities, so I could only imagine the unsettling thoughts running through their minds right now. I studied their speechless expressions, wishing there was a way to shield them from this.

"He spoke to you this time?" Noah asked, his voice seething with anger.

"Yes," I whispered, shuddering at the vivid memory of the stranger's wicked smile.

Noah took a deep breath, scanning all of us. "How long has it been since he left?"

"Assuming he actually left, maybe fifteen or twenty minutes. I'm not really sure."

"Okay. You guys stay here. I'm going to search the premises and make sure he didn't stick around." Noah glanced at Ethan before moving his gaze back to me. "Laken, can you turn on all the outside lights?"

"I left the back light on and the only other one is outside the front door," I told him. "Do you need a flashlight?"

"No. I've got one in the car. I'll be back in a few

minutes." He reached for the door handle and opened it. A sliver of blackness appeared between the door and the frame as Noah slipped outside. "Lock it behind me," he instructed before shutting it.

Silence loomed in the entry hall as we stared at the door before I stepped forward and snapped the deadbolt into place. *Be careful,* I thought, wishing I had told him that before he rushed outside.

With a sigh, I turned to Brooke and Ethan as they watched me, concern lurking in their eyes. "Why didn't you tell us?" Brooke asked.

"I didn't want to worry you guys," I explained. I knew Brooke wouldn't like my answer, but it was the truth.

"Laken, don't you get it? We're your best friends. You're supposed to worry us. We want to look out for you. Imagine if you were in our shoes. Wouldn't you want to know if someone was threatening one of us?"

"Well, when you put it that way, I guess so," I responded sheepishly. "Everything just happened so fast. I thought I saw someone out there a few weeks ago, but he was really far away and I couldn't be sure about it. I was just hoping it would never happen again." I paused before adding, "He's not after me. He said he won't hurt me."

Brooke's jaw dropped, and Ethan jumped at his opportunity to get a few words in while she remained speechless. "Laken, a stranger just confronted you in your own backyard. I'm sure he's not here for anything good."

I nodded, folding my arms across my chest as chills raced through me. I thought of Xander and his father, grateful they were thousands of miles away, at least for tonight. But I wasn't about to tell Brooke and Ethan who the man really wanted. The less they knew about all of this, the better.

"If he said he wasn't going to hurt you, did he say what he was doing here?" Brooke asked.

"Not really," I answered. "But he knew about Ryder."

"So he was here to meet you because of that?" Brooke mused, confusion in her eyes.

"He didn't say. He was really cryptic and I just don't want to think about it anymore," I said, shaking my head. "Can we talk about something else? This is really upsetting me."

"No," Ethan muttered. "Laken, this is our home. You know as well as I do that strangers don't go sneaking around someone else's house at night in this town. I hope Noah finds him out there and cuffs him. But if he doesn't, you are going to tell your dad about him, aren't you?"

I sucked in a deep breath, my eyes meeting Ethan's. "I haven't decided. I need to talk to Noah first. And I need you to trust me on this. If we decide not to tell him, will you both please keep this quiet?"

Brooke looked at Ethan, her blue eyes meeting his gaze before they looked back at me. "As long as this guy never shows up again and you swear you'll tell us if he does, we won't tell anyone," Ethan pledged. "But why wouldn't you tell your dad?"

"Are you kidding? If he finds out about this, I won't be allowed out of the house until I'm thirty, and maybe not even then."

"Okay, you have a point," Ethan said with a smile.

A soft knock tapped on the door. "Noah," I said, rushing to unlock it and pull it open far enough for him to squeeze through.

Holding a flashlight in one hand, Noah shut the door with his other one. Then he tucked the flashlight under his arm and rubbed his hands together. "Everything looks clear. There's no sign of anyone out there."

I smiled with relief. "Thanks. But I'd still feel a lot better if Dakota came home soon."

"Yeah. So would I," he agreed, meeting my worried

gaze. Then he shifted his attention to Brooke and Ethan. "Look you two, I hate to break things up here, but I think it would be best if you both headed home for the night. I'll stay with Laken. Ethan, is that your car out front?"

"Yes," Ethan answered.

"Good. Can you take Brooke home?"

Ethan nodded. "Of course." He and Brooke returned to the family room to get their shoes and coats. Ethan also grabbed his DVD out of the player and shut off the TV.

After our quick goodbyes involving hugs from both of them, Noah closed the door while they disappeared down the sidewalk. He clicked the deadbolt into place and turned, smiling softly at me. "Alone at last."

"Is that what you want?" I asked, wondering what he meant after telling me last week he couldn't see me for a while.

"What I want and what I can have are two very different things right now."

"What does that mean?"

"It means I miss you," he said, his eyes full of longing, tempting me to believe he spoke the truth. "I'm glad you told me about this tonight."

"I didn't have anyone else to turn to. You're the only one who knows about the wolves and the person I saw in the woods last month." I remembered Xander knew about them as well, but since he was thousands of miles away, there wasn't anything he could do right now. "Did you find anything out there at all? Was there any sign of him?"

"Not a trace," Noah said with a sigh before mustering up a smile. "You're still wearing your coat and you look awfully uncomfortable. You're not going outside again, so why don't you take it off and meet me in the kitchen? Do you have some tea I can make?"

"There should be some in the pantry. Middle shelf. I'll

be there in a minute." As Noah headed for the kitchen, I returned my parka to the closet and kicked my boots off. Then I wandered into the kitchen, the floor hard beneath my socks when I headed straight for the table still cluttered with pizza boxes. As Noah filled a teapot with water, I folded the boxes and stuffed them into the garbage can. When I turned around empty-handed, Noah ignited the back burner under the teapot. After three clicks, a blue flame erupted and he adjusted it to a medium setting. Then he turned away from the stove, his jacket now hanging on the back of one of the chairs at the table. His broad shoulders filled out the black shirt he wore with jeans, and the sight of him unnerved me. As if I didn't have enough on my mind tonight, I ran a hand through my hair, feeling a little self-conscious.

"Where are your mugs?" he asked, filling the awkward silence between us.

"In the cupboard above the stove and to the right."

"Got it." He turned and pulled two white coffee mugs out of the first cabinet he opened. They clanked together as he carried them and a box of tea bags across the kitchen. When he reached the table, he set the mugs down and dropped a tea bag into each one. Then he angled his head in my direction, glancing at me out of the corner of his eye. "Care to join me, or are you going to stand over there all night?"

I sighed, relaxing as I walked across the kitchen, still not sure what to say or how to act around him. All I wanted to do was melt into his arms, but I knew that wasn't likely.

"Sorry," I said, pulling out a chair and sitting down in front of one of the mugs.

He lowered into the chair next to me. "You have nothing to be sorry about. I'm the one who should be saying that. But right now, tell me what happened tonight. I got the impression you didn't want to say too much in front of Brooke and Ethan."

"I don't want them to worry. I've tried to keep this all to myself, or at least just between the two of us." I paused, gazing at him. "I recognized him."

"Really? Who was it?"

I shook my head. "I don't know his name, but I saw him once before and so did you." When Noah raised his eyebrows, I continued. "Remember the guy from the bar who helped you with those drunk kids on our first date? It was him."

Noah's eyes widened as he took a deep breath. "What did he say?"

"A lot." A chill rolled down my spine as the man's voice echoed in my mind. "He said he wouldn't hurt me. Then he thanked me for finding Ryder so fast. It was a trap, and I was the bait."

"Laken, that sounds crazy. Are you sure about this?"

"Yes, I'm sure. He set me up. He arranged to have Ryder taken so I would find him, and then Xander and his father would find me."

Noah shook his head in disbelief. "You mean the guy from school you're doing the History project with? The same one you had me run a background check on?"

"That's the one. You met him once, remember?"

"I do. So what does this guy want with them?"

"I don't know. He never said." I paused as the tea pot's whistle grew from a whisper to a high-pitched scream.

Noah jumped up and rushed to the stove where he shut off the burner. Then he carried the teapot back to the table and filled each mug. While he returned to the stove, I watched the water in my mug slowly darken to a caramel brown as I pinched the paper at the end of the teabag string, moving it up and down.

The teapot clanked against the burner before Noah returned to his seat beside me. I stared straight ahead, lost in my memory of the stranger. "I don't believe him," I slowly admitted, glancing at Noah out of the corner of my eye.

Noah played with his teabag, his eyes on me. "What don't you believe?"

After a few seconds, I turned to meet his gaze. "That he won't hurt me. I'm scared. I don't know what any of this means. He knew who my birth mother was."

Noah circled his mug with both hands and raised it to his lips, steam rising from the tea as he took a sip before placing it back on the table. "You're kidding."

I shook my head. "I wish I was. He knew she had an unusual way with animals and that I do, too."

"Did he say how he knew?"

"Not really." I sighed, my mind reeling with questions. "I'm also scared for Xander and his father. I don't know what this guy wants with them. And I have no idea what I had to do with bringing them here." I paused, raising the tea and sipping it, careful not to take big gulps and burn my mouth. "Should I tell them?" I asked when I lowered the mug.

"Tell who what?"

"Xander and his father." Frustrated, I shook my head, staring down at my tea. "What am I saying? Of course, I have to tell them. If something happens to them that I could have prevented by warning them, I'd never forgive myself. But if I tell them, I wonder if they'll go to my dad." I looked back at Noah. "Are you going to tell him about this?"

"I don't know," he said slowly with a sigh. "On one hand, I really should. On the other hand, there's no concrete evidence this guy was even here, and he didn't hurt you. Even if we find him, it's your word against his. And if he has a clean record, we won't be able to keep him. The best you can do is get a restraining order against him."

I shivered, knowing he was right. And what would a restraining order accomplish if the guy really didn't want me like he'd said?

Lost in my muddled thoughts, I snapped back to reality when a scratching sound at the back door broke through the silence. "Dakota!" I gasped, jumping up so quickly I almost knocked my chair over behind me. I ran to the door, unlocked it, and pulled it open. Dakota pushed his way into the kitchen, bringing a quick shot of cold air with him. After I shut the door, I knelt beside him, smothering him with a hug. "Thank goodness, you're home!" I said, releasing him and sifting my fingers through his fur, feeling for blood. When I found none, I scanned the floor beneath him, relieved to see that the white tiles were clean.

At least one thing the stranger had said came true. Dakota hadn't been harmed. My smile faded as a deep rumbling growl came from Dakota's throat, and my stomach dropped in fear. I stood and stepped back, noticing his eyes focused intensely on Noah. Dakota raised his head, the fur on his back standing on edge.

"Dakota," I scolded in a low voice. "It's only Noah and you know better."

Very slowly, without taking his eyes off Noah, his growl faded and the mohawk on his spine flattened into place. He looked at me, his gaze comforting me. Then, as if forgetting Noah, Dakota nudged my legs and I knelt next to him again only to receive a sloppy wet kiss on my neck under my black hoodie.

In spite of the evening's somber mood, I couldn't help smiling. "Okay, I'm not mad anymore." Then I pushed him away before standing up and wiping at my neck.

Dakota disappeared around the corner, the clicking of his nails against the wooden steps growing faint as he climbed up the stairs. I returned to my seat, trying to ignore the amused smile on Noah's face.

"What?" I finally asked, blushing.

"I still can't believe he understands you."

My smile fading, I wondered where Dakota had been while the man was in the backyard. "I wish I could understand him. I'd love to know what happened out there. The other wolves belong to that guy," I told Noah.

"Really? Did he bring them here to turn them loose on Dakota?"

"I don't know. It's almost like he put more questions than answers in my head tonight. The only thing that makes sense is why Ryder was taken. But even that opens up more questions." My thoughts heavy, I rested my elbows on the table, leaning my forehead in my hands. "Why is all of this happening?"

Dropping my forearms onto the table, I turned to look at Noah, my hair falling over my shoulder. "I wish I would just wake up and find that all of this has been a bad dream."

"All of what? Everything? Even your way with animals?"

I nodded. "Yes. I'd give that up if it meant some psycho wasn't hunting me down."

"Maybe he's telling the truth and he really doesn't want you."

"But if he is telling the truth, then he's after Xander and his dad. That's almost worse."

"Maybe that's how you look at it, but I for one am relieved he's not after you." He reached across the table to gently place his hand on mine.

My eyes met his as a familiar tingle crawled up my arm.

"Noah, please, don't," I said, whipping away from his touch. It hurt too much to be this close to him, to feel the warmth of his fingers, knowing how far away he really was. An awkward silence lofted between us and I shifted my gaze to look down at my tea. "Why did you come over here tonight?"

"Because, regardless of what you may think right now, I still care about you."

I looked back at him, not quite sure what to say. "Then why did you leave? If you really still cared, you would have been here tonight when that guy showed up. And then maybe, he would've just left without coming near me."

"I know it might be hard to believe, but I do still care. Things are out of my control right now. I promise it won't be like this forever."

I shook my head, not sure what to think. "Noah, that makes no sense. It's your life. You make your own decisions." At that moment, a disturbing thought occurred to me, one I couldn't believe hadn't crossed my mind over the last two weeks. "Is there someone else?" I blurted out before I could stop myself.

Noah looked away from me as an apprehensive look filled his eyes. After a long pause, he spoke quietly. "I'm not sure how to answer that."

I felt like someone had just punched a hole in my heart. Tears stinging my eyes, I fought to hold them back. "You just did," I said, then rose to my feet and carried my mug across the kitchen. After setting it in the sink, I placed my hands on the edge of the counter. Leaning on them, I took a deep breath, trying to steady my nerves. How could I have been so stupid? Xander had been right after all. I was naïve.

I heard Noah's footsteps approaching behind me. "It's not what you think."

Spinning around to face him, I bit down on my lip to keep from crying. "Then explain it to me," I said, my voice shaky. Swallowing back my tears, I took another deep breath.

"I can't," he said, looking down at the floor, avoiding my stare. After a few moments, he raised his eyes, meeting mine again. "I wish I could, but there's too much at stake. I'm trying to keep several people from getting hurt, including you."

"It's a little late for that."

"I guess I can't blame you for reacting this way. I know I'm being cryptic, but you have to trust me," he begged.

"I want to, but how can I?" I shuddered as a tear rolled down my cheek. "I know I'm younger than you and, of course, you've had girlfriends in the past. But if you weren't free to date someone new, then you shouldn't have."

"I thought it was over. And it is, but someone out there won't let it be. It's a delicate situation, and if I make one wrong move, someone's going to get hurt."

I desperately wanted to believe him, to trust him, and I found myself giving in. "How long am I supposed to wait? The Halloween dance is next weekend, and I really don't want to go alone."

"I thought you didn't like to dress up."

"I'll do it if you come with me."

He smiled and stepped toward me, closing the distance between us. "I'd love to see you dressed up in a costume."

"Then be my date."

"I can't. It's too soon." He rested his hands on the edge of the counter at my sides. "You have to know this is killing me. All I want to do right now is kiss you," he said, a deep longing in his eyes.

I wanted that too, but not now, not this way, not knowing there was someone else.

"I keep remembering the night you spent at my apartment," Noah continued. "It took every ounce of willpower I had and quite a few drinks to stay on the other side of that door. This is hard for me, too."

I glared at him. "Then fix it." As our eyes met again, he dropped his arms to his sides and stepped back.

"I'm working on it," he said.

I slipped to the side, brushing past him on my way across the kitchen. "Just don't make any promises you can't keep." I spun around when I reached the table. He had also turned, facing me from where he leaned against the sink. I felt the tears welling up in my eyes. "I told you everything. I told you things I've never told anyone. And I trusted you."

"I know. You can still trust me."

I shook my head. "No. Trust has to be earned. And now that I know you've been hiding something from me, you just lost it." I paused, my eyes searching his for any sign of remorse. "Why now? Why did you have to let this happen when I need you the most? The timing really sucks."

Noah nodded, his head hung low as he avoided my gaze. "So what now?" he asked.

"You tell me. Maybe I'll accept Xander's invitation to the dance. If I can find something to wear, that is." The words slipped out before I could stop them. I hadn't planned on telling Noah that Xander had asked me out, but I didn't mind the thought of him being a little jealous.

Noah jerked his head up, glancing at me in surprise. "Xander asked you to go to the dance with him?"

I nodded. "Yes. He's asked me out a few times. But he didn't waste any time asking again when I told him you decided you needed a break."

"Well, he has very good taste. And I can't say I'm surprised. I'd do the same thing if I was him." He paused thoughtfully. "So you talk about me with him?"

I shrugged. "Only when I need a guy's opinion."

"Is that why you're so worried about him?"

I folded my arms across my chest, grateful my tears had dried up. "No. I'd be worried about anyone that stranger's looking for."

"Of course, you would."

I stifled back a sudden yawn as fatigue came over me. The faint clicking of Dakota's nails at the top of the stairs trickled into the kitchen, and I suspected he was wondering what was taking me so long to join him. "I'm really exhausted," I said. "Now that Dakota's home, you can go. I'll be fine."

"No way," he objected. "I'm not going anywhere until your parents get back."

I frowned, knowing there was no point in arguing with him. "Fine. Suit yourself. I'm going up to my room for the night," I announced, ready to end this conversation before it got any worse. Then I walked around the kitchen table, not sure how he would explain what he was doing here when my parents returned. They both knew we were taking a break and surely they would be curious. But I quickly dismissed my thoughts. Noah would just have to figure that out on his own.

I stopped at the bottom of the stairs and looked at him one last time. "Good night, Noah," I said, as if it was a permanent goodbye.

Lifting my foot onto the first step, I heard him say, "Good night, Laken."

The sound of his voice brought more tears to my eyes, and I wondered when, or if, I would see him again.

To be continued...

Don't miss

Surrender at Sunrise

The conclusion of The Sunset Trilogy

Now Available from
Tonya Royston and Black Opal Books

ACKNOWLEDGEMENTS

I want to start this section by thanking my readers. Those of you who have taken a chance on my book mean the world to me! To anyone I met at an event, thank you for stopping by my table. I never get tired of meeting people at fairs and festivals and sharing this story. Words can't describe how I feel when someone's face lights up as I tell them a little about this trilogy. Lastly, thank you for your messages and feedback. Nothing makes me happier than to hear from someone who enjoyed my story!

To my husband for continuing to support me. Thank you for bearing with me as I've filled the calendar with more events than I thought would be possible. Thank you for not minding the basement full of books, bookmarks, and event supplies, and for helping me set up at fairs and festivals. It's been grueling at times, but getting out to these events and meeting people has meant so much to me. I couldn't have done it all without you!

To Veronica for being an incredible friend! Thank you for reading and helping with the final draft on this story. But more than that, thank you for believing in me and letting me share my fears and doubts along the way. You have been a kindred spirit in so many ways!

To my publisher, Black Opal Books, and the editors, Lauri, Faith, and Joyce. Thank you for all of your support and taking a chance on my story. I have learned a lot from all of you!

To Jenn Gibson for the beautiful covers. I said it last time, and I'll say it again. Thank you for your hard work and dedication. Your work is amazing! I appreciate everything you have done for me!

Lastly, to my family, coworkers, and friends as well as everyone mentioned above. Thank you for listening and supporting me. It's been an incredible journey, and it wouldn't be nearly as special if I didn't have all of you to share it with!

About the Author

Tonya Royston currently lives in Northern Virginia with her husband, son, two dogs, and two horses. Although she dreamed of writing novels at a young age, she was diverted away from that path years ago and built a successful career as a contracts manager for a defense contractor in the Washington, DC area. She resurrected her dream of writing in 2013 and hasn't stopped since the first words of *The Sunset Trilogy* were unleashed.

When she isn't writing, Tonya spends time with her family. She enjoys skiing, horseback riding and anything else that involves the outdoors.

More information about Tonya and her upcoming endeavors can be found at www.tonyaroyston.com.

43791894R00162

Made in the USA
Middletown, DE
19 May 2017